The World
(Book One)

Kenny (Paul) May

ISBN-13: 978-1490519289
ISBN-10: 1490519289

'The World' is a work of fiction—any characters'
resemblance to people living or not
is purely coincidental.
The locations in this novel, however, are/were real.

Any and all poetry and/or short fiction contained in these
pages are the original work of the author and are
copyrighted by the author. Some works of poetry have
appeared previously in his volume of poems, 'Test
Flights,'
and are also copyrighted by the author.

Authors Note:
I am fully aware that the Air Force police at Torrejon Air
Force Base and at the Royal Oaks housing area were
called 'AP's' (Air Police), not 'MP's' (Military Police).
There is a reason for this which will be revealed
in the final volume of 'The World.'

KERRY (PAUL) MAY

Acknowledgements:
I wish to acknowledge the following readers, because I
have been lucky enough to have found such readers, and
I thank them for their
encouragement and their support.
In no particular order:
Brett Z, Bill E, Joyce J, Fred W, Miguel S, Rose V,
Shari H, Julie D, Leslie B, Suzanne J, Lori D, Mary T,
Dr. C and Mr. Hoge

Special Acknowledgements:
go to the following individuals for their encouragement,
their insights, suggestions, corrections and great recall of
details:
Rob K, Jackie S, George T and Peggie L.

Very Special Acknowledgements:
go to Dave M and Pat R who have endured everything
I've written from the very beginning and
their smiles still speak volumes.

Supreme Acknowledgement:
I wish to extend the greatest acknowledgement of all, to
my parents, Albert and Josie May,
without whose courage to seek the supreme change in
their lives, 'The World' would never have been born. I
love you guys forever and ever.
(That's their photo on the back cover, circa 1955.)

Cover art & design by Rhonda Tiger.

KERRY (PAUL) MAY

Kerry (Paul) May lives in Eugene, Oregon with his awesome wife, two Chinese pugs, four cats, and composes poetry, fiction and screenplays on the 'magic' table. His previous publication is a volume of poems titled, 'Test Flights.'

KERRY (PAUL) MAY

Dedication

This book is for my wife, Rhonda Tiger: my editor,
my sounding board, my audience, my rock,
my soul mate, my lover, and my best friend.

J.D., Ernest and Ray—
much obliged, gentlemen.

Chapter 1: The Cargo, Part 1

"Get in," the pretty officer's wife said. "Are you going to the base? I'm going to the base." So I got in. Now if the officer's wife *hadn't* stopped, like she was *supposed* to not stop, then there's really no telling the alternate directions my day would have gone. I'm serious here.

The distance from the Royal Oaks housing area (called 'El Encinar de los Reyes' in Spanish, which was about a ten-minute ride on the P-5 bus from Plaza Castilla in Madrid), to Torrejon Air Force Base was some 22 miles, give or take, but the ride to the base could take 35 minutes to an hour depending on whether you were on a school bus or on whose car you got in to if you were hitchhiking. I know. I made this trip, back and forth, about a thousand times.

Hitching a ride from Royal Oaks to the base, or vice-versa, was the norm. If you had space in your car you picked up however many passengers you could. It was kind of an unwritten code among military personnel and dependants. Refusing to pick up hitchhikers didn't sit well with the brass. We were a community of Americans living in the dead center of a foreign country. Hitchhiking was an element of community. At least it was back then, in Spain, in 1971, Franco's Spain.

Just before our Christmas break, my high school held tryouts for the varsity and junior varsity basketball teams. Being a sophomore, and being a player of not so many skills, except hustle, I was as surprised as anyone when I made the JV squad. It was also our coach's first basketball coaching job. Actually, his first coaching job of any type, a man of even fewer skills than I, but because he was one of two geometry teachers our school employed, he showed the school board how he could diagram plays that utilized a player's specific skill set, limited or not. So, our first official team practice was to be held at the base gymnasium the first Sunday after Christmas at 8:00 am. Yeah, the first Sunday after Christmas, which meant the day *right after* Christmas. No joke.

Now, here's the key to hitching a ride from the back entrance of Royal Oaks out to the base. If you had to be at the base by 8:00 am, it was best if you were at the back entrance around 6:00, give or take 15 minutes or so. Especially during the holidays. The first shift changes at the base happened around 7:00. Someone on their way to work was bound to come along some time shortly after six and, hopefully, they had room in their car.

I walked from my house, up near the front gate, (which had an actual *gate*, unlike the back entrance, and which, in all the time I lived in Royal Oaks, I never saw closed), to the back entrance, in what must have been record time. Mostly officers and ranking civil servants lived up near the front gate and the closer you got to the back entrance, the lower the pay grade. But every residential building in Royal Oaks, except for the six or so single-family units right near the front gate, reserved for the highest ranking officers, were huge, four-family units called quad-plexes, all equal in size and all equally nice. To anyone who lived there, it didn't matter where you lived.

From the front gate to the back entrance was about a mile and a half. My father was in the Civil Service and he had rank. I walked through the thickest, deadest freezing fog ever, which was typical, from time to time, in late December. I bet I couldn't see 10 feet in front of me. Good thing was, I wasn't at the back entrance for more than a couple of minutes when a new, maroon, Seat (pronounced 'see-aught'), a small Spanish-made car, usually a second car used by officers' wives, stopped, though not so easily, and that's when I opened the passenger-side door and saw the late twentyish-looking woman who asked me if I was going to the base and I said I was and got in.

Yes, she was definitely pretty—short blonde hair, wire-framed glasses, a perfect and gratifying smile—someone I'm quite certain that on more than one occasion people mistook for that actress on the Mod Squad whose name escaped me at that particular moment. She had on a thin, red, tight, soft sweater that had sequins, arranged like snowflakes, sewn on just above her breasts, which were certainly wonderfully above average, and she wasn't wearing a bra. Her perfume smelled like strawberries.

Now, I know what you're thinking, but the answer is, no, nothing happened between the pretty officer's wife and me, though I'll admit that she did come to mind twice or ten times, give or take, in the following weeks, during a hot shower with a bar of Safeguard. This isn't 'The Graduate' here.

"My name's Clancy, Clancy Dunham," she said. "What's yours?" So I told her.

"We just rotated here from Ramstein a month ago. Is the fog always this bad?" she asked. I told her that fog like this only happened once or twice a year right around this time but, yeah, this was pretty bad stuff all right. I was so grateful for the heater in her car.

"Well, I need you to be my eyes so we don't get wiped out by some truck or something on this back road here. We just got this car and I'm afraid I haven't quite mastered this stick shift yet. My husband showed me and I've been practicing driving around the housing area but my footwork isn't up to par yet. Can you drive a stick?" she asked. I told her I could. I lied. God (or whomever), she smelled delicious.

"Well, good then. Off we go!"

Our drive to the base was fairly uneventful. The fog was just as thick on the back road as it was in the housing area. The back road leading up to the highway by the Madrid Airport was very curvy and with the thick fog, Clancy would just get her car into second gear then drop it back down into first gear again. The fog thinned very little by the time we reached the highway. Once Clancy got her car into fourth gear on the highway, it was clear sailing, so to speak.

"So, why are you going to the base at this ungodly hour?" she asked, while we were still on the back road. "Aren't you on Christmas break now or something?" So I told her about having our first team basketball practice at the base gym. The back road was definitely the best leg of the trip.

"Ah, a lesson in discipline," she said, trying, then succeeding, to down-shift. "I don't know anything about basketball, but I understand the motive behind discipline." I guess I didn't understand what she was getting at but I agreed anyway. The back road to the highway, while being very curvy, was also very bumpy. While Clancy concentrated on the road and her gear-shifting, I took the opportunity to watch her boobs bobbing up and down and swaying side to side, oh, ever so subtly, inside her sweater. I kept my gym bag in my lap the entire ride to conceal what was most certainly my finest hard-on in nearly a week.

The highway was deserted. We cruised along just fine. Then Clancy said, "Aren't you curious about why *I'm* going out to the base at this ungodly hour, on a Sunday?" I admitted I was, just a little, her not being Air Force personnel and all, but told her my father always said it was best not to pry into the affairs of others lest you be told something you're not supposed to know. And, yeah, I actually said 'lest,' if you really want to know. Unreal.

"Good philosophy. Your father is a smart man." I told her my father was a foreman at the base's power plant and she said she thought that was just fine. Then she asked, "Oh, say, do you like my hair? I just had it shortened a couple of days ago." She leaned forward a bit as she kept her eyes on the road, arched her spine, then ran her thumb across the middle of her back to show how long her hair used to be. "It used to be this long. Tell me you think it looks okay this way." But I wasn't looking at her thumb on her back. I was looking at her breasts jutting out inside her thin sweater. It took every ounce of discipline I had right then to not spontaneously spawn off in my shorts.

"It's called an 'officer's wife's cut,' or something like that. I'm just now beginning to get used to it." She settled back in her seat with a look I took to mean that she was still unsure about her decision. "So, is it okay-looking?" she asked. "You can tell me. Be honest."

Now, I should probably clarify something here. See, I'd had a secret thing for Doris Day ever since I was a little kid back in eastern Oregon. I never missed one of her movies when it arrived at the Liberty Theatre. While my friends would go on and on about Raquel Welch, Ann Margret, Sophia Loren or Brigitte Bardot, or even the latest Playmate of the Month, I would nod and agree with everything they said and never mention Doris.

When my friends asked me why I would go see one of her movies, usually by myself, I'd just tell them I was bored and it was just something to do. They always understood and they never caught on. It was a really small town. But there was no woman quite like Doris Day in my book. None. Something about Doris' short blonde hair, her light sprinkling of freckles, her sparkling eyes, (except when she cried—I always hated it when they made Doris cry in a movie), her perfect teeth, and the soft focus lenses they always used for her close-ups. The complete package. Clancy didn't *look* a thing like Doris Day, but Clancy had the same *effect* on me that Doris did. My gym bag stayed put.

And to be totally honest, I thought Clancy's hair was cut just a bit too short, but I did appreciate looking at the silky fine blonde hair on the back of her neck. The way each thin, golden strand lined up perfectly somehow reminded me of a school of tiny, shimmering fish all swimming in perfect unison. But instead, I told her what I knew would be the right thing to say—I told her that her hair looked really good, which pleased her and which pleased me for pleasing her—an opportune moment that I knew I'd never have with Doris Day. Clancy's expression of indecision was quickly replaced by her smile once more.

"Well, if you must know," she began again, "my husband called me from his work and told me to bring something out to him. He works in the Intelligence Building, the one with all the big, steel doors. God only knows what those boys do in there. Intelligence things, I suppose." I agreed with her. So much of the Air Force's goings-on were classified, or whatever, what with Vietnam and all.

"Anyway," she continued, "what he asked me to bring him is in the back seat there, under my coat." I turned and saw the edge of what looked like a medium-sized black suitcase beneath her red coat.

"Lift my coat up. Maybe you can tell what it is." I held my gym bag in place with one hand and with my other I lifted up her coat, which must have seemed an awkward thing to do, but Clancy didn't say anything. Beneath her coat was a kind of attaché case. The corners of the case were pretty scuffed and scratched and there were several pretty worn locking devices of some kind on the left and right side of the handle.

"My husband takes this thing to work and brings it home every day it seems. But last night, for some reason, he left it at home," Clancy said, "so he calls me this morning and tells me it's real important that I get it out to him at the base before his shift ends at seven." Then she said, "You know, seeing's how we're being honest here, and it's just us two, I'll admit I've tried to open it a time or two, but it wouldn't budge." I couldn't be sure, but I got the feeling that Clancy felt better for having told me that.

I covered the case with her coat again and faced forward. Clancy touched my knee and said, "I guess that means you and I are on some kind of a secret mission, huh?" She smiled. She was enjoying her clandestine operation. I determined that Clancy could have been in the movies or on TV if she wanted to be. She had an easy way about her. "In fact," she continued, "my husband told me that I should come to the base alone and not pick anyone up, but with this fog and my not being too used to this stick shift, I figured he'd understand. If he ever found out, that is." She looked over at me for a brief second. "*You* won't tell on me, will you?" Yeah, she was definitely enjoying herself. I told her I wouldn't say anything to anyone. "I know. I knew you wouldn't. Secret spies aren't supposed to rat each other out." Saying that made her smile. Then she looked at her watch then *patted* my knee this time, which made me jump.

"Anyway, we'll make it with about 10 minutes to spare. Not too bad, huh? My husband said he'd meet me out in front of his building so, if it's okay, I'll let you out after we get through the front gate at the base." I told her that would be good because then I could walk over to the cafeteria at the flight line and get something to eat before practice because the Service Club cafeteria, near the base gym, where I'd normally eat, didn't open until eight but that the flight line cafeteria was always open because pilots and crews came in at all hours, whenever they landed, which was all the time, and that I had a couple of bucks on me which was plenty enough to grab something for breakfast, maybe some cereal or something... Yeah, I was babbling, but you see, she'd touched my knee with her perfect hand, twice, and I was already on the edge as it was.

"Good. Then it's a plan." Then she said, "You know, what if that case has some kind of secret codes in it that could determine the fate of the entire world? Wouldn't that be something?" I told her that I wouldn't care to know either way and that made her Mod Squad smile appear again. "So, discipline, and a full understanding of the old, 'Eyes Only, Need to Know' protocol." She made quotation marks with her fingers while still holding on to the steering wheel. Her fingers were perfect and small and her fingernails had clear polish on them. Jesus (or whomever), it was almost too much for my groin to handle.

"You'd make a fine officer some day," Clancy said. "My husband's a lieutenant. He's been told he's been put on the 'fast track' [quotation fingers again]. To what, I don't know. That's why I decided to cut my hair." Then she paused for a couple of seconds, then asked, "Did you know that the first three letters of the word, 'lieutenant,' spell 'lie?' Interesting, huh?" I told her I'd never really thought about it. That made her smile again. I was beginning to get the hang of this whole smile thing of hers. Her smile was easy and comfortable, like nothing rotten had ever happened to her in her entire life, or that a lot of rotten things had happened to her and she'd learned to smile at everything, good or bad.

"I've asked my husband probably a hundred times what it is he carries back and forth to work in that case all the time, and you know what he says?" I told her I'd have no idea.

"Go on, guess. Try to guess." I told her that I'd really rather not know.

"Stuff," she said. "He calls it 'stuff.'" She looked over at me briefly again. I shrugged.

"Well, just so you know, unlike you and my husband, I'd have been a terrible officer." And that made me smile which made her laugh.

We pulled off the highway to the main access road that led to the front entrance of the airbase and, with a couple of tries, Clancy managed to get her car down into first gear as we got up to the MP shack at the front gate, then stopped.

The MP that stepped out of the guard shack was one of the biggest Black men I had ever seen. Even in his large winter coat, the seams of the shoulders and sleeves were greatly strained. Big, I tell you. He was carrying a clipboard. Clancy rolled down her window.

"Morning, Sergeant. Special delivery." She was facing the MP but I knew she was smiling. The MP looked at his clipboard, then at the car, then at Clancy. All business.

"Good morning, Mrs. Dunham, ma'am," the MP said. "Your husband called ahead. He's waiting for you now." Then he bent down and looked into the car at me. "Who's your passenger? I was told you were coming alone," he said. Every word the MP spoke hung together, briefly, then was carried away, slowly, with the slight swirling wind. The fog at the base was as thick and freezing as in Royal Oaks.

"He's been my co-pilot, Sergeant," Clancy said. "With all this fog and my just learning how to drive this car, I figured, what's the harm, you know?" The MP looked at me again. "You got your ID on you, boy?" he asked.

I took my ID out of my wallet and handed it to Clancy who handed it to the MP. He looked it over and handed it back.

"Sergeant, if you wouldn't mind, could you please not let my husband know that I picked this young man up?" Clancy asked. "He's really been a godsend. Without him I might not have made it here at all. It would really mean a lot to me."

The MP looked at Clancy, then at me one last time. His expression softened. "Sure thing, Mrs. Dunham. My lips are sealed. But you better hurry. It's almost seven. Drop him off at the corner up there. With this fog your husband will never know. Carry on, ma'am."

The MP saluted quickly and stepped back from Clancy's car.

"Thank you, Sergeant," Clancy said. "You're an angel."

Clancy found first gear and we left the guard shack which quickly disappeared behind us. We pulled off at the first corner and I got out, still holding my gym bag in front of my crotch. This had to be some kind of record for me. I managed to get one last good look at Clancy's fine bobbers, only this time she caught me.

"Oh, do you like my sweater?" she asked. "My husband gave it to me yesterday for Christmas. I love it. It's really soft. Here, feel it." She held out her arm so I could touch her sleeve. I told her that it was okay and that we should go so she wouldn't be late. I swear if she'd asked me to touch her sweater while I was still in her car I would have certainly spewed in Technicolor.

"Discipline, protocol *and* a gentleman," Clancy said. "You'd be a great officer." I told her I doubted it, but thanked her anyway.

"Maybe we'll do this again some time," she said. Then she said, "Oh, wait, where are my manners?" She reached behind the passenger's seat and brought out her purse. She pulled out her wallet and took out a ten dollar bill and handed it to me. I told her that that was okay and thanks very much for the ride. Every word I spoke materialized right in front of my face, then drifted slowly away in a clump, in the wind, just like the MP's words did at the guard shack.

But Clancy insisted. "We secret spies need to be compensated, you know?" she said. "Take it. You *earned* it. Our national security is intact." She leaned over the passenger seat, her breasts swaying perfectly inside her new sweater, and gently shook the bill at me. So I looked one final time at her boobs and took the money. Clancy smiled.

"Enjoy your breakfast, on me," she said. "See you around, maybe, I hope." I said likewise and then she was gone, grinding her gears until they caught, then disappearing into the fog within seconds. Gone.

The airbase sits on an expansive flat plain. The freezing fog swirled mildly around with the light wind which made it feel much colder and wetter than in Royal Oaks. I started walking toward the flight line cafeteria. Within five steps of walking through what felt like shaved ice, my hard-on was gone. But by now I was seriously too hungry and too cold to care.

Chapter 2: The Cargo, Part 2

The walk from the first corner of the base to the flight line cafeteria was about a half mile. The water particles in the fog were so crystalline, it felt like they were crackling as I walked through them. The air stung my face and ears and began to cling in layers on my coat and the front of my pant legs. I ended up walking backwards for part of the distance to try to balance things out.

As I neared the front entrance of the cafeteria, I could hear that a large transport jet of some kind had just landed and was being maneuvered toward the pair of large hangers at the far end of the airfield. Being an air base of notable size, jets of all types came and went all the time, but the only days that really mattered to a high school kid were Thursdays—every second Thursday, to be exact. Transport jets arriving every second Thursday from The World (meaning the United States) meant the base's book and magazine store, BX, and Class VI Liquor Store would be restocked with new magazines, paperbacks, records, blue jeans, sneakers, Tijuana Smalls and Canadian Mist early Friday morning. Every second Friday was the best day of the month.

When I entered the cafeteria I was instantly grateful for the warmth. The cafeteria was brightly lit and spotless and empty. I grabbed a tray and immediately looked for any bowls of fruit cocktail or canned, sliced peaches in the salad cooler. Nothing in an overseas Air Force base cafeteria said 'The World' to me more than fruit cocktail or canned sliced peaches. As luck would have it there was both, so I grabbed one of each, as well as a couple of single-serving boxes of cereal, a half-pint of 'fake' milk, and ate quietly. Practice still wasn't for another 50 minutes. I still had over seven bucks of Clancy's money, plus the two bucks I brought with me, so I knew I could eat an early lunch at the Service Club after practice before hitching a ride back out to the housing area.

Right as I finished eating, the pilots and other members of the transport jet flight crew came in. Gray jumpsuits, fur-collared, quilt-lined bomber jackets, mirrored aviator sunglasses and that walk they had—that confident, semi-bowlegged stride—it's no wonder these guys always married beautiful women and never had a problem getting laid. There were six of them and they all got coffee and sandwiches and took up four tables between them. No one lounges like a transport jet flight crew. Their air of elitism was always impressive. Pilots. Flyers. A row of stars on a uniform may carry weight behind a desk or a steel door, but everyone knew who the *real* studs were.

When I left the cafeteria, I saluted the group of six men and two of them saluted me back. Once outside I wrapped my coat around me as tightly as I could and put my arm through the handles of my gym bag and crammed my hands into my pockets. I decided to walk along the road that ran parallel to the fence outside the two large airfield hangers. I wanted to get a closer look at the jet that had just arrived, not that I could correctly identify it, not like some of my classmates who were completely gooey-eyed about military aircraft, but I was curious to see what the flight crew that had swaggered into the cafeteria had been flying. The base gym wasn't quite a mile away. I had some time to kill. The fog continued to swirl about me and stick like glue.

I walked maybe 100 yards down the road before I began to see the huge tail of the transport jet now parked off to the side of the first hanger. The loading ramp underneath the tail was lowered and there were plenty of men going in and out of the plane. I could make out two forklifts also moving in and out of the back of the plane, extracting large loads each time. Each forklift would take its load to one of two large flatbed trucks that were parked nearby. Through the fog, it was all murky, like the frequent bad TV reception in eastern Oregon, so I got off the road, stepped over one of the large double steam pipes that crisscrossed every direction on the base, jumped over a drainage ditch, then crossed the short field up to the tall, cyclone fence for a closer look. For some reason I had to know.

Each time a forklift exited the plane, it carried three long, matte, silver-colored cases, stacked one on top of the other. Once on the tarmac, the forklift driver would stop and another man would look at the boxes then check something off on his clipboard. Then the forklift would proceed to one of the two flatbed trucks where two men attached large plastic bags to the ends of each box. Even though the fog was as thick and as swirling as before, and all this activity was taking place nearly 100 yards away, I could still make out what was in the plastic bags the men were attaching to the large boxes— American flags.

Right then was when I was made aware that an MP had showed up—a different MP than the guy at the guard shack at the base entrance, a white guy, but just as big and just as firm in his business. And he had a tan. It's the beginning of a high plains Spanish winter and this guy is walking around with a goddam tan. I had no idea he had even driven up in a jeep or that he was even standing just on the other side of the fence until he spoke.

"Who the fuck are you, kid? And what the fuck are you looking at?" he yelled. So polite. These guys weren't all like this guy or the guy at the guard shack. Some of them were actually just guys. But, I'd bet as high as this MP made me jump, my 5'8" ass could have dunked a basketball backwards with both hands. I practically dislocated my wrist trying to get my gym bag off my arm.

"Can't you read the sign?" the angry MP yelled. Yelling was apparently his thing. He pointed to the metal sign that was hanging on the fence right next to where I was standing, that read 'Absolutely No Trespassing Beyond This Point.' So I told him, of course I could read, but I also told him I wasn't trespassing, that I was, as he could see, on *my* side of the fence. That didn't please him.

"That sign also means 'No Looking' either, you little wise ass," he yelled. This is the first time I can recall thinking how simple logic was totally lost on some people. No use. The fall off of Idiot Mountain is a short one.

"This is a matter of national security," the MP yelled. "I suggest you move your skinny little ass on out of here and I mean like right now!"

Now, this was the second time, in less than an hour, that I'd heard someone mention 'national security.' Time to go. I grabbed my gym bag, turned and took a couple of steps, but turned back around in time to see the two fully-loaded flatbed trucks driving into the first hanger. The ramp beneath the plane was being raised again. The men who were working there were now gone. But, I had to know. I don't know why. I just did.

The MP was almost back to his jeep when I yelled at him. He turned around. I asked him how many there were. He started back toward the fence and motioned for me to do the same, so I did.

"How many what?" he yelled, as we both reached the fence at the same time. The fine ice crystals in the fog were clinging to his tanned face. "How many what?" he repeated, so I asked him how many caskets were on the plane.

"Listen," the MP yelled, "and listen good. There were no caskets. There was no plane. And you were never here, you got that? You saw nothing!" He put his hand on his holstered pistol and leaned forward until his face was practically touching the fence. Then he yelled, "You got that? Am I getting through to you? You were never here and this never happened." His words clustered together then drifted slowly away. I nodded that I understood but, to be honest, I was focused on the hand on his holster.

"Good," he yelled, "now get the fuck out of here before I shoot you in the neck!"

The base gym was nearly a mile away. I bet I made it there in six minutes.

Chapter 3: The Cargo, Part 3

Our first team basketball practice was a dog-ass bitch. I played football on the school's JV team, and even got into a couple of the varsity games during the fall season, and we did a lot of running in our practices—grass drills and wind sprints—but nothing like this. Our new coach called them 'Turkey Trots.' We'd start at the out-of-bounds line at one end of the court, run to the first foul line and back, then to the mid-court line and back, then to the opposite foul line and back, then run all the way to the out-of-bounds line at the far end of the court and back. Full speed. We did that at least 20 times during our two-hour practice. My legs were burning and rubbery. It didn't help that the sadistic base gym manager refused to turn on the heat either. Everyone would get hot and sweaty from all the running but when we stopped, we'd immediate get cold. Definitely a dog-ass bitch practice.

Our new coach showed us some of his diagrammed plays but he also insisted on demonstrating the proper mechanics of standard basketball moves such as lay-ups, jump shots and free throws. I mentioned earlier that this new coach had even lesser basketball skills than myself and this was true, stylistically speaking. Everyone on our team pretty much had the basic skills down pat. We'd all played on teams in the base league or Royal Oaks league the year before or had played rat-ball pick-up games plenty of times, not to mention in PE classes. A couple of my teammates had been bouncing a basketball since they could walk, but our coach insisted on his instruction and he insisted on our paying attention.

He was Coach—a nice man, a lovely man really, who looked a little like Wally Cox from Mission Impossible, a man who myself and my teammates would determine, throughout the course of his first coaching season, to be an overall wonderful inspiration for personal growth. But, not a basketball player of any discernable athletic skills whatsoever. And it didn't help that the man showed up in a powder blue jogging suit with yellow piping, and wearing a pair of Red Ball Jets (Run faster! Jump Higher!) tennis shoes. Unreal, really.

Coach began his instruction by demonstrating a proper right-handed layup. That's what tipped us. The most difficult part of Coach's instruction was our struggle to not laugh out loud. When Coach ran up to the basket for his right-handed layup, he properly planted his left foot, rose up off the court smoothly, but then he kicked up both of his heels like a Doublemint Twin on a trampoline in one of those chewing gum commercials back in The World. Now, though that was bad enough, it was Coach's follow-through that sealed it. Once Coach laid the ball perfectly off the backboard and into the basket, he'd leave his shooting arm extended above his head for a good three seconds, like a synchronized swimmer just going under. Coach Esther Williams. The discipline employed by my teammates and I was legendary. Coach repeated the same goofy mechanics when demonstrating a proper left-handed layup (he made this shot as well). When it was our turn to follow Coach's lead, we all did our usual layup forms and Coach was pleased.

Coach also demonstrated a proper jump shot, kicking up his heels as before, and dropped in a perfect, net-snapping swish from the side court line. His foul shot technique utilized the back board perfectly (one foot raised, arm extended for three seconds on his follow through) and, just for shits and giggles, Coach fired up a two-handed set shot from near mid-court and hit nothing but net. Coach received no style points but his geometric bottom line held true—he made every shot. None of us could make that claim. We had a coach. A good coach.

As our season progressed coach stopped kicking up his heels and keeping his arm extended on his follow through. Coach began looking more and more like one of the guys.

At the end of practice, after a couple of final Turkey Trots, we were completely gassed. Coach gathered us together for a short chat, though he did most of the talking. He laid out his training rules of keeping our grades up, no smoking, and no drinking of alcohol. Now, back in The World, the 'no drinking' rule was a complete no-brainer that was reinforced by state legal-age limits of 18 or 21. The legal drinking age on the base or in Royal Oaks was also 18, but anywhere else in Spain there was no drinking age limit. To an American teenager the temptation was more than obvious. If you had the money you could drink alcohol anywhere in Spain. The Franco Spanish government believed they successfully curtailed any alcohol abuse by not allowing their citizens to drive automobiles until they were 21 years old. Give the youth of Spain a chance to get their ya-ya's out, so to speak. A shrewd plan on the part of the General and good for the Spanish grape industry. Plus, there was the whole mandatory two-year military service for post high school Spanish males to consider. I'd seen many a group of Spanish youth under the influence of 'vino.' I loved Spain...seriously.

But then Coach said something to us that has stayed with me for my entire life—he said that if any of us were to consider partaking in 'liquid spirits' that we should always use a mixer. He left it at that. No explanation. I remember initially thinking that what an odd thing for an adult to say to a bunch of over-hormoned fifteen-year olds. Seriously. But I realized then, that in his own lifetime, Coach must have surely exorcized his own demons successfully with his own advice, original or not. His statement was delivered with such sincerity that it bordered on being a warning, as well as a concern. Since that moment I determined that the best sign of a good teacher was how they utilized their personal histories to educate without preaching. Preaching meets deafness with a fifteen-year old. Also, there's the whole give and take factor between instructor and pupil. While we were given the life-long secret to preserving our livers, Coach followed *our* lead and eventually lost his powder blue jogging suit and bought himself a pair of Converse All-Star sneakers (white canvas, low top).

After practice, in the locker room, I told a couple of my teammates about riding out to the base with Clancy. I didn't tell them about her husband's black case in the back seat but more about how she wanted me to ride shotgun because of the fog. I went into *great* detail (captivating detail, if you really want to know) about Clancy's new Christmas sweater and the gentle bounce and sway of her perfect, bra-less boobs, while traveling on the back road. My audience clung to my every word, mouths agape. Then I told them how Clancy had given me a ten dollar bill once we made it to the base. That was when my teammates called, 'bullshit.'

"You're so full of shit, man," one of them said.

"Admit it, man. You got a ride out here from your mom, like I did," the other one said, then hiked up a leg in my direction and ripped a slender, but impressive, steamy locker room fart. I told them it was the truth, though I couldn't prove it because I spent part of her ten dollar bill for my breakfast, but that they could go screw themselves if they didn't believe me.

Now, there's one thing unique to being a military brat stationed somewhere outside of The World—you were saying, 'good-bye' as much as you were saying 'hello.' You could make a friend one minute and in the next minute their parents were packing up to leave. Spain was no different. It happened all the time. One thing an overseas military brat developed was the ability to adapt to their surroundings when their surroundings were constantly changing—and the ability to handle the change. I thought about telling my teammates about my encounter with the MP and the transport jet but I was sure that would have gone over equally well. I still had seven of Clancy's dollars left, plus the two bucks of my own, and I might have shared my good fortune with them at the Service Club but, screw them, I thought. So, after our first practice I went to the Service Club alone.

The Service Club was a place for enlisted men to hang out in, but anyone was welcome. There was a cafeteria, a juke box and a game room. Now, as much as fruit cocktail or canned sliced peaches represented The World to me, a plate of steaming chili con carne ladled over a mound of rice would always remind me of the nearly five years I spent at the air base. A full plate of rice soaked in government-issue chili con carne for 99¢, a handful of complimentary, saltine cracker packages and a glass of ice water, not only tasted great and was quite filling, but was easy on the wallet as well. It meant I still had eight bucks left over, which meant my next trip to the base book and magazine store on Friday would be a generous venture.

Chapter 4: The Cargo, Part 4

There were three hitchhiking stands, actual stands with a bench and a cover, alongside the main road that exited the base. One stand was marked for hitchers going to Torrejon Village, a small Spanish village a couple of miles off base which had apartment complexes that were built specifically for American personnel and their families, one for those going into the suburbs around Madrid or into Madrid, and one for Royal Oaks. The fog had lifted just slightly by the time I left the Service Club. With a belly full of chili on rice, I didn't pay much attention to the icy air on my way to the hitching stand. I had just barely sat down on the bench when a faded, lime green, rear engine, smoking, ridden-hard-and-put-away-wet 1967, 4-door, hard top, Chevy Corvair skidded to a stop a few feet in front of me. Instant ride. Twice in one day. What luck.

I opened the Corvair's passenger-side door and inside was a staff sergeant I'd seen many times sitting in the stands at the Royal Oaks gym. A husky, intense man with a crew cut named, Murphy. And yet, there was something else about him that I recognized, or *somewhere* else that I placed him, though I'd never actually spoken to him before, but the familiarity of his face and his demeanor meant I *knew* him, somehow. That was another element of community in Spain, in 1971—everyone knew everyone else whether you actually *knew* them or not. And sometimes you knew them *best* when they were no longer there. But with Murphy there was something I just couldn't quite remember about him, but it seemed important.

"Get in, kid, I'm runnin' late," Murphy said. "C'mon, c'mon. If my car idles for longer than five seconds the engine cuts out."

I jumped in and we took off before I shut the door and then I immediately became aware of the sweet scent of gasoline and the acrid taste of exhaust fumes.

After going through the front entrance, Murphy pushed his Corvair up to 70 mph before we were even off the base's access road and on to the highway.

"Do you smoke, kid?" Murphy asked. "Well, don't smoke or you'll send us both to hell. I have a bit of a gas leak problem and my exhaust system needs a bit of work." I told him I didn't smoke.

We kind of had to shout due to the loudness of the engine growling behind us. "Good! And keep your window rolled down or we'll both be passing out."

In another five minutes was when things began to go really south for us. First of all, Murphy felt it was necessary to vent a bit concerning the events of his shift, which had led to his being detained from going home for nearly four hours and, second, his impatience with Spanish drivers.

"Do you know what the military is, kid?" Murphy asked. The knuckles of his thick fists had gone transparent from gripping the steering wheel so tightly. I started to answer him, as if I really knew anything, but he interrupted me. "Whatever you think it is, I'm here to tell you that you don't know shit about what the military is." Murphy was on a roll. He continued, and the more he spoke, the more wild-eyed he became. "The military is nothing more than a fucked up class system. That's what it is. And you can trust me on that." I thought Murphy was going to rip the steering wheel right out of the car, he was gripping it so tightly. Then he said, "You know what a class system is, kid?" Now, I was pretty sure that I knew, based on what I'd learned in Mr. O'Neil's social studies class in the ninth grade, but this was Murphy's show, so I just shook my head, no.

Murphy gritted his teeth and pressed into his steering wheel. We were going almost 80 mph by now. "A class system," Murphy continued, "is when the people at the top hold the people in the middle responsible for some stupid shit stuff the people at the bottom do. That's what it is. The military is a class-A, fuckin'-A, mother-fuckin' class system where the shit rolls downhill only until it reaches the people in the middle and then lands in the lap of yours-fuckin'-truly." Murphy paused and took a breath, then said, "Son of a bitch!"

Perhaps I shouldn't have, but I did, ask him what he meant.

"Check out that box in the back seat. You'll see."

I turned around and saw a medium-sized, wooden, khaki-green crate in the back seat and froze. Apparently my expression gave away my immediate concern. Murphy looked at me and chuckled. "It ain't what it looks like, kid. It's just a box," he said. "Cut me some slack, will ya?" Murphy shook his head.

The box in the back seat had a bunch of letters and numbers stenciled on it, but one word was clearly visible—'GRENADES.'

"Put down that gym bag and reach back there and open the lid. You'll see what I mean." I did what he said and opened the box. "Grab that canvas bag in there." So I took the canvas bank bag out of the box and set it on the side of my bucket seat. The bag was heavy and tied shut with a piece of wire. I looked at Murphy and he looked back. "Well? Open it."

I took the piece of wire off the bag and looked inside. Inside the canvas bag were hundreds, maybe over a thousand, perfectly round, flat pieces of metal, mostly steel, but some made of copper. Every piece was exactly the same size.

"Do you believe that shit?" Murphy asked. So I asked him what they were.

"Slugs, kid," he said, and he was gripping his steering wheel very tightly once more. I told him I didn't follow what he meant and took one of the pieces of metal out of the bag to look at it more closely.

"They're slugs, kid, shaped just like a quarter. Some genius in one of the dozen or so machine shops on the base apparently had too much time on his hands." My confusion couldn't have been more obvious, I guess, because then Murphy asked, "Kid, do you have any idea how many vending machines there are on the base?" I said I didn't, not exactly, but I knew they were everywhere.

"Fifty-eight, not counting the ones in the Intelligence Building. One of the jobs me and my crew are responsible for doing is emptying the cash boxes in these machines once a week. We emptied the boxes last night and I reported what we found to my LT and he told some colonel who then told the boys behind the steel doors."

Murphy paused again and took a deep breath. "I mean, fuck." Then he said, "Most of these slugs came from the beer and cigarette machines in all the barracks. Must have been quite a party, those fucks."

Now, I knew a little bit about the beer machines in the barracks. More than a few times, while attending one of the dances at the base Teen Center, my friends and I had paid some airman to get us some cans of beer from one of the machines in the barracks. I didn't say anything about that to Murphy and just asked him what happened next.

"What do you think happened?" he said. "Some asshole lieutenant from intelligence called me in just as my shift was ending and I had to spend the last four hours explaining this shit. They blamed *me*, kid! Do you believe that? They fucking blamed me because I was the one who reported it. Unreal fuckers, I tell you." So I asked Murphy why they would blame him when it was obvious that he had nothing to do with it.

"Because, like I said, kid, shit rolls downhill and they need someone to pin the blame on so they can wrap up their neat and tidy investigation." Now, I wasn't trying to be naïve on purpose. I guess I was just trying to understand the workings of *this* class system. I guess. So I asked him why they picked *him* to blame. Murphy took a breath, a contemplative breath.

"Because I was handy, kid. Use your head here." So then I asked him if he got in trouble. Murphy had a way about him. I instantly liked Murphy, for some reason.

"All they said was that this was gonna go into my file. I still get to keep my stripes. I mean, whoop-de-do and how-do-ya-do, huh? The lazy knee-knockers." I told him that I thought it sucked. Then I asked him what he was supposed to do with all the fake coins in the bag.

"They gave me a bunch of those paper bankrolls for quarters to roll these things up like they were real quarters then bring them back in tomorrow." So I asked Murphy why he thought they wanted him to do that. What were *they* gonna do with them?

"How the hell should I know, kid? Maybe pass them off to some bank or something, or maybe they'll use them themselves. Who knows how these guys think?" Then he paused and looked at me. "You know, kid, you ask a lot of questions. I'll bet your dad's a civilian." I told him my dad was a indeed a civilian. Murphy clicked his tongue.

"Figures," Murphy said, but now he was visibly perplexed as to what end his assigned task would come to, but then he said, "Tell you what, kid, if you decide to join the military, don't be an officer. They're all dicks, I'm here to tell you." I told him I'd remember that.

"But, do yourself a favor," he continued, "don't even consider the military. That bullshit in Nam won't last forever and it's all bullshit anyway." So I told him I'd remember that as well.

"Good. You do that. Put that bag back in the box now. That's evidence." I re-secured the wire tie on the bag and opened the lid to the box again and this time I saw that there was a pistol in the bottom of the box. So I put the bag on top of the pistol and shut the box lid.

We rode in silence through the thick fog for the longest minute of my life, doing 80 miles an hour, when we quickly came up behind three cars traveling significantly slower and traveling side by side, taking up both lanes. "Oh, fuck! Now what?" Murphy said, as he braked quickly and began slamming on his horn.

Two Spanish cars were in the right lane and one was in the left. All three were doing about 40 mph. All three were full of people. Murphy moved over to the left land behind the single car and hit his horn again. No use. The driver in front of us did not speed up to allow us to pass. So Murphy swung his Corvair back over to the right lane again and leaned on the horn.

Murphy gritted his teeth. "Spaniards drive like old people fuck." Now, as much as I wanted to disagree with him, having been inside many a Spanish taxi in downtown Madrid, I kept my mouth shut. I saw zero benefit from agitating Murphy any further.

We rode behind the two cars in the right lane for another slow mile when the rear car slowed even more to take an exit that led up to an overpass. Murphy veered his Corvair suddenly off the highway and followed the car. He had an expression on his face: the expression of the only man on a firing squad who *knows* that the bullet in *his* rifle is real. I doubt right then that if I *had* said anything that he could have heard me. If a trial lawyer were to ask me if I thought Murphy had become psychotic, or whatever, when we took the exit, I doubt anything I said could have benefitted Murphy's case. He had a cold and determined look in his eyes and the slightest of smiles at the corners of his mouth.

Murphy followed the car up the off-ramp. He got right up behind the car as close as he could. He leaned on his horn and waved his arm out his window trying to signal the other driver to stop, which, at the top of the overpass, the other driver *did*. Murphy put his car into park. "Put your foot on the gas, kid. Just tap it lightly every three or four seconds or so, so she doesn't die. I'll be right back."

I reached my left foot over to the gas pedal and began tapping and counting after Murphy got out. Through the fog I watched him jog the short distance up to the other car and signal the driver to roll his window down, which the driver did. Now, as demonic looking as Murphy had become, I more than halfway expected him to take a poke at this guy and clock him where he sat, but what he *did* do was something I'd never seen before and haven't seen since. Murphy reached inside the driver's window, turned off the car's ignition, yanked out the car keys and threw them somewhere, far down into the fog below the overpass. Then he jogged back, got in, put the Corvair into gear and drove around the other car without saying a word. I can't be sure, maybe because of the fog, or because I may have been hiding below my window, if the stunned driver of the other car, or the other people in the car with the driver, truly understood the middle finger gesture Murphy flipped them when we passed by.

Once we drove around the other car Murphy turned

right on the overpass which meant we were going to go up and through the small village of Paracuellas, known to harbor gypsies and miscreants, then down again on the other side, around the Madrid Airport, then come in at the halfway point of the back road to Royal Oaks. Or so I'd been told. I'd never gone through Paracuellas before but I'd heard all the rumored story variations about how some airman had been beaten to death by villagers on the main street over a 200 peseta debt to a prostitute back in the '60's. Paracuellas wasn't off-limits but more of a recommended avoidance, not to mention that the road leading to and away from Paracuellas was narrow and steep. Paracuellas was easily the highest point anywhere around Madrid. So I asked Murphy, though I already knew, if this was where we were going.

"It's a short cut, kid," was all Murphy said.

We were two-thirds of the way up the narrow road to Paracuellas when we drove out of the fog. Once we got to the town's main cobblestone road, all around us, in every direction, was a flat, pristine, brilliantly white blanket of fog that concealed everything beneath it. Paracuellas was floating on a cloud.

We were barely 50 feet into the center of the village when we found ourselves behind a large flock of sheep moving casually in the same direction we were going. Even over the loudness of the Corvair's engine, I could hear the bells some of the sheep were wearing clanging as they walked. Murphy's attempt to move through the sheep slowly was futile. Too many. The back of the flock filled the entire street from one side of the street to the other. He had to stop many times to avoid hitting any of the animals as we inched along. There were two men walking in the middle of the flock guiding the sheep who turned around briefly when we approached. Both men carried long, polished, heavy wooden staffs. One of the men was missing an eye. He reminded me of a photo of some famous one-eyed poet, whose name escaped me right then, that I'd seen in an anthology in the high school library one lunch hour when I was just killing some time.

Murphy leaned on his horn. The two sheepherders turned briefly and threw Murphy a look—one of those looks that, depending who you were, could mean many things, but usually meant, "Fuck off." That's the look Murphy got.

Now, if a flock of sheep is called a 'flock,' and a sheepherder is called a shepherd, or whatever, I just then wondered why these two guys weren't called 'sheep-flockers.' I decided to file my puzzlement away for further inquiry because right then was when Murphy did what I'd hoped he wouldn't do. He sped up slightly and bumped one of the sheep in the butt with his bumper. That was when the one-eyed guy whacked the front hood of the Corvair with his wooden staff. I mean, he hit it hard, too.

We were nearly halfway through the village by this time, nearly to the top of the steep road. Murphy stopped his car, slammed it into park, and leaped out. I expected him to grab the one-eyed guy's staff and maybe throw it or break it, but the one-eyed guy met Murphy's assault and expertly countered Murphy's every move with a barrage of skillful swipes and jabs with his staff, then the other herder got involved and they were both poking at Murphy and Murphy was cussing a blue streak at the two men, in English and Spanish. Then the Corvair died.

Murphy backed away from the two herders, still cussing away. The two men were now more concerned about their sheep than Murphy, but that's when I realized that there were now *other* men, a couple dozen to be more precise, who, with all the ruckus Murphy had created, had come out of the numerous doorways that lined both sides of the narrow street behind us and who, by all appearances, were just waiting for the American to do something else.

Murphy came back to the car. The flock of sheep had gone further up the street and were now heading down the other side of the hill followed by the two herders. The men from the doorways began to congregate in the street about 90 feet behind us.

Murphy got into his driver's seat and tried to start the Corvair. The ignition clicked but the engine wouldn't turn over. He pumped the gas and tried again. Nothing, just a clicking noise.

"Get out, kid," Murphy said. "We gotta push her up over the top of this street, then jump start her on the way down the other side." So I did what I was told. Murphy pushed from his side and I pushed from mine. We were almost to the top of the street when the first rock bounced off the top of the Corvair. Murphy looked at me and I looked at him. Then another rock hit the car, banging off the back engine hood and hitting the rear window.

"Hold on to my car, kid," Murphy yelled. He let go of his side of the car and started walking toward the group of men from the doorways. Murphy got about five steps down the street when the group of men launched a full barrage of rocks at him. All of the rocks missed him but one and that rock caught Murphy just above his right eye. Murphy grabbed his head and bent over, briefly, then raised back up and, with the most fluid motion you'll ever see, flung a perfect strike with a golf ball-sized rock and nailed the guy out in front of the pack of men right on the point of his chin. The guy went over backwards, immediately, like he'd been shot. That's when it hit me, where I recognized Murphy elsewhere besides in the stands at the Royal Oaks gym—Murphy was a home plate umpire for Little League baseball games.

"Eat *that*, fucker!" Murphy screamed.

Murphy hustled back to the car, the welt above his eye already as big as a 50-cent piece. "Push, kid! Push, goddamnit!" he yelled.

We pushed. We got the Corvair almost over the crest of the main street when a hail of rocks began pelting us and the car. I got hit twice, once on my shoulder and once in the back. I don't know if Murphy got hit again or not but his car took a lot of hits. We pushed until we finally reached the top of the street.

"Get in, kid!" Murphy yelled. So I did. But Murphy didn't get in. Instead he opened the back door, opened the lid of the grenade box, moved the bag of fake coins and took out the pistol that was underneath the bag. "Fuck this noise," he said, once he had his pistol in his hand.

I was in the Corvair. I couldn't see what Murphy was doing. I could see that he was just standing beside the car. I looked back and could see that the pack of doorway men were now 50 feet behind us, all holding rocks, all waiting to make a move, but all standing still. I figured Murphy must have been pointing his pistol at the men, no doubt with that psychotic grin on his face. It was a standoff, but for some reason, I figured we'd never get any further out of this village unless I did something. So I did the only thing I could do. I grabbed Murphy's bag of fake coins, took the wire tie off and got out of the car.

It was then that I could see that Murphy was, indeed, pointing his pistol at the pack of men behind us. And he was grinning. He was grinning ear to ear. A great big American grin. Then Murphy looked at me but I didn't give him a chance to say anything. I stuck my hand inside the bag, grabbed a handful of the fake coins and threw them at the pack of men behind us. The fake coins were no sooner airborne than the men in the pack dropped their rocks and waited for what they must have surely thought was real. Then I threw a second handful and then a third. Then Murphy yelled, "That's my evidence, kid!" So then I threw the whole damn bag of fake coins as far and as high as I could and when the bag hit the street, the hundreds of round pieces of metal scattered in all directions on the cobblestones and every man in the pack was now on their hands and knees in the street scrambling around like crazy. I looked at Murphy. He sucked his breath through his teeth. "One more push, kid, goddamnit! C'mon!"

Together, Murphy and I pushed his Corvair over the top of the street until it started to roll down the other side of the steep hill. We both jumped into the car and shut the doors. Murphy tossed his pistol into the back seat. "That was evidence, kid!" he yelled again. So I told him that the Air Force could go fuck themselves and that no way was I gonna die in Paracuellas for some punk-ass lieutenant's stupid investigation, which made Murphy smile for some reason.

I turned around and could see that the pack of men from the doorways were now running after us. They began throwing the fake coins. Fake coins were banging off the Corvair and landing in the street all around us. I turned back around to face forward and could see that the sheep-flockers and their sheep had already disappeared completely into the white wall of fog about 200 feet in front of us. I couldn't see the sheep, but I swear I could still *hear* them, their bells, their bleating.

The thick blanket of fog stretched out in front of us for as far as I could see. The only things visible above the fog were the red, blinking lights on top of two radio towers far off in the distance. We picked up some speed and Murphy tried to jump start the Corvair. The car jerked violently but the engine didn't kick and we slowed, briefly, then quickly began to gain speed again on the steep incline. In front of us was the oncoming wall of whiteness. Behind us were the shouts and curses of the pack of angry men closing in on us. Murphy was waiting until we gathered more speed than before. The wall of whiteness was rapidly approaching. So, I propped my feet against the dashboard, hunkered down in my bucket seat, grabbed my thighs, put my head between my propped up knees and began to pray.

"Jesus Christ, kid! Are you praying?" Murphy yelled. So I told him to shut up, and then he yelled, "Tell me you're praying, kid!" So I told him I was. We were really gathering speed now so I started praying faster. Now, I'm no religious nut, not by a long shot. But I was praying like I was the greatest believer that ever lived. I prayed to the god of above-average, firm breasts that bobbed and swayed ever so perfectly inside tight, soft Christmas sweaters on Spanish back roads. I prayed to the god of perfect jump shots launched from the top of the key that went through the hoop and snapped the net cleanly. I prayed to the god of remorse and closure for the families and friends of young men delivered home in silver boxes like so much cargo. I prayed to the god of all poets, one-eyed or not, whose effects on me I was just beginning to feel. I prayed to the god of rundown Corvairs with leaky gas lines and compromised exhaust systems. I prayed to Doris Day and promised to never have another carnal thought about her for the rest of my life. I was praying my ass off. I'm serious here.

When I opened my eyes we were 20 feet from the wall of whiteness. I could no longer hear the angry pack of villagers behind us. I could no longer hear the sheep bells in front of us. I could only hear the wind coming through my open window. Then I spread my knees even further and barfed. Now, I don't have a weak stomach, not really, not like some people I know, but I ralphed my chili-on-rice, my cereal, my canned sliced peaches and my fruit cocktail all over Murphy's floorboard and all over my gym bag. I mean, I sold the biggest Buick of my life right then. I didn't look to see if Murphy was looking at me as I was puking. I just knew he was. I could tell. Sometimes you just know if someone's looking at you. But right then I couldn't have cared less if he was, so I yelled at him to kick it, kick his son-of-a-bitchin' car for all she was worth and Murphy yelled back, "Fuckin' A, kid!"

Then he kicked it and it caught and the engine behind our bucket seats roared to life and it held, and Murphy slammed his foot on the gas pedal. And then we heard a 'pop' and then a 'hiss' and then a 'whoosh.' That's when the Corvair's engine caught fire. I had my head between my knees. My eyes were closed. But I knew that the flames that came up out through the rear engine hood vents shot up a good five feet by the amount of heat I felt on the back of my neck.

"Oh, perfect!" Murphy yelled. "Isn't that just fucking perfect! You *bitch*!"

Murphy began banging his fist on the horn. Then he screamed, "Hold on, kid! We're going in! Don't stop praying!" And we did, and I didn't.

Chapter 5

Murphy's Corvair engine burned for maybe five minutes before the gas tank exploded. Actually, it didn't really explode, it just sort of *whooshed* really loudly then all the gas spilled out of the gas tank underneath the car and then caught fire and pretty soon the whole car was one big lime green blaze. You'd think the gas tank was made out of cellophane the way the gas just spilled out all at once like that. It's no wonder old Ralph Nader had such a conniption fit over these cars.

Now, once Murphy and I reentered the wall of fog, our visibility was maybe 20 feet at best. There were no sheep in front of us on the road and I was very grateful for that, as was Murphy, who kept repeating, "Oh fuck, oh fuck, oh fuck…" until we made it to the bottom of the long hill down from Paracuellas before the engine died a final time and we got out. Murphy was able to grab his pistol from the grenade crate in the back seat and I got my gym bag out. Actually, because my gym bag was covered in half-digested chili-on-rice, fruit cocktail, sliced peaches, cereal and milk, I took my sweaty clothes and my Converse All-Stars out of my gym bag then threw it back through my window into the car. Murphy just looked at me and shook his head. Then he went around to the front of his car and popped open his trunk with a fist-slam.

"Help me get this stuff out of here," Murphy yelled.

I came around to the trunk and looked inside. There was a tool box, a spare tire, a tow rope, an old blanket and a pair of boots. We threw everything on the side of the road just as the big *whoosh* hit and jumped back. Then we just sort of stood there and watched the Corvair burn. It burped and sizzled like an Alka-Seltzer, but I'm pretty sure I could also hear the sheep bells clanging and some bleating somewhere off the side of the road in what must have been a wide, sloping field. But, I knew for a fact that somewhere, out there, in the thick fog, there was laughter—not the long, sustained kind of laughter, just laughter, sort of like 'told-you-so' laughter, no doubt coming from the two sheep-flockers. I don't know if Murphy could hear it or if he even cared. He was too busy rocking heel-to-toe watching his car burn. He wiped a tear from his cheek and caught me looking at him when he did.

"It's the smoke, kid. It's the smoke," he said. He was lying, of course. Then he wrapped the boots in the blanket and tied the blanket with the tow rope. He tucked his pistol into his belt, picked up his toolbox and began walking down the road. I grabbed my clothes and my Converse and began to follow him. I asked him what about the spare tire.

"Forget it, kid. It's flat," Murphy said, without turning around. "Let's go."

We walked for about 20 minutes when the fog suddenly burned off completely—just like that. The sun was shining, the air was crisp and clean. It was just barely twelve noon now. There was a whole half of this day left.

Murphy and I walked for another 20 minutes or so, in silence. I wanted to ask him again about the spare tire from his car, even though he said it was flat, which it wasn't because it bounced when he dropped it on the side of the road, but I could already hear his answer—"Waddaya wanna do, kid? Roll it all the way to fucking Royal Oaks or something?"—so I didn't. I could tell that the man already had a lot on his mind—the investigation, his now *lack* of evidence, his burned up car, and probably also thinking about the headache he had from the large lump above his eye. I mean, I could actually *hear* him thinking, so I clammed up. Two cars passed us during our walk—Spanish cars, full of Spanish people. It *was* Sunday, after all, and back then, if you were Spanish , and you owned a car, and it was Sunday, then what you did was cram as many family members into your car as you could and take a drive somewhere. I loved Spain with all my heart.

The third vehicle that came by was a pickup, the MP pickup from Royal Oaks, to be exact. I was never so happy to see an MP as I was then, or so I thought, until another time when I was even happier to see an MP's pickup, about a year later.

When the pickup rolled to a stop next to us, the driver, a thin, handsome Black guy, whose name I found out later was Sergio, motioned for me to hop in the back of his pickup and for Murphy to get into the cab with him. When Murphy opened the door to get in, I heard Sergio say, "Murphy! What in fuck sakes are you doing way the fuck out here? Is that your old piece of shit car I saw back there all burnt to shit on the side of the fucking road? Murphy, you one crazy fuck, man! This oughta be fucking good! Boy, howdy, I'm tellin' ya? Get in, man!" Then Murphy got into the cab. In the back of Sergio's pickup was Murphy's spare tire.

Now, before I continue, I should probably point out some particulars about 'colorful' language and the military—well, the Air Force, at least. Before transferring to Madrid, my father was stationed in eastern Oregon, at an Air Force radar station, a small installation that was put there to keep an eye on the Russians and their nuclear testing. At least, that's what everyone in my old hometown, Condon, a town in the middle of nowhere, said. I lived there for 13 years. The buddies that I hung out with throughout grade school all cussed—amongst ourselves, that is.

I mean, if you think about it, what do ten or eleven-year old boys, in a little dusty town, in the middle of nowhere, do in the summer except swim at the town's swimming pool, ride bikes, play baseball and football, sneak cigarettes and beers, look at Playboys, read comics and cuss? All of us cussed. One of my best friends, a kid who lived up the street, named Darren, had decided one summer that he was cussing too much and so declared that he would only say 'fuck' ten times a day. Only ten. The rest of that summer was spent counting Darren's 'fucks' to make sure he didn't exceed his daily limit. I mean, we weren't bored or anything, but that was a bit taxing.

But, as for the military and its euphemistic nature, my father, like I said, a civil servant with rank, who worked in the radar base's power plant, tacked a sign up on the wall in my bedroom, above my dresser one summer day, while I had been gone all day dicking around with my friends, that read—"The continued use of profane language reveals a definite lack of intelligence." My father had nailed the sign on my wall, no doubt with good reason. He'd brought the sign home from the power plant on the base. I think I remember his saying something about them getting some new signs for their wall. Subtle, to be sure. My father was like that, extremely subtle.

I don't think I ever heard my father say 'fuck' all the time he was alive. A few other cuss words, not many, but definitely not that one. It could have been the result of his having spent so much time in such close quarters on his submarine during World War II, that he came to loathe the most-used expletive in the English language. I never asked. I had never cussed in front of my father or mother, but, no doubt, he must have heard me cussing with my friends, thus the surprise sign nailed to my wall. Now, to be exact, this *was* a sign formerly tacked on the wall of a power plant on an American military base. I'd guess that if it *was* a mandatory sign posted on the walls of many other buildings on many other military bases and posts all around the globe, then it was either the *most* ignored posted sign of all time, or the sign actually spoke of the blatant truth that everyone already knew—a definite lack of intelligence. That said, if I had a dime for every time I said, 'fuck' in my lifetime, I'd be toolin' around town in a brand new Subaru Outback. If I had a dime for every 'curse word' I'd spoken in my lifetime, I'd own an NFL team. With two dogs and five cats to tend to daily, I'd have made a buck and half yesterday. I counted.

So Murphy gets in the cab of Sergio's pickup and I jump in back with Murphy's spare tire and off we go. Sergio asks again what was going on and although I couldn't hear all they were saying because I was too busy freezing my ass off in the back of the pickup as we drove, I *was* fully aware when the two men began laughing—I mean, laughing their asses off. Seriously. Twice Sergio swerved and nearly ran off the back road before getting into Royal Oaks. He was laughing up a storm and banging on the dashboard as Murphy was telling his story and goddamn Murphy was cracking himself up as well. The one time I raised up and looked through the back window into the cab, I could see tears running down the faces of both men.

When we got to Royal Oaks, Sergio stopped in front

of Murphy's house, which was about 50 yards inside the back entrance. Murphy got out with all the stuff he'd been carrying.

"See ya around, kid," was all Murphy said. And he started walking down the sidewalk to his front door.

Sergio opened his driver's side door, stood out on the pickup's running board and yelled, "You still the man, Murph! Don't fuckin' let anyone else tell you otherwise!"

"Fuckin'-A!" Murphy yelled back, without turning around.

Then Sergio yelled, "Oh, hey, Murph? I got your spare tire back here! You want it, or what?" To which Murphy flipped Sergio the bird and kept walking. Then Sergio shrugged and looked at me and said, "You live up by the front gate, right?" I told him I did, though my teeth were still chattering. "High Road or Low Road?" he asked, so I told him my house number. "Ah, the dead girl's house," he said. "Sit tight, my man. You're almost home."

Then Sergio giggled to himself. "That must have been some kind of fuckin' trip ya'll had. I mean, damn, man! That Murphy's one crazy fuckin' dude in my book." Then Sergio got back inside the cab of his pickup and took me home.

Of the over seven miles of paved roadway in the Royal Oaks housing area, there were two main roads that led from the front gate to the back entrance. When you entered the back entrance, you were on the Low Road, named such simply because, geographically speaking, it was lower than the High Road. From the back entrance moving toward the front gate there was a gradual rise in altitude. But the High Road, starting from the front gate, started high, dipped down really low about halfway to the back entrance, then climbed steeply until the end where you turned left and went sharply down to the Low

Road and the back entrance. There was just one other road, about halfway through the housing area, that connected the two main roads.

At this point, there was a 'circle' where you could turn right on to a road where there were more quad-plexes, turn left down to the Low Road or continue going straight on the High Road. This circle was pretty good size. It was grassy and had four or five large boulders embedded in it and some kind of medium-sized tree that I'd swear never grew an inch during the entire four years I lived in Royal Oaks. Many a summer night was spent on this little patch of land, drinking beer, making out, cracking wise. You know. We called it 'The Circle.' Genius. I suppose someone tried to call it the 'Grassy Round Place,' but it didn't catch on.

I got out of Sergio's pickup on the road in front of my house. He tipped his MP hat to me. "Count your blessings, boy," he said. And I told him it was a good thing Murphy had a gun.

Sergio un-holstered his own sidearm and showed it to me through his window. Then he smiled. "Damn that, my man. Damn that," he said, and drove off toward the front gate.

When I walked into my house, which was the upstairs portion of our quad-plex, I walked into the living room. My father was sitting in his chair, smoking a cigarette, drinking a beer and listening to Christmas music. My mother was in the living room, in her chair as well, and reading the latest Stars and Stripes newspaper. My mother looked up from her newspaper at me.

"There's some leftover turkey from last night in the fridge if you want. It's all cut up. I think there's a leg in there," she said. "How was your first practice?" she asked. I told her I was tired.

"Where's your gym bag?" my father asked. He nodded at the fact that I was carrying my still sweaty clothes and my shoes in my hands, so I told him my gym bag had got covered in barf. And he said, "Okay, but where is it?" So I told him that it got burned up in the car fire.

My father never blinked. Not once. I figured that there were three distinct scenarios that could have gone through his mind at that point: 1) He knew about Murphy's car before I got here and what I said made sense, 2) He didn't really care or, 3) He was capable of putting together the most minute of details and coming to solid, logical conclusions in a matter of seconds. I knew the answer had to be #3. He said, "Well, I'm sure it's for the best. We'll get you another gym bag this week."

See? Subtle. Subtle as hell. Two and a half years later, when I was preparing to get on the jet back to The World and to college, my father didn't say, "I love you, son," or, "I'll miss you." No. Nothing like that. What he did say was, "Just be the man that you are." It's no wonder that when he died in 1985, it took me well over a year to come round again.

"Well, if you threw up then you must be hungry," my father said. "Go get yourself some turkey. It's really good cold."

I went into the kitchen, dumped my sweaty clothes into the washing machine, grabbed a turkey leg and went to my bedroom. I was eating the turkey leg while lying on my bed and fell asleep. When I woke up three hours later, the half-eaten turkey leg was stuck to my neck. Fuck.

Chapter 6

Now, there's no real reason I started this novel out half way through my sophomore year and not when I was in the 8th grade when we moved to Spain from Oregon. It's not like nothing happened in the first two years. A lot of stuff happened. I think it might have to do with school sports though. Sports seemed to have brought all things together for me—team sports like football, basketball and some baseball. Wrestling never interested me and neither did track and field though I did throw the discus and shot put when I was a senior.

When we arrived in Spain, in late September, 1969, my sister and I had already lost about a month of school. She was two years older than me and had big boobs. Her transition was much easier than mine. Big boobs can open a lot of doors to friendship, both male and female. But, here's the deal with our late arrival in Spain—in the years before there was a high school, grades 9-12, and a middle school, grades 5-8, the high school was a large, converted, three-story barracks and the middle school had its own building over by the front gates of the air base. 1969 was a huge rotation year at Torrejon and because there were so many more middle school kids, the 8th grade was moved over to an annex barracks next to the high school. A total bitch, if you want to know.

We 8th graders went from top dogs at the middle school to the lowest shits at the high school. The 9th graders couldn't have been happier. I, for one, was totally confused. There was no one in any class below me and everyone above me hated me. Hell, even half of my own classmates hated me. I think that's why sports were so important. Sports was the great leveler. If you tried out for a team and then made the team, it actually *meant* something. It meant someone approved of you. Not something to be taken lightly, by any means.

Now you were not only a student but you were also a representative of the school. Classmates, parents, and in our case, some of the highest ranking officers in the Air Force, were now watching what you were doing and hoping you would do well. There was no telling how important that could be when it came to being some kind of *somebody* in your own eyes down the road. Everybody likes heroes and many of those who were watching you play knew that they could no longer be that kind of hero ever again. It was weird, I tell you. It's kind of like driving a car—if a person ever really actually *thought* about sitting behind the wheel of a half ton of steel and traveling at 60 or 70 miles per hour, it should scare the daylights out of them.

Also, considering the veritable tossed salad of kids in my school—kids from all over the world— from Japan, Germany, England, Turkey, Italy, shit, just name a country where The World has some kind of base—then it only seemed natural that you'd want to be part of some special niche within the student population. Being a hick from a little community out in the middle of nowhere, and not being a Jesus-nut or a musician or a scholar (by any stretch) then sports seemed to be the only path. The only problem was that there were no organized school sports, other than PE, for 8th graders. Other than Little

League baseball and league basketball, which meant lots of commuting to and from Cannillejas, a suburb of Madrid, where we lived our first year in Spain, to either Royal Oaks or the air base, for practices or games, there was nothing. My 8th grade year in Spain sucked...totally.

For the first three months in Spain, my family and I lived in the Motel Osuna in Cannillejas. A nice place with two twin beds in every unit. My parents had one unit and my sister and I shared another. Not much happened while we were there except the time my father had to dance his flaming twin mattress over the terrace railing, buck naked, at 2 am, because he'd fallen asleep while smoking in bed. Not his finest moment, to be sure. My mother gave him the silent treatment for a day and took all the ashtrays out of the bedroom.

The only other thing about the Motel Osuna (besides the chocolate ice cream in the restaurant, which was the best in the country) was that it had a swimming pool. My sister and I would swim nearly every day after school until the end of October. One time some ogling pervert lieutenant was also staying at the motel and he had my sister going off the diving board again and again to go to the pool bottom for 50 peseta pieces. See, my sister had big boobs, like I said. She knew what was up. She figured giving this guy a few bounces in her bikini for 50 pesetas a pop was like stealing. I mean, the guy could have looked for free. What an idiot. Unreal.

When we finally moved from the motel, we rented the lower floor of a duplex on the other side of the highway, the same highway that went past the air base. See, Cannillejas was split in two by the highway—there was *this* side and *that* side. We were now living on *that* side. No difference between the two sides—just kind of an oddity. 1969 was a major rotation year for Air Force personnel and their families, as I've already said, what with Vietnam and all, and Torrejon being a primary flight squadron base, not to mention the back door to Vietnam.

With the increase of people, housing wasn't that easy to come by quickly. We were on the list to move into a house out in Royal Oaks, but we had to wait another six months until we were at the top of the list, plus because of the government's whole rank and file BS, and because my father, though a civil servant, still had an officer's pay grade, we had to wait for one of the lower numbered units up by the front gate to become open—that whole class system thing that Murphy got so bitched out about.

There was a kid named Eddy in my 8th grade class who'd been here since he was in the 5th grade. His older sister graduated from the high school the year before and had decided to stay with her family in Royal Oaks until they left for The World in the summer of 1971. She started dating some GI on the base and after six months he asked her to marry him and she said, "No." So this guy drove out to Royal Oaks from the base, knocked on her front door, came inside to the living room, pulled out a pistol and shot her in the head. No shit. The girl's father then wrestled the lovesick guy's gun away from him and then shot *him* in the head. To keep the pending investigation as efficient as possible, with the whole military protocol thing and all, the rest of the family was transferred back to The World as quickly as possible. Eddy's father was a captain, which meant, despite his rank, he would go through the usual proceedings for crazy things like this, but would do so across the pond. We were given their unit as soon as they were gone and the place had gotten cleaned up. Unreal. But, if there was a bright side to any of this, our unit *did* get new carpeting in the living room. Everyone likes getting new carpeting. That was the summer of 1970, before my freshman year.

KERRY (PAUL) MAY

~~~~

A Place of Good Standing
(A Short Story)

The boy sat at a table on the far side of the hotel lounge by the row of large, round windows that had been fashioned to look like the portholes of a large ship. He sat by the windows so he could watch the other hotel guests walking on the beach. The sun was just now going down behind the city limits of Valencia. Between the times that the boy would look out the window, he would drop deep into thought as he carefully composed messages on the complimentary postcards he had selected from a spinner rack out in the lobby.

On the opposite side of the lounge, at another table, sat a man and a woman. The woman sat motionless, erect in her chair, while the man jiggled the ice in his glass, fidgeted, smoked and readjusted his sitting position often. Other than these three, and the waiter's captain in his white shirt with his sleeves rolled up, sitting behind the bar reading a newspaper, the lounge was empty, as it usually was, the hour before the evening meal preparations began.

The boy looked up from his postcards at the man and woman across the room. He knew they were Spanish. The woman wore a blue dress of silky material and a darker blue scarf wrapped about her neck and shoulders. She was a large, big-boned woman with long dark hair that seemed to shimmer from the lounge's many decorative brass lamps. Her dark hair matched her dark, deep-set eyes. From where the boy sat he determined the woman must be pretty. The fidgeting man wore a plain brown suit. The sleeves of his suit jacket were too short and exposed his skinny white wrists. Whenever he crossed and uncrossed his legs, the boy could see that

58

the man was not wearing any socks with his dress shoes. The man nervously twitched about and was constantly attending to his slicked-back hair.

The lounge in the hotel was large. The smooth, red floor tiles were polished to a deep shine. Large clay pots with ferns and other foliage were placed in the corners and beside the ceiling posts. The table tops were made of thick, amber acrylic and floating inside the acrylic were shiny, one-peseta coins as if suspended in air. The boy had counted nearly a hundred coins in his table top. The walls were hung with black and white photographs of old steamer ships and fishing vessels as well as a variety of large fishing nets with blue or green glass floats woven into them. The lounge was peaceful and quiet. The boy continued to write on his postcards.

The boy and his family were on a week's vacation. They had lived in Spain for nearly a year now. His father was a power plant foreman stationed at the American Air Force base outside Madrid. This transfer to Spain was their first as a family. Before they moved from Oregon, the boy's friends told him that living in Spain meant riding to school in a donkey cart. Americans can be so naïve. The boy didn't know it then, but he knew it now. Madrid has millions of people, the boy told his friends, before the military movers arrived. No use. Spain was donkey carts and bad water. Don't drink the water, his friends told him, and each month since his arrival the boy had written to his friends to let them know how wrong they had been, how much he had seen, how different, yet similar, things really were, even though he never drank Spanish water, unless it was bottled, just in case.

The boy's postcards all had the same picture on them—a long flat beach with large, thatched beach umbrellas and the sun just rising behind them. Across the tops of each postcard was written, "Valencia,

España." Of course, the boy would not mail his postcards until after he had returned to the air base. One never knew about the Spanish mail service.

Two men in uniform entered the open lobby doors and selected a table near the center of the lounge. The waiter's captain was quick to their table to take their orders then quickly returned bring each man a steaming cup of espresso. The boy watched the men in uniform with interest then turned his gaze out the large round window to watch his mother, father and sister walking on the beach down near the waterline. Their hair blew crazily about as they walked slowly, as inland people were prone to do, against the warm wind. After their evening meal the boy would take his own walk on the beach, out beyond where the floodlights, mounted on top of the hotel, could reach.

The interior of the lounge became brighter as the sunlight waned. The boy finished writing his third postcard then reread all three. He was carful not to repeat himself on any of the postcards as his friends in Oregon would certainly compare the news. Each postcard had something different to say about the hotel where he was staying, about the shops in Valencia, the people, the fountains, the weather, the food. The boy was running out of ideas.

At their table in the center of the lounge, the two men in uniform conversed quietly. Occasionally, one man would point to a picture on the wall and the other would respond. When the two men finished their cups they rose and walked toward the exit. The big-boned woman in the blue dress across the room rose from her chair as well and quickly followed the men in uniform out into the lobby.

The waiter's captain looked up, briefly, from his newspaper, at the woman in the blue dress as she left the lounge. Then he looked at the fidgeting man who was also watching the woman. The fidgeting man was not fidgeting any more as he watched the woman leave.

The woman in blue walked by the boy's table. The boy watched her as she spoke with the two men in uniform. She would touch and twist her long dark hair as she spoke. She touched each man on his sleeve. Finally, both men shook their heads and bid the big-boned woman good evening and continued out of the hotel lobby leaving her alone in the doorway to the lounge.

The woman in the blue dress stood for a long minute in the doorway before reentering the lounge. She paused near the boy's table and looked at him. The boy thought she looked afraid but he couldn't be sure. Then she lowered her eyes and walked back to her table and the fidgeting man. Immediately after the woman took her seat, the fidgeting man hit her across the face with the back of his hand, sending her and her chair toppling to the floor.

The big-boned woman in the blue dress sat stunned on the floor. The boy looked at the woman, then at the waiter's captain. The waiter's captain looked at the man and woman then at the boy. He shook his head and continued reading his newspaper.

When the boy looked back at the big-boned woman, he caught the fidgeting man's eye instead. The man's face was twisted. He craned his neck and tugged at his shirt collar as he stared back at the boy. Immediately, the boy feared the fidgeting man. The boy looked back at the woman who had now righted her chair and was sitting once more. She dabbed her lips with her scarf. She did not look so pretty to the boy now. She dabbed her lips then dabbed beneath her eyes. The man fidgeted in his chair. He raised his hand as if to strike the woman once again and she cowered away from him. The fidgeting man made sure the boy had seen him do this. Then the man slammed the acrylic tabletop with his palm as if to dislodge the floating pesetas. "Cabrone!" he said, loudly.

On his fourth postcard the boy wrote, "Love is not for the foolish." He looked at these words carefully. Then, after this sentence, he wrote, "or the wise." This postcard he would not send.

The fidgeting man and the big-boned woman across the lounge rose to leave. When they reached the doors to the lobby the man turned and came back to the boy's table, pulling the woman along by her elbow. The woman's cheek was still reddened by the man's backhand, her lip now swollen. The fidgeting man lit a cigarette.

"¿Como se llama, chico?" The fidgeting man said. The woman stood beside him. She wrung her hands and smiled nervously. The boy could see that the woman's teeth were deeply stained.

"Robert," the boy said, he lied. He did not understand much Spanish, yet, but there were a few things he knew, and no way was he going to tell this guy his real name.

"Robert," the fidgeting man said. "Roberto," he said, slowly. He puffed on his cigarette and blew the plume of smoke over his shoulder. "You are American, boy?" the man asked, in English. His tone was stern. He glanced briefly at the waiter's captain behind the bar then back at the boy.

"Yes," the boy said.

The fidgeting man smiled. His teeth were white and well-cared for. "Would you like to become a man today, Roberto?" He pulled the big-boned woman closer to the table.

"I *am* a man," the boy said.

The fidgeting man laughed loudly. He threw his head back as he laughed. Then he said something rapidly in Spanish to the woman who also laughed, but not so loud.

"A man, eh? So, you are a man?" the fidgeting man asked. Then he said, "Tell me, man from America, do you have money? All men from America have money, no?" Then, "You have money for a girl? You are a man who needs a girl?"

The boy looked at the big-boned woman who smiled at him with her stained teeth, then looked down at the shiny pesetas floating in his tabletop. He hated the way the man looked down at him. He hated the woman for making fun. But, he hated the man more. When he looked up again, he looked into the fidgeting man's smiling face.

"I have money," the boy said, "but no money for you."

The fidgeting man stopped smiling. His face changed to anger as he looked down on the boy. He leaned forward and put his hand on the boy's shoulder and squeezed it hard. He leaned close to the boy's face.

"You think you are too good, eh?" the fidgeting man said, in a whisper. He squeezed the boy's shoulder again, even harder. "Little American man and your money. You are better than us all?"

"I didn't say that," the boy said. He shook himself loose from the fidgeting man's grip.

"I didn't say that," the boy said, again. "Go away."

The fidgeting man blew a last plume of smoke over his shoulder then crushed his cigarette underfoot on the shiny red floor tiles. He placed both of his hands on the boy's table and leaned close to the boy's face again. "You remember something for me, eh, American boy? You remember where you are, eh?" the man said.

The boy felt as if he could cry but he would not let himself. The fidgeting man stood upright once more.

"No, you are not a man," the fidgeting man said. "You are a boy. All American men are boys. Which is why you make so much trouble for the rest." The man reached out and tapped the boy lightly on his chin. "You remember who you are, eh, boy?" he said.

The fidgeting man took a step back from the boy's table and grabbed his crotch. "Cabrone!" the man said to the boy.

The big-boned woman started to say something to the boy but the fidgeting man pulled her roughly by her arm as they exited the lounge.

The boy closed his eyes, briefly, to calm himself. He decided he would tell no one about his encounter with the fidgeting man and the big-boned woman.

Waiters and kitchen staff began entering the lounge. Large white tablecloths were laid on each table. Candles were placed on each table as were napkins, silverware, stemware and wine lists, all under the expert eye of the waiter's captain who went from table to table to inspect each setting. The waiter's captain made sure that the last table to be set for the evening meal was where the boy was sitting.

In Oregon, the boy had seen his father hit his mother, once, across the cheek during an argument. They had come home late from the bar. Both of them were drunk. Afterward, his father sat at the kitchen table and cried. Then his mother sat with his father. She put her arms around him and cried, too. The decision to put the paperwork in for the transfer to Spain was made the next day. The decision was made by them both. There had been problems in Oregon. Things, the boy imagined, every couple must go through. But, that was when he was 12. Now he was 14. A distance had been created from then until now. Through the large window, the boy watched his parents walking on the beach, holding hands, his older sister happily trailing behind them. Tonight, before taking his own walk, out beyond the rooftop floodlights, when his father ordered his usual after-dinner peppermint Schnapps, the boy would request the same. There was much to learn about becoming a man. Soon they would all sit down to decipher the menu with their dictionary, but first the boy had to go up to his hotel room to wash and to put his postcards into a book in his suitcase for safekeeping.

The waiters' captain watched from behind his bar as the American boy gathered up his postcards and departed, then he motioned for the boy's table to be prepared. Perhaps, he thought, he should have intervened when Rufino and his whore approached the boy.

He finished folding the last of the freshly laundered wine towels and came from behind his bar to inspect the table settings a final time. Each utensil had its order as each piece of stemware had its proper position. He nodded to himself in approval. To be a good host in Spain was to be in a place of good standing, a place of security. It was common knowledge. Perhaps the two soldiers Rufino's whore had spoken with might someday seek his tutelage, he thought, once their tour of service to the general had concluded. In a few minutes he would put on his dark, barman's coat hanging in the cabinet behind the bar and his narrow cummerbund. Then he would inspect the dress of his crew, right down to the young men's fingernails and teeth.

But, the American boy came back into his thoughts. He didn't mind so much that that crazy Rufino brought his whore into the lounge in the afternoons from time to time. Afternoons were rarely busy and Rufino always left a tip. And if Rufino had no fares for his whore in the afternoon he would do her himself after the evening desserts. Besides, the American boy had done well for himself, the way he had stood up to Rufino. It was true, the Americans had been increasing in numbers for some time now. Not only here, at the hotel, but everywhere in Spain. Spain was a safe place to vacation, a place of safety for strangers.

The waiter's captain stepped back behind his bar and opened the cabinet. He removed the shirt he was wearing

and took out a fresh, white shirt and put it on carefully ,
tugging the sleeves and careful to tuck the tails smoothly
into his trousers. He wrapped the cummerbund around
his waist and slid his arms into his dark barman's coat.
Soon, he thought, soon Americans will be everywhere in
the world and all people will learn English and speak
English. Spain would have its share. There had already
been talk about changes in Spain.

And maybe it wouldn't be so bad, the waiter's captain
thought, as he adjusted the strap to his cummerbund to
make sure it was perfectly secure. It's already 1970. Not
even the General can live forever.

~~~~

But, there were a couple of other incidents of
significance that took place while we lived in Cannillejas
for that first year—the kinds of things that can stay with
a person for their entire lifetime—one for the innocence
of its magic and one because it was perfect revenge.

Revenge. Our duplex in Cannillejas was at the top of a
long sloping hill from where the American kids in the
neighborhood caught the bus to school. There were two
ways to get there—down a cobblestone street for three
blocks, then hang a right for two more blocks or, down a
wide, dirt alley that was no kind of real road because it
was deeply rutted from years of streaming rain water.
The alleyway was nearly a straight shot, three blocks, to
our bus stop. When it wasn't raining, the dirt alley was
the route all the American kids in my neighborhood
took. (I say, 'all the American kids,' but actually we
were less than a dozen or so in our neighborhood on our
side of Cannillejas.) About halfway down this dirt alley
was a house with a low stone and concrete wall that had
a high, iron-bar fence embedded in it, with some serious
spikes at the top of each bar. Some old guy lived there

and he had a huge garden plot inside the fence.

In Spain there were a lot of high fences around a lot of houses, usually some kind of stone masonry with lots of glass shards embedded in concrete along the top. The fences were everywhere you went. Now, I'm sure there were crimes of theft or break-ins in Spain, just like anywhere else, but, considering the executioner façade employed by Franco's Guardia Civil, why anyone would risk it put me at a total loss, not to mention the guarantee of getting your body ripped to pieces while attempting to scale these walls.

The old guy that lived on this dirt alleyway had two dogs that had to be the devil dogs from hell. Every day, when it wasn't raining, that myself and the other kids walked this shortcut, if the old man was outside in his garden, which was more often than not, he'd send his dogs running and screaming to the iron fence, and these dogs were psychotic to the max—some sort of cross between a Doberman, a jackal and a T-Rex, with huge yellow teeth, Charles Manson eyes, and probably 70 lbs. each. Wicked animals, straight from the puke pits of hell. It was as if these dogs could smell the blood pumping through your body. So, naturally, the path best taken down the dirt alley was on the opposite side, as far away from the iron fence as physically possible.

Now, this old guy that lived there, I never found out what his story was, but he took great delight in scaring the shit out of us kids—he'd be cussing and screaming and laughing at us all at the same time. A total dick, in my book, whose total dickness was never warranted in regards to us. I don't know what this guy was growing in his garden that so needed to be protected by the hell hounds, probably plutonium or platinum (work with me here), but every chance he'd get, he'd send his snappers to speak their piece then stand back all cocky and shit, like he had some kind of final word on our existence.

Creep.

Now, while this old guy's stone and concrete wall was only about three feet high, it was also about a foot wide and with the iron rods embedded in its center, there were still about four inches on either side—a four inch shelf. After about the 40th time of being terrorized by the old fart and his dogs, a couple of friends and I hatched a plan for payback. So, this one night, a Wednesday night, a school night, we snuck down the alley as quietly as we could, making sure the old man and his Lucifer-bred twins were inside his house, and began to spread three double-sized packages of chocolate Ex-Lax along the inside of the stone wall's shelf.

The next morning, having told the other kids in our group what we'd done, we made sure that everyone made a little more noise than usual as we went down the alley. Sure enough, the old guy set his dogs on us and they proceeded to scream and snap their drooling jaws, but then caught the scent of the chocolate and gobbled up every bowel-loosening morsel we'd left for them. It took them about five seconds, if that. Success.

The next morning, on the way to the bus stop, we passed by the old guy's place. He was out in his garden with a shovel in his hands and a bandana wrapped around his nose. The two devil dogs were outside but they were just sitting on their haunches, quite uncomfortably, I might add, and couldn't have cared less that we were even walking by. And we walked by as innocently as angels. I raised my hand to the old guy and wished him 'good day,' in Spanish, but he just looked at me. From that day forward, the old guy never sent his dogs after us but he did make sure that they were in the yard each school day morning, just in case one of us had decided to steal his plutonium or whatever the hell it was that he had such a major bug up his ass about protecting. Magic.

The weather in Central Spain wasn't all that different from what I'd known in eastern Oregon. There were four distinct seasons. About the only difference was that the quantity of snow that fell in Spain each year was far less than what fell in my hometown. In eastern Oregon, we could get three feet of snow in one night. In Spain, if we got six inches at any one time, it was not only rare, but magical. Once, in my hometown, after an extremely dry autumn, it snowed three feet on Christmas Eve after my sister and I had gone to bed and it was still snowing when we woke up. Storybook, to be sure. The only crappy thing was that once it snowed, then froze, then continued to snow, off and on, for the next two months, I couldn't ride my new stingray bicycle outside until it was almost March. I rode my new bike in the living room. Being a kid can be a real bitch sometimes.

On New Year's Eve, our first year in Spain, while in Cannillejas, it snowed. It started to come down lightly in the early evening, but then picked up speed around 9:00. By 10:30 there was a good six inches.

Down the street from our duplex lived a guy who worked at the air base with my father. He, his wife, and my parents had decided to spend New Year's Eve at a tiny bodega, just off the main street that ran through the middle of our side of Cannillejas, called Angelo's. Angelo's was a quirky little dive that seemed to always have someone around who could play guitar. It was a small bar and, like all small bars, they had their own special 'house liqueur' reserved for tourists, special guests, or anyone who wanted to quickly strap on an alcoholic buzz to set the mood for the remainder of the evening. Angelo's house liqueur tasted like a cross between bananas, licorice, with a touch of cayenne pepper—guaranteed to kick anyone's ass by the third shot glass. I know. I'd had mine kicked on three or four occasions while I lived in Spain.

So, the adults were gone. My sister and some of her new friends had gone into Madrid to Puerta del Sol, to pound down some cheap champagne and to eat twelve grapes, one for each of the last twelve seconds of the old year in order to bring good luck for the new year—a lovely time spent with a couple hundred thousand other half-drunk crazies all crammed together, assholes to elbows, exchanging spit and grabbing ass. Another time, perhaps.

But on this New Year's Eve, I was saddled with the task of watching over my father's co-worker's son, who was three years younger than me, which meant he was ten years old. The kid's name was Nickel. No shit. Nickel. Who in their right mind would name a kid 'Nickel' for Chrissakes? I never got the total skinny about that. It may have had something to do with the fact that his older sister's name was Penny, but I was never really sure. And this kid was the ultimate when it came to delinquents. I'm serious here. This kid was always getting into trouble, from setting fire to their front room curtains using a can of bug spray and a cigarette lighter, to finding out what happened if he put his father's bowling ball in the clothes dryer. A crazy ten year-old if there ever was one. And I was slated to babysit the nuclear little shit.

So, what does one do with an out-of-their-mind ten year-old on New Year's Eve? You go with the flow. You do what he wants to do, and what he wanted to do was sneak some cigarettes, grab something from his parents' liquor cabinet and ring in the New Year. I didn't mind so much. Not really. As long as he did what he wanted to do, and it didn't involve fire or explosives, I figured we were safe. For his tenth birthday, this kid's parents bought him a pellet rifle. I couldn't ever figure out who was crazier, the kid or his parents. Besides, I wasn't being paid to babysit. I was just given the agenda so the adults could go off on their toot to Angelo's dive to make their own memories, worry free. No doubt, I could have used a couple shots of Angelo's house liqueur just to ease into my assignment.

After sampling a couple of Nickel's mother's menthols and kicking back a couple of shots of his father's Canadian Mist, Nickel decided we should venture outside to see what was shaking. I was feeling warm and feeling fine. Nickel was bouncing off the walls. If there was ever a mixed drink which included three tablets of Sominex, Nickel could have used it. So we go outside and wander aimlessly around in the six inches of snow and wait for something to happen—and it does.

About a block from Nickel's house, while walking slowly, watching the snow falling beautifully in the streetlights and absorbing the silence that accompanies a fresh snowfall, four Spanish teenage kids, probably the only Spanish teenagers in our entire side of Cannillejas that didn't go into Madrid to cut loose, came around a corner and began walking toward us.

I believe a brand new element for the Periodic Table was born that night and it came from the pores in Nickel's skin. You could smell it, taste it and feel it as it oozed from his body. The four Spanish teenagers were probably 16 or 17 years old. They walked on one side of the cobblestone street, four abreast, and Nickel and I walked on the other. They were conversing quietly amongst themselves and when they walked by, they nodded politely to us and continued on. They got maybe 20 feet beyond us when Nickel let out a squeal of delight, packed a big ass snowball and pelted one of the Spanish kids, walking in the middle of the four, squarely in the back of his head. We were dead meat.

With expressions of total shock and surprise, the four Spanish guys turned around and faced us. No suspense here—Nickel bent over, packed another snowball and clocked a different guy in his chest. The Spanish teenagers looked at each other. Then they spread out. We were *so* dead meat. In unison, all four of them began packing snowballs. Nickel had already made another, so I thought it best I should join in. The stand-off lasted maybe six seconds before the fight was on. Now, despite the fact that baseball was not a widely-played sport in Spain back in 1969, these four Spanish kids had no trouble pounding the shit out of Nickel and I with their salvos all while Nickel is jumping around like a sadistic prison guard during a prison riot. We were being summarily hammered.

Now, here's where the magic steps in. After about five minutes of pummeling, against unbeatable odds, one of the four Spanish guys pulled out a white handkerchief and yelled, "Espera!" Everyone stopped. The guy continued waving his handkerchief and walking slowly toward us.

"What the hell is he doing?" Nickel said, and I told him I had no idea. The Spanish kid kept walking until he was right in front of us. Then he winked at Nickel and I, put his handkerchief away, bent over, made a snowball, then turned and fired it at his three friends. Suddenly, it was three against three and our new-found turncoat began chanting, "USA! USA!" as his three friends began chanting, "Viva España! Viva España!" The snowball fight resumed with great vigor, excitement and happiness for another ten minutes. Unreal, I tell you.

When the war ended, the four Spanish teenagers were all talking at once and slapping each other on the back and slapping us on the back and re-enacting our battle with great enthusiasm. Then, just like that, after a few exaggerated handshakes, we said our 'adioses' and they continued on their walk as the snow continued to fall and dance about in the streetlights. Nickel and I went back to his place. Both of us fell asleep on his living room couch until morning. The last thing I remember hearing in 1969 was Nickel saying, "Well, that was fun. Hey, I got a chemistry set for Christmas. Wanna try blowing something up?" Hello, 1970.

Chapter 7: 'Hero'

When I woke up from my nap it was just after 4:00 pm. Being Christmas vacation, I knew there would be an early movie at 5:00 down at the theatre. And even if I decided against going to the movie, I could just hang out at the Teen Center, which was underneath it. Maybe I could play some foos-ball, ping-pong or maybe a little bumper pool. There were always plenty of kids around to get a game of spades or hearts going. So, I splashed my face, washed my neck, smeared on a little Canoe cologne, grabbed my half-eaten drumstick and began walking.

One thing about Royal Oaks was that it didn't matter if you had to walk somewhere, anywhere, because it was always so pleasant visually—white picket fences, low stone walls, red tile rooftops, perfectly mowed lawns, overgrown fields with bushes and wildflowers, laundry lines with clothing flapping in the breeze, probably 30 different kinds of trees (mostly oak)—the housing area was beautiful, no matter where you went, no matter how long it took you to walk to wherever you were going, even in winter.

When I got down to the Teen Center everyone was talking about how Sgt. Murphy had been attacked by a large band of militarized gypsies and his car had been blown up with a bazooka. Unreal. The first person who told me was a teammate from my JV basketball team— an excitable kid, he could barely contain himself. He said, "Shit, man, did you hear what happened?" and before I could answer he told me all about how Sgt. Murphy had to run for his life, guns a-blazing, and how the gypsies stole all his gold *bullion* before they blew up his Corvair with a perfect bazooka shot from the top of Paracuellas. I guess my laughter didn't sit well because then he said that we (meaning all of us) were about to go to Red Alert Level Three, and that the new base commander was considering a squadron of F-4's to blow the shit out of Paracuellas and send them fuckers back to the Stone Age and what did I think of that, smart ass?

Yep. Excitable as hell, he was. So, I told him that he needed to calm himself down and get the real story, that I was with Murphy, that we were, indeed, attacked, sort of, but that there was no bazooka, that Murphy's car blew up all by itself. So then he said that I was full of shit and I told him he could fuck off if he didn't want to know the truth.

The movie that was playing was 'The Dirty Dozen.' I'd seen it twice already over the Christmas break but thought it would be a good way to kill a couple of hours. Besides, resting my tender turkey-trotted-out legs seemed like a good idea. So, I slapped down 50¢ of my hard-earned Clancy money for a ticket and another 55¢ for a bag of popcorn and a Coke and watched Lee Marvin, Charles Bronson and Jim Brown kick some Nazi ass one more time.

By the time I got out of the movie, two hours later, people were now discussing how *Murphy* and *I* had been captured and tied up by machete-wielding militant gypsies, that Murphy's car had actually been pushed over a cliff (after the gold *bars* had been removed) and somehow we'd managed to chew our way through our ropes and were picked up by some soldiers on maneuvers who were, right now, as we were speaking, planning their full-on assault on Paracuellas at midnight. No less than two people, two people I didn't know from Adam, came up to me. One said, "Way to go, man," and the other said, "It's good to have you back." I'll say this much about military dependents—first, you had to love their loyalty and, second, you had to love their enthusiasm, especially in a semi-closed, close-knit community where it seemed that so many of the movies shown were a bit on the testosterone-pumping end of the scale.

One time, while living in eastern Oregon, in Mr. Schultz's 5th grade class, something else happened. There was a military brat named Taylor in my class who sat in the front row. All smart kids sit in the front row. Something to do with forcing oneself to have to pay attention, or something like that. I don't remember if Napoleon Hill said something about front-row sitters or not. It's been awhile since I've read any of his books. I didn't start sitting in the front row in any classes until my junior year in college, which probably explains my GPA in my freshman and sophomore years.

So, Taylor sat in the front row. We'd get these work-page assignments in class after our lunch recess a couple of times a week and when we'd finish them we'd take them up to Mr. Schultz's desk at the front of the classroom, then sit back down. Whenever someone finished their worksheet, they'd say, out loud, "Done!" God (or whomever), I *hated* that. Taylor was always the first one to say, "Done!" Then, while he was waiting for the rest of us slackers to finish, he would doodle in his notebook. He would doodle battle scenes—planes, tanks, stick soldiers, all with dash-lines that showed gunfire or missile launches, and explosions with dead stick soldiers with X's for eyes. Taylor was possessed by warfare. No doubt the very second he got his high school diploma, he'd be standing in some recruiter's office hyperventilating to beat the band.

So, there's Taylor, sitting in the front row, up by Mr. Schultz's desk, doodling his battle scenes, when I completed my worksheet and took it up front. Just for shits and giggles, on my way back, I swung by Taylor's desk. I tapped Taylor's desk as I passed by and he looked up at me. I showed him my hand, then pulled the imaginary pin out of the imaginary hand grenade I'm holding, complete with sound effects, and tossed it beneath his desk. I got two steps back toward my desk when Taylor blew himself up, complete with sound effects (very loud sound effects, I might add), turned over his desk and laid out on the floor.

For a brief three seconds you could have heard a pin drop before the class went bananas. Mr. Schultz was laughing so hard he had to leave the room. The other 5th grade teacher, Mrs. Meyers, in the classroom right next door, came over to see what all the commotion was about, as did her entire class, all crowded in our doorway. A classic moment. Enthusiasm at its pinnacle. Taylor and I had to spend half an hour in Principle Warren's office being lectured about the sins of drawing undue attention to oneself. And, of course, *everything* was my fault because hand grenades, imaginary or not, are serious business.

So, after the movie let out, I was all set to stand at the top of the stairs in front of the theatre and make an announcement in regards to the truth about what exactly had transpired with Murphy and myself when this girl walked up to me—a fairly pretty girl with blonde hair and green eyes, a girl I'd seen many times in the hallways at school my freshman year, a girl I'd seen on the football field twirling a stick with a ribbon attached to it with the school's drill team, a girl who I knew was a year ahead of me in school, a junior, a girl who, in all reality, I wouldn't have had a popsicle's chance in hell of ever spending any time with—and handed me a folded note.

"That must have been awful," the junior said, as she touched my arm and smiled. Then she said, "I also heard about you and that officer's wife this morning, too, dirty boy." She wiggled her eyebrows at me then disappeared into the crowd of departing movie-goers. Jesus, how can anyone dole out the truth if no one is willing to listen? I was all in. I realized I had to just let it go, whatever *it* was. I opened the girl's note. It was scribbled on a torn piece of a popcorn bag. The note said that she was babysitting on New Year's Eve and which quad-plex she'd be at. It also said to make sure that I came over *after* 10 pm. I looked up from her note to see if I could spot her but she was gone.

To say I was intrigued would have been the understatement of the year. I mean, for Chrissakes, she *wiggled* her eyebrows at me. She had some sizable bazooms. Guess I *was* a celebrity. Holding her note made me realized I had no choice but to clam up. Seriously. Besides, the junior was wearing a short skirt that was made of white fur. No shit.

After deciding to scrap my stump speech for truth, I decided to go into the Teen Center to see what was shaking. Now, the theatre area was a tiny cosmos within the semi-cosmos of Royal Oaks. Within the over seven miles of paved roads and driveways in the housing area, was a one-quarter mile stretch of road that led down a long hill from the High Road. There were two longish buildings for day care, pre-schools and a grade school, the large theatre building which had the Teen Center beneath it and a snack bar cafeteria in the back, a small commissary if you wanted to spend twice as much for things that were available in the BX on the base (a great place to shop for emergency boxes of Jell-O if the need ever sprang up), a large basketball gymnasium, a tennis court and four separate baseball diamonds—three behind the gymnasium and one on the other side of the theatre.

Two of the baseball diamonds had actual dugouts made of concrete and corrugated metal roofing. I mention the dugouts for two reasons—first, the military will build anything at the drop of a request and, second, the dugouts were the perfect hideaways for a little slap-and-tickle if you and your current squeeze didn't want to be Exhibit A at a teen dance. A couple of times, in the next couple of years, there would actually be a waiting line outside the dugouts. I always believed that, compared to any townies, wherever military bases were located back in The World, military dependents somehow packed a reserve chute of hormones. The kids in my high school were some of the horniest people on the planet. I think it had something to do with that whole, 'hello/goodbye' thing and the strong potential for 'missed opportunities.' Anyone who lived in Royal Oaks, who claimed they were bored, just wasn't paying attention.

So, I went into the Teen Center and the place was jamming. There were kids at every game table. There was a sign-up sheet· for ping-pong. All the tables were full of spades players, hearts players and game boarders. One table had four people at it who had been playing Monopoly since 2:00. I saw Sgt. Slater and waved.

Sgt. Slater was part Polish, part German, part Hispanic and, somewhere in his gene pool, from way back, was a DNA strand from a tribe in Africa. He was the only 'Black' guy I ever knew that had freckles and a short-cut Afro of red hair, which he always insisted was its real color. Sgt. Slater was in charge of the Teen Center in Royal Oaks and oversaw the gymnasium as well.

Sgt. Slater waved back at me then motioned for me to come over to him. He was sitting at a table on the upper stage, checking out games. Now, it was called the 'Teen Center' but there were always kids in there of all ages. There was many a time when, after winning a game of ping-pong, the next kid on the sign-up sheet could barely see above the edge of the table. The only time the Teen Center really became the 'Teen' Center was when there were 'Teen Dances'—high school freshmen and above, only. So, I went over to Sgt. Slater to see what was up.

Slater finished checking out a game of Chutes 'n Ladders to a couple of 4th graders then turned to me. He smiled. Three of his front teeth were gold.

"So, the hero returns," he said. I told him to stop messing around.

"Relax. I've been in this man's military too long not to know the difference between shit and bullshit, you know?" I told him that was good because this had all gotten way out of hand. Then I asked him what he wanted me for.

"I was wondering if you'd be interested in picking up a few extra bucks." So I asked what he meant.

"I've been able to allocate a buck-fifty an hour, each, for two people for six hours a week to keep this Teen Center properly cleaned to spec, you know? I thought you might want the job. You interested?" he asked. "You got a friend maybe, who might want to get in on this?" So I told him that actually I *was* interested and that I actually *did* have a friend who'd be interested and, actually, anyone I knew would have been interested in a few extra bucks because jobs of any kind were hard to come by in Royal Oaks but, one guy, Alverez, would be my first choice because I'd known him the longest and actually, he and his family came over on the same C-141 converted transport jet to Spain with me and my family back in '69. I say *converted* transport jet because the seats we sat in while crossing the Atlantic had been installed backwards so we crossed the damn ocean flying backwards and not many people can say that. Alverez and I became instant friends and, as luck would have it, we were both on the JV Basketball team.

"Good. Then it's settled," Slater said. "Bring him down here tomorrow afternoon sometime and we'll take care of the paperwork." So I told him thanks a lot and thanked him for thinking of me.

"No problem," Slater said. Then he paused and looked at me kind of funny. I asked him if there was anything else and he said, "No, not really." But then he said, "So, just how *did* you and Murphy get away, really?" I told Sgt. Slater I'd see him tomorrow and he said that sounded good.

I decided to leave the Teen Center right then and walk back home. With the way my day had gone, I was sure to see a big-ass UFO on the way, or find a $50 bill lying in the street, or end up talking to a burning bush. I was ready for anything. But my walk home was totally uneventful which gave me a chance to run down the laundry list of the events.

Lists are good. Lists are important. If everyone made a list of everything they did at the end of the day, and maybe tacked on some emotional response to each item on their list, they'd be able to evaluate what *kind* of day they had. Call it an 'inventory.' Perhaps a daily list could help determine if one were truly a contributing member of society (which is probably why most people don't make lists).

Now, a list at the beginning of the day could serve anyone well, but a list at the end of the day was far more important if, for no other reason, than to determine just how valid or important their list at the beginning of the day truly was. My mother's always making lists. I think smart people who make lists make lists to help themselves stay smart for some reason. I'd bet that kid in my 5th grade class, Taylor, was a huge list maker. You don't get straight A's in school without making lists, either written or in your mind. Though a *mind list* can be a tricky thing because everyone is always being bombarded with so much external stimuli.

But, the most important list would be the one at the end of the day—a chance to size oneself up to oneself. I'm not talking about some kid of self-analysis or gauging one's self worth here, I'm talking about discovery of the *reality* of oneself, period.

And then again, a list of any type can be taken too seriously, if you know what I mean. Lists shouldn't be serious, they should just serve as a kind of guideline for accomplishment, plentiful or not. I'd bet that black attaché suitcase in the back seat of Clancy's car was just a bunch of lists, not some sort of nuclear silo codes, just lists, secret lists. But, come to think of it, it *could* have been lists of nuclear silo locations or codes, or whatever. I'm trying *not* to sound like I'm talking out of my ass here—lists are important. If one really looks around on any given day they'd see that lists are everywhere and these lists can determine nearly every move they make. Not their own lists, but someone else's lists.

So, on my walk home from the Teen Center, I began my mental list. I'm not saying I'm smart or anything, I'm just saying that maybe some day something on this list could become important down the road—a turning point, a beginning, like what can happen when I accept a ride out to the air base from someone who wasn't supposed to pick anyone up. But I still believe that smart people make lists and the smartest people make a list at the end of the day as well as at the beginning of the day and the very smartest people end their end-of-the-day list with the words, 'make tomorrow's list.' The lists I make are always the abbreviated kind because my mind has a tendency to wander off in a bunch of different directions all at once, if you haven't yet noticed, so I try to keep it short, so I won't start bleeding from my ears.

For instance, I'm walking home from the Teen Center, and it's cold, but not too cold, not like earlier when I about froze my nuggets off walking through the freezing fog here in the housing area and then out at the base. Just cold. So, I start thinking about the cold and how cold I was, how cold the ice particles were when they stuck to my face and clothes. A detailed list would include something about how cold it was. List-making can drive a person crazy which is probably why so many geniuses end up either in padded rooms or with rifle barrels under their chins—their lists were *too* detailed.

Then, as I'm walking, I pass by the swimming pool, which is just down the street from The Circle on the High Road, and start thinking about all last summer and all the hours I spent there—how big and beautiful and blue the pool was, how soft and green the sloping lawn down to the stone tile walkway around the pool was, how great the cheeseburgers frying on the grill in the snack bar smelled, how wonderful all the boobs of all sizes in all the bikinis looked as all the girls lounged about in groups of three or four or alone on their beach towels. See? Wandering. To stay sane one must stay focused. Details are important but too many details can make you walk into a street sign or make you feel like you're falling over backwards.

Now, before I continue with my list, I guess I should point out something in regard to a reoccurring image in these pages—boobs. Blame Hugh Hefner. He glorified boobs in his magazine (thank you, Jesus, or whomever) and sucked impressionable ten year-olds into his world with as calculated a spell as Snow White's poisoned apple. He made a lot of money (he probably makes lots of lists, too) and, in my opinion, gave girls the right to be over-the-top proud of their features. My references should not be viewed as lewd, but as expressions of admiration. I hope that clears things up. Not my fault. I can be as accountable as the next guy, more so more often than not, but it was Hef that gave girls their rightful, elevated status of self-appreciation. But, I guess if you've gotten this far, then you're either already okay with all this, or your tolerance level should be commended. And, as to the variety of labels I attach to breasts, consider this: 'breasts' is such a clinical word. When a woman gets her boobs radiated during a mammogram, it's called a 'breast exam.' All business. And 'tits,' well, every animal on the planet has tits or 'teats' or whatever. You won't see a female gorilla or a lioness with 'bobbers' or 'bazooms.' They're tits, period. Ever heard of a 'bobber exam?' Didn't think so. Call it poetic license. So, if the term "garbanza floogers" should show up, it's meant as a compliment. All good in my book. Blame Hugh. He started it and bless him until the end of his days.

I always felt a little sorry for our school's cheerleaders and drill team members. My high school bounced back and forth a couple times between being Torrejon High School and Madrid High School, but it didn't matter because these girls had to wear either a 'T ' or an 'M' on their chests. No doubt they all heard the same lame comment a thousand times each: "Hey, what's the 'T' (or) 'M' stand for?" (guffaw, guffaw). Brilliant. But, in my opinion, bobbers are one of the few things god (or whomever it was that started this mess) got right. And if for some reason you happen to be a female and you're reading this, and you still find yourself offended, then take this short test, please: reach up, grab a couple of handfuls (doesn't matter how much is there, never did) and then tell me I'm wrong about any of this. Of course, the next best thing god (or whomever) got right was his creation of cleavage—any amount works.

THE LIST

- With the successful transfer of the mysterious, black attaché case the safety and security of the free world remains intact.
- Being paid as a National Security Agent is money well-earned.
- Being freezy-ass cold sucks.
- Air Force pilots have it all.
- The war sucks.
- MP's can be scary, or not.
- Corvair is not my car of choice.
- Making fake coins: genius.
- Spanish drivers don't really drive like old people fuck—just when it's foggy.
- One-eyed sheep flockers are actually kind of cool if you really think about it.
- 'Sheep Flocker'
- Being attacked by a mob of angry men can be just a little exhilarating.
- Puking on your gym bag is not a good thing, but on the bright side, puking on your gym bag when it's zipped shut, is better.
- Flaming cars: not good.
- Seeing a tough-ass sergeant cry can really affect your personal outlook on the world.
- Eating a turkey leg in bed: bad idea.
- Being told you're some kind of hero, even though you do your best to deny the accolade—advantage and disadvantage, at the same time.
- Trying to tell the truth—always a good approach.
- Getting a date with a junior because of the whole 'hero' thing—call it luck.

- Being tabbed as a 'hero,' even when you weren't *really* a hero, is not such a bad thing when you consider that so many men throughout history that were tabbed as heroes, weren't really heroes, they just happened to be in the right place at the right time but, that said, I'm convinced that every woman in history who was ever tabbed as a hero was no doubt the genuine article.
- Having to wait five days before experiencing my date with the junior—the reason why god (or whomever) invented bars of Safeguard soap.
- Getting offered a job that will give me nine extra bucks a week (which could have had something to do with that whole hero thing, not sure)—good.

I made it home after some meandering. I got up to The Circle, then decided to go down the street to the Low Road and walk up to the front gate then down the High Road to my house. Royal Oaks was the best place to take a walk, especially if you wanted to clear your head or make a list.

When I walked in the door, it was almost 9:00. My father was already in bed as he had to leave for work around six in the morning, but my mother was still up, sitting in her chair in the front room writing something in one of her steno notebooks—the woman could go through five or six of these, front and back pages, in a month—that whole "list" thing.

"Ah, there you are," she said, as I walked in the door. "Did you know that after you left we got about a dozen phone calls about you?" I told her I wouldn't know about that.

"Well, apparently you had yourself quite a day, no?" she said. I told her it was just one of those kinds of days. So then I asked her who had called and she held out her notebook to me.

"A lot of people. Here, look, I made a list," she said. So I asked her if Alverez called and she said, "He's on the list. I think he's number three or four."

I took the notebook from her and scanned the list she'd made. Alverez's name was there, as was Sergio's, for some strange reason, and my basketball coach's. I didn't recognize anyone else's name.

"Everyone wanted to know if you were okay," she said. My mother had a concerned look on her face, but not too much of a concerned look because I was standing right there in front of her and she could see I was perfectly fine. Right then, my sister and two of her friends, came through the front door. My sister looked at me from the hallway and just shook her head.

"I heard about you, ya crazy little shit," was all she said to me. She was a senior. She could get away with some stuff that I couldn't get away with yet, like cussing around our parents, not that she did that a lot. I think she and her friends were a little bit drunk as well. My sister, who was quite a looker herself, hung out with some of our school's most gorgeous girls (big boobs opened doors). These girls would come over to our place now and again and I always made sure to let my presence be known. They'd flirt with me and tousle my hair, you know, just to be friendly and all, but this one time, at a teen dance out at the base, when one of my sister's boyfriends went to the can, I asked her if she wanted to dance a slow dance with me (no bump and grind, just a dance) and she agreed. When the song ended, my sister's friend, who was also a senior, whispered to me, "You know, when you're a senior, you and your friends will be running this school like we are now." I told her that that sounded like something to look forward to. Then she said, "Don't fuck it up for those of us who were seniors before you." Then she kissed my cheek and went back to sit with her boyfriend. Unreal. It didn't dawn on me what she was getting at until almost two years later.

Going to school at Torrejon/Madrid was special and deserved special consideration. Special care. My sister's friend had really nice lips. The kiss she planted on my cheek was warm and sincere. I had no idea it would last for nearly four decades.

So, my sister comes in, says what she says, then goes down the hallway to her bedroom to get some money or something and her two friends are standing there giggling between themselves. Then my sister comes back and pokes her head into the front room. "Bye, Mom, we're going into Madrid," she said.

"Curfew is 2:00. Don't forget that the last bus from Plaza Castilla is at 1:15," my mother said.

Then my sister and her friends were gone. God (or whomever), how I couldn't wait to be a senior.

Then my mother said, "Have a seat." So I did, and for the next hour I tell her about my day. The whole time I'm talking my mother is writing stuff down. Genius.

Chapter 8: Working Men

On Wednesday, we had our second JV basketball practice at 8:00 am again at the base gym. No hitchhiking drama this time. I caught a ride with my father's car pool group. One of the guys was still on vacation so I got his seat.

I had called Alverez back on Monday and had gone down to the Teen Center to sign the work papers for Sgt. Slater and he gave us each a key to the place. The Teen Center closed at 8 pm each night except Fridays and Saturdays (10 pm, unless there was a teen dance), so we could pick any two days to put in our three hours each of cleaning time. Alverez and I decided on early Sunday mornings (the Teen Center opened at 11 am) and Wednesday nights after closing. Slater showed us the 'To Do' list that was necessary to keep the place up to military code and the janitor's closet where all the cleaning supplies were kept. He casually warned us to expect a few 'surprises,' as he called them. I asked him what he meant by surprises and all he said was, "You'll see." But Alverez and I were working men now and we were already planning what to do with our new-found wealth. So, Wednesday night would be our first official janitorial duty. Alverez and I were cautiously excited, though Sgt. Slater had sufficiently spooked us both.

My father's car pool dropped me off at the Flight Line Cafeteria a few minutes before 7 am. He gave me a couple of dollars and told me that it might be best if I went straight to the gym after I ate. I told him he could count on it. Interesting thing is, my father never gave me money. If I needed money for something, like a new gym bag, or if it's Friday, when I got my weekly allowance ($3), it always came from my mother. I don't know what compelled my father to lay a couple of breakfast bucks on me and I didn't ask. It could have been one of those 'bonding' moments, I'm guessing— something just between us guys.

Basketball practice was another hairy-assed bitch. I was just getting over the soreness in my legs from all the goddamn Turkey Trots we had to do on Sunday and Coach hits us with nearly as many during our second practice. Other than the conditioning, most of our practice was spent on fundamentals. Coach would sit in the bleachers watching us and writing shit down on his clipboard (list!), and from time to time, blowing his whistle to change from one drill to another. Fundamentals, fundamentals, fundamentals. Then he came out of the bleachers and showed us the proper way, with the help of his exquisitely-drawn diagrams, to execute a full-court press, a half-court trap, how to break a full-court press and a half-court trap, a couple variations of pick-and-roll, and then three plays he had diagrammed for when we were on offense.

After our last round of Turkey Trots, there were still 20 minutes remaining of our three-hour practice. We were all expecting another chit-chat session with Coach, but he surprised us. For the last 20 minutes, we were going to play full-court, five-on-five, rat ball so Coach could analyze how much we'd learned. We had twelve guys on our team. The two players on the sideline only had to sit out for one minute then got to pick which player on the court to replace. No one would be off the court for more than five minutes during the game—non-stop, no foul shots, full speed. Coach would yell out one of the three play numbers to whichever team had the ball and that team had to try to execute it. It didn't matter to Coach if the players on defense knew what play was being run, Coach wanted it to be run anyway. I was dog-ass tired after the first practice we had, but I thought I was gonna faint dead away before the end of this one. But, I'll admit, it was fun.

When the big, screen-covered clock on the wall high above the basketball court hit 11:00, Coach blew his whistle and told us all to lay down on the court to rest (gladly). Coach had an announcement. He had made his decision as to who his starting five, as of right then, would be. He told us that he'd come to his decision after much careful analysis and observation, even though we'd only had two practices thus far. He read the list off. I was on it and so was Alverez. When Coach said my name, I'd bet every player on the team, including Alverez, looked at me than looked at Coach like he'd lost his mind.

But, here was the key to Coach's magic—this starting five he had selected would remain so, but at any time any other player wanted to challenge for one of the starting five positions, they could—they just had to say so. The starting five had to work their asses off to keep their starting five status and the other players had to work their asses off to try to take that status away. A perfect ploy, a perfect working condition, everybody works to improve. Nothing, throughout the entire season, was carved in stone. Everybody would work as hard as they could. Coach was one sly, smart, son-of-a-bitchin' genius, if you ask me. From that moment forward, until the end of the season our practices were even more spirited and competitive. For a bunch of 15- and 16 year-olds, we had more than our share of temper flare-ups, name-calling and excessive elbows, but no actual fights. Coach wouldn't tolerate fisticuffs, for any reason, on or off the court. We were teammates, first and foremost, and that fact was to be remembered at all times. We were a self-policing, miscreant band of potty-mouthed post-pubescents, with only one objective—to be competitive.

In the locker room after practice, I overheard much in regard to my sudden good fortune, but I let them slide. I was as screwed up about this as anyone. Just as I left the gym, coach took me aside.

"You're probably wondering why I put you on the starting five," he said. Duh. I told him I was.

"It's simple. Your endurance. Nothing more." I told him I didn't quite follow.

"You recuperate quicker than anyone else. Your ability to keep going, full speed, is your best asset." So I told him, thanks, I guess.

Coach responded. "Your job is to make those players on the bench keep up with you, and to make them come after you, to challenge you." Then he smiled. "Now, we both know you're not one of the best five players on this team." True, I was thinking, there were at least six players who could shoot better than I could. Then coach said, "But no one seems to want this more than you do. Don't let my decision make me look foolish, okay?" So I told him I'd do my best. The man was a smooth manipulator, hands down. Then I asked him just what my actual role on the starting five would be.

"To pay attention," Coach said, and he left me standing there like a stump, wondering what the hell he meant.

Right then Alverez came out of the gym and we began walking toward the hitchhiking stands. We walked for a few moments in silence, then Alverez said, "I can't believe I'm on the starting five." Alverez was 5' 11" tall. I was only 5' 8". He was a shoo-in to start—everyone accepted this fact from the beginning. But, for him to say what he did somehow lifted a huge weight off my head. I determined right then that, when you're 15- or 16-years old, being surprised must be a daily occurrence or something—that whole, 'People will work for a living but die for recognition' thing. But, some people will sell their souls to *keep* their recognition. I began wondering right then where I'd fit, if anywhere, into all of this.

That night, Alverez and I got down to the Teen Center right at 8:00 pm—our first night of janitorial duty. Sgt. Slater was just about to lock the doors when we walked in. He'd left the cleaning list on a table for us to check stuff off.

"You guys can play the juke box as loud as you like [movies in the theatre above the Teen Center only ran Friday through Sunday]. Just be doubly sure you lock up when you leave," Slater said. "You guys know where everything is." Alverez and I were ready to go, but then Slater paused.

"You know, the last six people who had this job all quit on me. Of course, they were volunteers," Slater said. "At least you guys will get paid. I've had to do most of the cleaning myself for the past month, but I'm afraid I haven't had much time to do any real cleaning for over a week with all the Christmas break stuff going on, you know?" And I'm thinking, 'How bad could it be?'

Then Sgt. Slater said, "I hope you two boys decide to stick around. I really could use the help." Sgt. Slater's face was totally sincere. "See you guys later," he said as he left. Alverez and I began putting games away and stacking chairs on tables to sweep and mop the large, lower deck dance floor with Stevie Wonder's

'Superstition' rattling all the locks on the doors and the windows.

Now, janitorial service is an honorable profession, in my book. It takes a *very* special mindset to clean up the messes left behind by perfect strangers. One never looks at, nor thinks about, the conditions of a public restroom. You do your business, then get out. But everyone on the planet should have to clean a public restroom for at least a month during their lifetime if they truly want to comprehend the nature of humankind. And there's a certain skill to sanitizing—don't let anyone tell you differently. My best friend's father, back in eastern Oregon (Darren's, my friend who wanted to limit himself to saying, 'fuck' just 10 times a day) was the head custodian at the high school and everyone loved him. As a matter of fact, after I went back to The World to college, two years later, my first work study job was as a janitor in an off-campus art school and gallery. Hard work, but gratifying work, and if anyone tells you that being a janitor is a 'loser's' job then just tell them to make the loser's job easier by not pissing on the floor.

So, once Alverez and I finished sweeping and mopping the lower deck, as well as the upper deck portion where the two entrances were, we'd only been there a little more than an hour and thought how we were making great time. The last things to clean were the boys' and girls' bathrooms...the 'surprises' Sgt. Slater spoke of.

Alverez took the girls' bathroom and I took the boys'. Neither of us were in either bathroom for more than a couple of seconds before backing right back out again. We stood there, just looking at each other for a few seconds. Alverez's caramel-brown skin had gone four shades lighter and, by his expression, I knew my face had gone as pasty as the inside of an éclair.

Now, I've mentioned the 'puke pits of hell'—think of

THE WORLD, BOOK ONE

the worst campground outhouse there ever was, multiply it by ten and take away any kind of ventilation (both bathrooms had windows that had been painted shut by good old-fashioned military-issue lead paint) and you'd have one tenth of an idea as to what we experienced.

All over the ceiling in the boys' bathroom were weeks-old, once soggy, now dried, wads of toilet paper that had been thrown up and stuck to it. From the sheer quantity, and the various levels of deterioration of the wads, it was apparent that this activity had gone on for some time. I mean, goddam, who looks at the ceiling when they walk into a restroom unless they're assigned to clean it? Then we found that some kid had taken a crap in one of the two wall urinals. The steam radiator, on the far wall, was covered in what looked like spit, while someone was consuming a Hershey bar, not to mention the dried green globs from someone's bout with influenza. The floor was literally covered in piss and in the corners, was a crystallized, bright yellow crust, a quarter of an inch thick. The two sinks looked like someone had dyed their hair in them (reddish-brown) and on top of the color was a crop of fine, transparent fuzz in full growth mode. At least 50 boogers had been smeared on the two mirrors. The boys' bathroom had two toilet stalls. Alverez and I, having both suppressed the desire to blow chunks, each took a stall door and opened them at the same time. Both toilets were loaded to the max, and in one stall, someone had left poopy toilet paper stuck to the back of the stall door. Nice touch. On three, Alverez and I flushed the toilets with our feet and ran out of the room.

On to the girls' bathroom. The first things that were evident upon opening the girls' bathroom door were the three mirrors above the sinks. One of the mirrors was covered in a still-glistening, brown smear that someone had finger-painted, "77 Rules" in. The second mirror had lipstick graffiti written all over it, but the third mirror was the one that set Alverez and I back—someone had slapped a used Kotex pad to the mirror and made sure it stuck. This had to be some kind of competition. Two of the three sinks were clogged and filled to the point of overflowing. There were three toilet stalls in the girls' bathroom. One stall was virtually pristine but the other two had overflowing toilets with bits and pieces of whatever one could imagine collected all around on the floors, including a half dozen tampons that had swelled up and discolored and looked like corndogs. These toilets we didn't dare flush. Alverez and I needed a plan.

Fortunately, Alverez had spotted that both bathrooms had floor drains, but due to the tilt of the floor in the boys' bathroom, any liquids on the floor ran to the corners rather than to the drain. We filled a bucket with water from the big basin in the janitor's closet and poured it into both drains to make sure they still worked. Success—both drains flowed freely. We had a plan.

We found an old 50' garden hose underneath the big basin that had a brass spray nozzle attached to one end. We cranked the hot water tap all the way and began blasting the bathrooms top to bottom. We emptied a half-gallon of bleach onto each bathroom floor and sprayed and mopped and scooped until the hot water ran out, then continued spraying with cold water and more bleach. I took apart a wire hanger and pulled out everything I could that was clogging the two toilets in the girls' bathroom. I found a pair of socks and a training bra in one toilet and in the other toilet was a green, wool scarf that must have looked nice at one time. Both toilets flushed freely after that. What Alverez and I were doing was ridiculous and absurd. This was beyond 'out of control.' We got there at 8:00 pm and didn't leave until almost 2:00 am. We were gonna make sure Sgt. Slater put us down for the extra three hours.

While it was very apparent that Slater had totally avoided the Teen Center bathrooms for quite some time, I didn't know if I could pick which group, boys or girls, should have taken the 'gross-out' award—but somehow we were going to have to figure out how this sort of behavior would come to a screeching halt. And, shit, I was starting to think like someone's dad. I mean, seriously, we had to use an old snow shovel that we found in the janitor's closet to scrape the toilet paper wads off the ceiling in the boys' bathroom. Unreal.

Alverez and I locked up the Teen Center and began walking home. We started up the long hill to the High Road then took the shortcut path off the road that ran through a deeply, rain-rutted field that came out right next to the back wall of the swimming pool. We walked in silence until we came up to the High Road once more. I have no idea what Alverez was thinking as we walked. Hell, I wasn't even sure if I knew what I was thinking. At this point, all I could smell was bleach. Then Alverez stopped beneath a streetlight and turned and looked at me. He took a second to form his sentence, then he said, "If I ever see another goddam Kotex or a tampon again for the rest of my entire lifetime, I'm gonna slit my fucking wrists, you know?"

I doubt I had ever laughed that hard before or since in my life. Tears, I tell you, lots of them. Together we had stared down an enemy of overwhelming proportions and had come out victorious.

"It's too bad *we're* not volunteers because I'd fucking quit." I was so ready to pee my pants I had to relieve myself on the swimming pool wall.

Just before Alverez and I separated at The Circle (he lived on the Low Road) he said, "I can't believe I made the starting five." I told him I couldn't believe I'd made it either.

"Damn that," Alverez said. "I'm gonna go home and

take a fucking shower."

The next afternoon Alverez and I went down to the Teen Center and gave Sgt. Slater a blow by blow of what we had to deal with the night before. Slater listened carefully and kept nodding his head. No doubt our frustrations came through loud and clear (snow shovel—ceiling, etc.).

"I didn't sign up for *this* shit," Alverez said. Sgt. Slater took everything in, then he shook both of our hands.

"You guys are the best, you know that?" Slater said, "and to show you how good I think you guys are, I'm gonna reveal something that is totally off the books and could hang my ass from the highest tree, you know?"

Sgt. Slater was suddenly in a deadly serious mood. He shuffled a couple of papers on his table then motioned for Alverez and I to lean in so as to speak privately. Of course, we leaned in.

"What you boys need to know is that the funds I was able to allocate for your employment are National Defense funds," he whispered. He paused and looked us both directly in the eyes, first me, then Alverez. "National Defense funds," he repeated slowly.

Then Alverez and I looked at each other like, 'So fucking what?'

Slater caught the exchange. He said, "Do you have any idea how many swinging dicks I had to bullshit to get you two guys a measly six hours of pay a week, each, for a measly buck-fifty an hour?" We shook our heads, no. Slater was getting just a little bit peeved.

"Over two dozen, boys, two dozen. I kissed a lot of white, brass ass to get this for you," he said. Then he said, "These funds you're getting were *originally* meant for bombs, armaments, bullets—shit, even first-aid kits for our guys over in Viet-fucking-Nam—but I got them for *you*. Now, you think about that for a fucking minute."

I don't know what Alverez was thinking, but I started thinking about all the caskets I saw being stacked up like so much cordwood off the transport jet and thought for a second that I was either gonna start to cry or start singing the Star Spangled Banner. Then it hit me—we were responsible for cleaning a relaxation facility for the dependents of personnel in a housing area of a strategic, tactical air field that supplied necessities to the soldiers engaged in battle to keep our country free—or something like that. It made perfect sense. But, I didn't say a word. I looked at Alverez and he was a little stunned by what Sgt. Slater had just revealed. Alverez's hands were shaking a bit.

"So, here's the deal," Slater said, "you don't say a word about what I'm about to do and I won't mention your mutiny and impropriety for demanding unauthorized overtime pay to the higher-ups. Deal?" Alverez and I both shook our heads up and down vigorously. Then Sgt. Slater took his wallet out of his back pocket and gave us each a five-dollar bill. Then he put his finger to his lips.

"Shhhh….." he said. "Now, get out of here before I change my mind." Could Alverez and I have boogied out of the Teen Center any faster? I doubt it.

Chapter 9: New Year's Eve

I bet I combed and re-combed my hair at least eight times between 9:00 pm and 9:45. I'd taken care of every visible zit and then made triple sure that I didn't have any bleeders. I brushed my teeth at least five times as well. I smeared what I thought to be the proper amount of Canoe cologne on, not too subtle not too overwhelming, and managed to get some in my eye which was definitely no fun.

The junior girl with the fur skirt was babysitting at a quad-plex about three-quarters of the way down to the back entrance of Royal Oaks on the Low Road. Her note on the piece of the popcorn bag, which I'd reread maybe 100 times, said to make sure I got there *after* 10:00 pm. So, I calculated my walking distance to make sure I'd arrive around 10 minutes after 10:00. I figured it would be best if I didn't appear too eager, you know—that, for all appearance's sake, I'd give her the impression that this kind of tryst happened to me all the time. Oh, *hell* yeah. Call me Casa-fucking-nova. The last five minutes before I set out were the longest five minutes in recorded history.

It had started snowing about an hour before I began walking toward the back gate. A light and delicate kind of snow that was just beginning to stick to the grass, the trees and the weeds. There was no wind and the small flakes were coming straight down. A car drove by and a man an woman inside waved at me so I waved back. Then another approached and the passenger, a middle-aged women, rolled down her window.

"Happy New Year, hero," she said. So I told her that I hoped it would be and the same to her. One thing about Royal Oaks was that there were over 200 quad-plexes and then there were the six or seven single-unit homes. That meant over 800 families—and kids...shit-o-rover, lots of kids. Usually, if you walked from the front gate to the back entrance you could spend half your damn time waving at people. It was more so in the summer, or when the weather was warm, because there were always people looking out their big front windows, which every unit had, or they were out on their terraces, in their yards, walking their dogs, riding bikes, driving around— you could get 'waver's cramp' by the time you walked down to The Circle. In Royal Oaks you waved as a sign of familiarity—we were all in this together and waving merely established that *visual* familiarity with each other. No way could a person know everyone in Royal Oaks. Besides, families were always coming and going—hello/goodbye. Back in eastern Oregon, in my home town, people would wave because they *did* know you. They practically knew everything about you. That was one of the reasons my father put in for a transfer. Too many problems because of other people knowing too much. Well, that and the whole excessive alcohol consumption thing. So many plusses and minuses to living in a small town. But, waving *was* important in my home town. You'd wave because you actually *saw* someone. A wave in eastern Oregon meant, "I know you, and you're not alone." A wave in Royal Oaks meant, "I may not know you, but I know you're one of us."

So, the lady in the car rolls her window up and they drive on. Yes, Happy New Year's. I intended to somehow send this year into history with a 'bang' of some kind.

Another thing about living in Royal Oaks back in the early seventies, and perhaps why there were always plenty of people waving at you, was because there was no television. Okay, there *was* television, but it was Spanish TV, which meant about only four or five hours of viewing a day—state-run TV with a couple hours of state-run propaganda, a state-run soap opera, complete with propaganda messages, which was a total hoot the couple of times I tried to watch it, and soccer. Soccer was easily the most watched programming, especially if the Spanish national team was playing.

Now, Royal Oaks and the air base dependants could have had some kind of cable system installed to bring in American TV stations, but the budget vote was between two things—American TV or a golf course built next to the base. The top brass voted in the golf course, naturally. This was shortly before we got there. I'll admit that I did miss television, somewhat, but most of what was on TV in eastern Oregon was pretty crappy. We only got two stations, and really, the only two things I really missed were watching pro football and 'Dark Shadows.'

One of the coolest things the overseas military brass *did* get right was their contract with NFL Films during the season. Every Friday night, at both movie showings, the first half hour was a recap film of all the NFL games from the previous Sunday and Monday nights. A full half hour of the slow motion ballet of grown men tearing each other's heads off. Pure heaven. The lines at the theatre for Friday night movies were always long during football season. People would slap down their money, watch the half hour battle, then usually about half of the people in the theatre would get up and leave, totally satiated, their football fix for the week complete.

There were a lot of different kinds of movies shown in the Royal Oaks theatre and at the base theatre, but there were certain *types* of movies that were shown more than others. Clint Eastwood westerns always played to a packed house, as did movies starring Charles Bronson, Vincent Price, Christopher Lee and Raquel Welch ('One Million Years B.C.'—saw it four times). Any Peter Sellers Pink Panther movie would stick around for a couple of weeks, as did any John Wayne picture—didn't matter what genre or what year—but the longest movie line there ever was at the Royal Oaks theatre was when the Dark Shadows movie 'House of Dark Shadows,' came in. One topic of conversation, that could always be started and then continued for hours, was Dark Shadows. Back in The World, our grade school let out at 3:00 pm. Every day I'd beat feet to get my fat little ass home to tune into Dark Shadows at 3:30 pm, usually with two or three buddies in tow. A half hour of Jonathan Frid and that creepy kid named David, made the whole tedious day spent at school worth it.

The line to get into the Dark Shadows movie went all the way over to the gym from the theatre. They held the movie over for three weeks which was still the record when I left to go back to The World. So, in all actuality, I didn't really miss television for the five years I lived in Spain. No TV meant a lot of waving to a lot of people and there was something very good about that.

The snow was still coming down fairly steadily when I got down to the Low Road from The Circle. I looked at the house numbers until I found the one where the junior said she'd be. It was an upstairs unit. I did my best to calm my breathing as I climbed each step.

I was halfway through my knock when the junior

yanked the door open. She was holding a sleeping baby that couldn't have been more than five months old. The baby was wearing a pink nightgown of some kind, so I figured it was girl. Then the junior opened the screen door and pulled me inside.

"You're late," she said. "Do you know what time it is? They've been gone for nearly half an hour. Did anyone see you?" She looked around outside briefly, then shut the door. So, I told her that she had said *not* to come until after 10:00, that I didn't know what time it was and that I didn't think anyone saw me because it was dark and also snowing.

"I know it's snowing," she said. Then she smiled and said, "Okay, look. Wait here. I'm gonna put the baby down, okay? Don't move." She was wearing one of those real fuzzy kinds of sweaters with a large turtleneck collar (turquoise) and, as luck would have it, she also had on the same skirt made of white fur. Blood was already beginning to drain from all other parts of my body. Her perfume was soft, musky and flowery. I could smell some kind of alcohol on her breath, which didn't surprise me. She *was* a junior, after all, and it *was* New Year's Eve and all.

When she came back, a couple of minutes later, she had a half bottle of champagne in her hand. She held the bottle out to me. "Want some?" she asked. I told her, thanks, but I couldn't because of my being on the basketball team and all (I said 'basketball team,' not 'JV basketball team' you'll notice).

"No biggie," she said. She took a drink and set the bottle on the floor. Then she grabbed me and we were kissing. Now, they don't call it 'tonsil hockey' for nothing. This girl had her tongue jammed so far down my throat, she was banging my uvula like a speed bag. I backed away for a second, to catch my breath, and then we started going at it again. Then she grabbed my hand

and put it on her boob. "Feel me up," she said, so I did and we kept on making out like a couple of yaks. Her bra underneath her sweater felt pretty padded, which I thought was odd considering the size of her bobbers and how she certainly didn't *need* any extra padding, but I keep feeling her up anyway, first with one hand, then with the other, then with both hands, while trying not to choke on her tongue.

Then she pulled away from me for a second and took a swig of her champagne. "How old are you?" she asked, so I told her I was 16. I lied. I wouldn't be 16 for another five months. "Good," she said. So, I asked her how old she was.

"Eighteen." So, I asked her how could she be 18 and only be a junior. "We moved around a lot when I was a kid and I got held back a couple of times," she said. It made perfect sense.

"Don't stop feeling me up," she said, "That really feels good." So I did what I was told. Then I asked her how long she'd been going to our high school. "I'm a junior," she said. She took my hands and put them behind her, on her butt. Her fur skirt was even softer than it looked. So, in the spirit of getting to know each other, when we stopped kissing and I could take a breath, I told her I didn't remember seeing her at all at school last year when I was a freshman.

"I was gone for the year, but then I came back," she said. I was going to ask her why she was gone, but then she reached her hand down to my crotch and felt my hard-on and said, "Oh, perfect. Lie down." I gave her what must have been an absolutely perfect 'confused dog' look. We were in the short entrance hallway that all the quad-plex homes had and standing on a plush red rug. So she then took off my winter coat and threw it on the floor and said, again, "Lie down on the floor. Just lie down. I've already taken off my panties." So I did.

Within seconds she'd unbuckled my belt, undid my jeans, and pulled my pants and my Fruit-of-The-Looms down around my ankles.

"Ah, there he is," she said, and pulled her fur skirt up to her hips and climbed on top of me. She quickly slid my dick up inside her which was wet, warm, soft and snuggly. She sat upright on top of me and started sort of rocking back and forth like a little kid on one of those mechanical horses or elephants that I'd see just outside the entrance of a supermarket back in The World—5¢ a ride. I'd already ejected once just as soon as she'd slipped me inside her. The junior closed her eyes and kept rocking back and forth and I kept playing with her bobbers over her soft sweater. Then she put her right hand underneath the front of her skirt and began to rub herself, somewhere down there, slowly.

"Were you in the car when it was burning?" she asked, her eyes still closed. I told her I was. "Oh, god," she said, then she groaned. She started rubbing herself a little faster.

"Were you really attacked by gypsies?" she asked and I told her that I didn't really know if they were gypsies or not, but yeah, I was attacked and there were probably 50 of them. "Oh, god, oh, god," she said, and groaned again.

"Guns?" she asked, and I told her, no, they had rocks and sticks. "Oh, my god, my god," she said. The junior was rocking faster and then going up and down and rubbing herself between her legs so vigorously that I thought for sure her fur skirt was gonna start smoldering. She was breathing really heavily by now. In a single move, with one hand, she pulled her sweater off over her head and I could see that, indeed, her bra had some kind of extra padding. She put my hands back on her boobs. "Feel me. Feel me hard," she said, so I did what I was told. "My boobies are so sensitive right now. Squeeze them," she demanded. So I squeezed.

Then she said, "Oh, screw it, wait a sec." She took her hand out from underneath her skirt, unhooked her bra in the back and took it off. I was sure I was gonna pass right out. Her bobbers were firm and poked straight out. Her areolas were as big as Kennedy half-dollars and her nipples were dark and erect and as big as an eraser on a Ticonderoga #2 pencil.

The junior put her hand back underneath her skirt and began rubbing herself again.

"Squeeze my boobies," she said, her eyes closed once again. So I did, and when I did, her boobs squirted at me. Okay...hold the phone. They *squirted* at me. She kept her eyes closed and continued rocking and rubbing and bouncing.

"Now," she said, quite breathlessly, "Last question. Could you have died?" And I told her, yes, absolutely, and it was a good thing that Murphy had a gun.

"A gun? That other guy with you had a gun?" she asked. Man, did I not have a clue as to just what was happening. "Oh, my god," she continued, "Oh, my ever loving, breathing god!" And with that she moved up and down and back and forth, very fast, four or five more times, then collapsed on top of me groaning into my neck and holding my head tightly as wave after wave of shaking came over her. We stayed like that, on the rug, on the floor, for nearly five minutes.

Finally, I nudged her, because I thought she might have gone to sleep or something, you know. She sat upright and put her bra back on. I took one more good look at her boobs which made her smile.

"Bet you didn't do this with that officer's wife, huh?" she said. I started to say something about that, but then she said, "No, no, don't tell me. I don't want to know." She got off of me, leaned up again the wall, and took a long swig off of her champagne bottle. She looked at me then took a second swallow. "You sure you don't want some? It's New Year's Eve, ya know?" I told her, thanks, but I'd better not. In actuality, I was already loopy from her tongue. "Sit up," she said. So I did.

"Scoot over, closer to me," she said. So I did. "Put your fingers inside me. Two fingers. Move them slowly," she said. She sat back against the wall with her legs propped up sort of like a frog and I slid my fingers up inside her like she asked. "Slowly. Yes, like that," she said, as I began to move my fingers in and out slowly. She stayed still like that for a moment with her eyes closed. Then she said, "You have a really nice touch, you know that?" I didn't say anything, not that I knew what the hell I was supposed to say.

Then the junior said, "C'mere. Get closer." So I scooted over closer to her and she began pulling gently on my still slippery, half-hard dick and in a matter of seconds I was fully erect again.

"Lie down again," she said. So, I did and she climbed on top of me once more. I asked her if she wasn't worried about waking up the baby and she said she wasn't and said the baby would sleep for at least a couple of hours, so I asked her if she could be sure and she said, "Of course, I'm sure. She's my baby."

Then she started rocking back and forth and up and down again and said, between breaths, "Tell me about Murphy's gun." So I did and she went through her whole, 'oh, god, oh, god, shiver, shiver, shake, shake and collapse thing' and I shot off whatever I had left in me and then she stopped. She held on to me tightly with her face crammed into my neck. Then she whispered something, not to me, but no doubt to herself. She said something like, "Boy, howdy, I needed that," but I wasn't positive because it was muffled, what with her face buried in my neck and all. After a couple of minutes she got off, stood up and handed me my coat. I pulled my underwear and pants up, stood up and put my coat on. She looked at my shirt and giggled. "Sorry about your shirt," she said. "Try explaining *that* to your mom."

And then the junior gave me the softest of kisses on my lips and said, "Now, we're not gonna be telling a bunch of people about this, are we? None of our little basketball buddies or our other girlfriends, right?" I told her I swore I wouldn't say anything to anyone.

"Good," she said, "but, just so's you know, my father's a double black belt and if you *do* say anything to anyone, well, you know, it just wouldn't be very good. I mean, you know how rumors are, and all, around here." Boy, did I. So, I told her I promised. Then she opened the door and I walked outside.

"See you around some time, maybe.....eh, hero?" she said, and I told her, yeah, maybe, and maybe we could..., but then she shut the door, gently, in my face.

I started walking home. It was still snowing, but for some reason it all looked a whole lot different now.

Chapter 10

Deflowered. De-cherried. De-virginized. Pitted. Released of innocence—and no one to tell due to the threat of a pair of razor-claws cutting me up into itty-bitty pieces. I was now in a new kind of agony. The best thing about having an experience is being able to turn it into a *shared* experience with a close confidant or, actually, with anyone who will listen. Twice on New Year's Day my mother put her palm on my forehead to see if I was running a fever or something.

"You look tired. Are you sure you're okay?" my mother asked me. So I told her I might be a little tired. One time my father caught my eye, then just winked at me. Shit. How'd he know? Or did he know? It was apparent he'd figured something out. Though he never said anything, I did notice that he had a little bit of bounce in his step. Once, later in the afternoon, he and my mother were in the kitchen whispering, thinking that I was out of earshot, and I heard my mother say, in just above a whisper, "Oh, my god, are you sure?" and my father then *shushing* her.

All the snow had melted and I thought about maybe going for a walk or something but the sun was shining and there were others all out and about wandering aimlessly around saying, "Happy New Year," and "Isn't it a glorious day?" and all that other happy crap, so I decided I'd just hole up in my bedroom with the new stereo I got for Christmas and listen to my sister's 'Rare Earth In Concert' album, which is, and will remain, the greatest live rock and roll concert recording of all time (though Deep Purple's, 'Made In Japan' runs as close a second as there ever could be when it came out a year later, and then a couple of years after that, the live version of Grand Funk called, 'Caught in the Act,' especially the song, 'Closer to Home/I'm Your Captain'). I already practically had Rare Earth memorized, but still it was comforting to know I could connect with *someone*, mentally, spiritually, about my experience, because I was in some kind of goddam misery. Unreal.

Now, I listen to a lot of Motown, but listening to the sweet, hormone-laden, slow, bump-and-grind songs of Marvin Gaye, The Temptations, The Four Tops, or any of these artists, would have driven the stake of unshared experience through my devilish heart permanently. Okay, I know what you're thinking. Rare Earth *was* a Motown recording artist, but they weren't really soul, at least not Black soul, sort of white soul, maybe, but more rock and roll and, without a doubt, the best of genius contract-signing ever by Barry Gordy.

Is it possible to feel exhilarated and depressed at the same time? What sort of clinical terms could be assigned to my symptoms? I got laid. No, not laid, but *laid*, like a transport jet pilot laid, the laying-laid of any school boy's most intense, possible, carnal dream kind of laid. Okay. *Get a grip*, I kept telling myself all damn day. Now it's history. Time to move on. Boo-fucking-hoo, and woe is me and my fabulous good fortune. The rest of my day was destined to be spent just lounging about (more like wallowing about) and re-visualizing the night before.

Then I got an idea. The junior said she'd been going to our high school from the time she started high school. At least that's how I interpreted what she'd said. And she said she wasn't at the school all of my freshman year, which meant she was there, here, the year *before*, which would have been my *first* year in Spain, 1969-70. Genius. I got off of my ass and went into my sister's bedroom to find her yearbooks. I knew she had them hidden from my parents in a box in the back of her closet—I knew where all my sister's hidden shit was. If I ever wanted to make a few bucks, if my sister ever *had* a few bucks, which she didn't, I could do well with a bit of blackmail, but you really can't blackmail someone if you know they don't have any money. Something I deemed worthy of filing away with that whole 'sheep flockers' thing, for future reference.

So, I find her yearbook and take it back to my room and begin looking through it. I look through the freshmen pictures, but don't see any girl who looks like the junior. I keep looking. Nothing. I go into the kitchen and grab myself a Fanta Naranja (Spanish orange soda pop) and go back to my room. I search page by page for over an hour. Still nothing. I start over. The phone rings. My mother knocks on my door. It's Alverez on the phone. I tell her to tell him that I'm doing something and that I'll call him back. I keep looking. I look at sports. Nothing. I look at the drill team and cheerleader pages. Still nothing. For some reason, I have *got* to know what this girl's name is. I mean, the very least that any young man deserves is to know the name of the girl or woman who was responsible for their graduation into non-virgin status, right? It only seemed fair.

I should have asked her what her name was. I didn't. I don't know why. Maybe I didn't want to know, you know? Maybe, at the time, I just got all caught up in the whole mysterious moment, that whole mysterious stranger bullshit stuff and thought myself to be so aloof that something like this could happen to me and I could be just fine and dandy with whatever came next. Crap. I could really have snuck a beer from the kitchen right about then to try and calm my nerves. Or better yet, I could have used a couple of shots of St. Angelo's house liquor, but I knew I needed to stay focused. I needed to know her name. At the very least, if I saw her at school on Monday and she decided, because of our age difference, or our responsibility differences, that it was in her best interest to totally ignore me, then I probably wouldn't fall apart right there in front of the whole goddam school, which wouldn't be a good thing because I *am* on the JV basketball team's starting five and all. But the least I could garner from this was her name. You know, a name, because maybe we could just talk—not about *that*—but maybe just talk about stuff, anything, it wouldn't matter. Maybe we could be friends, as much as two people *can* be friends.

And then I found her. It was the only picture of her in the whole yearbook—a kind of inner-school club picture on the lower left side of the page—Future Accountants of America. I'd never heard of this club. I think it was disbanded or something. There were only four people in the picture—some guy wearing a Nehru shirt, a girl with big glasses, the junior wearing a large coat and, oddly enough, my JV basketball coach. A club. She was two years younger, and I'll admit, a little bit mousy looking. Her hair was shorter and bit darker. Her bobbers were smaller (I can only assume based on the coat she was wearing), but she was only a freshman then. And she was smiling. She, the guy, the other girl, and Coach were all smiling. They were standing beside our school's brick entrance sign that read, 'Torrejon High School— Home of the Knights,' looking so proud, so confident, so self-assured. And a year later she's 'in trouble,' so to speak, and goes back to The World to give birth because military personnel have a strong tendency to want to hide their histories, their humiliations, if one wanted to call it that, but she then comes back to Spain to live with her parents and get her high school diploma but no longer *fits in* because she has a daughter of her own now (pink nightgown) and what high school guy would want to hang out with a high school girl who already has a kid, and I'm guessing that she's fully aware of this, so to save any awkward complications, she rejects any and all askers until they no longer ask and now she has her casual acquaintances and her drill team stuff and no doubt the only people who are truly aware of what's happened to her are a couple of friends and a couple of administrators and maybe a teacher or two. Shit. This was deep. So much to consider, because, for some whacked-out, crazy goddam reason, she chose me to help her come back out of her shell, if only for an hour or so.

I look at the names beneath the photo and there it is. Now, I know. I have a name to go with the junior's face. And I can remember that name for as long as I live. I can remind myself that it wasn't love, but it was something special that we shared—something that made her feel good, and made me feel good, and felt perfect in its moment, and not the least bit awkward like so many experiences like this truly are—the fumbling, the blubbering, the guilt. But, damn—I couldn't tell anyone and it was killing me. But, now I knew her name, and someday I hoped to have the chance to say it...*to* her.

Okay. A bit overboard here with the emotional firestorm, but being a gentleman about this whole kiss-and-don't-tell crap wasn't going to be easy. I had to get a grip, but no way was I going to convince myself that it never happened. I fell asleep with my sister's yearbook that night and managed to sneak it back into my sister's secret hiding place the next morning without her knowing.

Chapter 11

On Sunday morning I started walking down to the Teen Center around 7:30 am. Alverez and I agreed to hook up on Sundays at The Circle and walk the rest of the way together. When I get to The Circle, Alverez is already standing there waiting.

"You're late," he said. "Do you know what time it is?" And I'm thinking, crap, I was just beginning to get comfortable with filing 'New Year's Eve' deep into the Rolodex in the back of my brain and he has to go and say what *she* said, "You're late. Do you know what time it is?" I had to fight like hell to quell the urge to spill my guts about the junior and my de-frocking.

"Where were you yesterday? You never returned my call." He was a bit miffed, I might add. So, I told him I was sorry about that but I was catching up on some reading.

"Reading what? School doesn't start until tomorrow." So, I told him never mind, and it didn't matter, and what did he want anyway?

"There was a dance at the Teen Center last night, numb-nuts, and you missed it. Everyone was wondering where you were." So I told him that of course everyone was wondering and I didn't know what happened but I had completely forgotten about the dance—very unlike me—'fool's names and fool's faces often found in public places,' as usual.

"Seriously, man. What are you, sick or something?" So, I decided to turn the conversation around and asked him what he did on New Year's Eve. I wanted to tell Alverez about the junior. I really did.

"Bunch of us went into Madrid. We did the whole grape-eating thing and were all crammed together like sardines." I told him it sounded like a lovely time. Then he asked, "What did *you* do?" and I told him, not much, just sort of hung out.

Alverez stopped walking and looked at me. "Bullshit, man," he said. "You went somewhere. Someone told me last night at the dance that they saw you around 10:00 walking in the snow down on the Low Road." So I asked him, what was the big deal about that?

"They said they could smell your cologne from a block away. What's her name?" he asked. So I told him it was no big deal and to just let it go.

"Well, fine. Suit yourself. Be all Mr. Secret Squirrel," Alverez said. "But if it were me, I'd damn sure tell *you*." And, boy-howdy, did I want to spill my guts, but the visual of having a finger-tip karate chop planted deep into my ribs and having one of my lungs pulled out was enough of a deterrent to keep me clammed up. So, I told him I was just walking—nothing more. I told him I was still thinking about being on the starting five and all, and that seemed to do the trick.

"Yeah," Alverez said, as we began walking again, "I hear that."

We got inside the Teen Center and the upper stage and dance floor looked like someone had dropped a bomb in the place—papers, wrappers, confetti, confetti streamers from those little popping things, spilled drinks—total mess. Alverez looked around the room and said, "It wasn't this bad when I was here. Seriously."

We got out the brooms, buckets of water and mops and began stacking chairs on the tables after we'd cleaned the tabletops which all seemed to be covered with sticky stuff. Alverez moved one table and stepped into a large, congealed pile of barf that looked like someone had consumed about a half a gallon of elbow macaroni salad. He jumped back and actually let out a scream. When I saw what it was, I nearly hurled both of my morning Pop Tarts.

Now, when Alverez screamed, it was funny—a pure and natural response to being grotesquely surprised. See, Alverez was a virtual master of sound effects. He could imitate any car, any make or model. One time he imitated Murphy's car—it was perfect. He could imitate any kind of aircraft the Air Force had to offer, as well as any make or model of helicopter. It was genius. And, after hearing it only once, Alverez could imitate any kind of weapon or explosion from any movie. Attending a Clint Eastwood western was always a hoot because right in the middle of one of Sergio Leone's dramatic close-ups, when he's trying to be all serious-like, Alverez would launch into a Gatling gun or some kind of cannon-type projectile. It always brought a laugh.

Alverez looked at me and then at the pile of barf and then at me again.

"Flip you for it," he said, all hopeful and all, but I told him no way—he found it, he had dibs. "Well, all right then, I get the boy's bathroom this time." Deal. It took us an hour and a half of sweeping and wiping to just get to the point of mopping the upper stage area and the lower main floor. Next to come were the bathrooms. Pure dread, I'm telling you.

Now, before I continue, I think it's fitting to bring up the subject of humans, Americans in particular, American dependents to be even more specific, and their unbelievable capacity to be pigs. I single out American dependents (in this case, the children of) for two reasons, 1) That's who Alverez and I were dealing with, and 2) Because of the nature of their fathers' or their mothers' engrained military work ethic. Being a pig at one's military workplace was never tolerated and more often than not, that attitude spilled over to the family residence as well as family members—usually—or, which seemed to be the case here, set the benchmark for rebellion. My sister's bedroom *always* looked like it was inhabited by a gaggle of badgers. My bedroom was always neat and tidy—perhaps a bit dusty from time to time, but neat and tidy. I've always thought that if one were to see another's private dwellings, then it would give one a good window into how the other person's brain worked.

The kids who came into the Teen Center were serious candidates for counseling, or at last some kind of weekly booster shot of gray matter. Now, I'm not saying that myself or my friends were without fault. I have no idea how much of a pig I was at the Teen Center, or anyplace else, before I became a janitor. Last autumn, after football season ended, a bunch of us came down here to a teen dance and someone had swiped a bottle of gin from their parents' liquor cabinet. Problem was, the only soda pop left in the Teen Center's vending machine was grape soda. Gin and grape soda—lovely combination. One of the girls that was with us, drank way too much of this stuff then politely projectile ralphed underneath our table all over my red, suede Converse low-tops. Oh, and for emphasis, her family's meal before attending the dance was spaghetti, with clam sauce. My shoes were filled but I wasn't giving them up. My socks were soaked so I took them off and left them somewhere in the Teen Center for whoever it was who cleaned up. And to clarify something—I never drank any alcoholic beverages while I was on any school sports team—

except when I was on the track team as a senior, which I'll explain later. *Between* sports was a different story, though. Play hard, party hard. One thing for certain, unlike so many others I knew, I never smoked pot, hash or did any other drugs. Never tempted to, either, for the obvious reason—the Guardia Civil.

So, I squished my way home in my puke-filled shoes. Just dandy. I washed them three times but ended up having to throw them away because when I tried to wear them, if my feet started to sweat just a smidge, I would still smell grape soda, gin, clams, garlic and stomach acid. Note to self—never buy suede Converse again.

When I entered the girls' bathroom, I was delighted to find that only *one* of the three toilets had overflowed and the residue had to have been Sangria by the sticky, acrid sweetness that covered over half the floor. Imagine being delighted that a toilet had overflowed because it was only *one* toilet that had overflowed. The mirrors and the sinks were surprisingly clean but there must have been over a dozen used or unused tampons stuck to the ceiling with their strings all hanging down.

In the boys' bathroom, Alverez discovered that only one of the two toilets had overflowed but on the floor in the stall, next to the toilet, was the slowly melting, soppy remains of what must have been about a 13" turd. A work of art, to be sure. In the other stall, Alverez found, on the toilet seat and the floor, what looked to be the results of four guys who'd jerked off, or one guy who had jerked off four times. The urinals and wash basins were fairly clean but one of the mirrors had been punched and there was glass everywhere. Alverez and I broke out the garden hose, the ammonia (ran out of bleach) and the snow shovel and were still finishing off the bathrooms when Slater came in.

I think Slater was as disappointed and disheartened as Alverez and I were. He did his best to stave off our complaints, but after Alverez said, "I don't goddam care if you goddam send the goddam MP's to my goddam house, I'm gonna goddam quit right goddam now!" (Alverez had a way with cursing when he was pissed.) It got Slater's attention and you could see the gears in Slater's brain begin clicking away.

"Boys," Slater said, "finish up here then disappear. Come back in an hour. I have a plan." He went to the locked arts and crafts cabinet and pulled out some pieces of sign board, stencils and magic markers, then sat at this table on the upper stage and began working. Alverez and I finished our work then went down to the small snack bar that was right behind the Teen Center.

Now, I don't want to brag, but I will confess to being the one who started the whole new way of eating French fries in Royal Oaks and at the air base. At least, no one was eating French fries this way until *after* I started eating French fries this way and then *everyone* was eating French fries this way. It was something I did at the Shoe String Drive-In in my home town back in The World. You'd get one of those little pink and white cardboard boats of French fries, go to the condiment bar where the mustard, ketchup, pickles and onions were kept, spread onions on your fries, then ketchup and salt, and you were good to go—practically a meal for fifty cents.

Now, I'm positive I couldn't have been the one who originated the idea of chopped or sliced onions on top of French fries, but I'm certain I was the one who brought the recipe to Spain. Alverez and I got two boats of fries each, with onions and ketchup, and a can of Coke— $1.25, and filling. There was one other variation to French fry consumption that I never witnessed until after I began doing it and that was dipping one's fries into tartar sauce. The only aspect of French fry eating that I did consistently, but never fully caught on, was eating

French fries with a fork instead of with my fingers. Even Alverez, with whom I shared many a meal during my five years in Spain, ate French fries with his fingers. He'd watch me eat my fries with a fork and say nothing, just shake his head at my oddball practice.

From the cafeteria, we wandered over to the gym to maybe shoot some baskets or something. There were a lot of players from different Royal Oaks league teams that were in our class that were playing three-on-three pick-up games. Alverez and I walked in like we were royalty—not because we had better overall skills than any of these guys (especially me), but because we had mustered up the courage to *try out* for the JV squad in front of about a third of the high school student body, knowing full well there was a chance we wouldn't make the squad (especially me). But these 'gym rats,' as they were called, of which I used to be one, were all playing their pick-up games and doing their best to ignore us 'big shots.' One major difference between being on a high school JV or varsity basketball squad and being on a Royal Oaks league team, was that the high school squads had full uniforms—jersey, shorts and socks, all matching—and if you were on a league team you just got a jersey or a T-shirt. Our JV uniforms were sweet, and they were brand new.

So, we went over to the opposite side of the gym where a bunch of pee-wee leaguers were trying to get a game organized and asked them if they wanted our help. Of course, these little guys all told us we could stick our help up our *asses*. Then they said, 'Corte tu bajo,' which meant, 'Cut you low,' (sort of), and came complete with a sideways hand-slashing motion.

Okay, so maybe Alverez and I weren't royalty. The little shits, anyway. To my credit I can say that I never picked on kids younger or smaller than me. Never. There were older and bigger kids in my neighborhood in my home town who seemed to make it their daily task to knock me around or flick me crap when I was growing up, so I knew what it felt like. Not that I didn't *want* to knock a few little kids' heads while I lived in Royal Oaks, the mouthy little clowns, but I never did it. Besides, one never knew if one of them wouldn't hold a major grudge for being picked on or knocked around by you and then confront you ten years later when they were 6'4" and 240 lbs. Then again, I didn't especially go out of my way to be nice to them, either. They were more satisfied with being smart asses to you, to show off in front of their little buddies. That said, I believe that the guff I took from these little punks that never resulted in a poke in their noses, may have contributed to their self-confidence toward pursuit of their future careers. You're welcome, and *corte tu bajo* yourselves, ya little fart-necks. (Unless, of course, your smart mouth helped to land you in prison to which I say, touché, bitch.)

After a little more than an hour, Alverez and I went back to the Teen Center. It was the last day of Christmas vacation and the place was full of kids of all ages. When we got there. Sgt. Slater was sitting at his large table on the upper stage, with his arms folded across his chest and sporting the biggest shit-eating grin of all time. When we walked in he flashed us his shiny gold teeth, obviously quite proud of his plan, so I asked him what was up.

"Stick around, boys. Should only be a few more minutes. I just finished putting up the new signs," he said.

"New signs?" asked Alverez.

"In the bathrooms," Slater said. "Go check 'em out."

Alverez and I went into the boys' bathroom and there, on the wall, next to the broken mirror, were the two signs Slater had made. The larger sign, in bold, black letters, read:

ANYONE CAUGHT MESSING UP
THIS BATHROOM WILL ANSWER
TO THE GUARDIA CIVIL!

The second, smaller sign read:

ANYONE WHO TURNS IN SOMEONE
WHO MESSES UP THIS BATHROOM
WILL GET A 1,000 PESETA REWARD!

Impressive signs, to be sure, but some kid had already wiped a fresh booger on the second, smaller sign. We went back out to Slater's table.

"Signs?" Alverez said. "That's it? You made a couple of lousy signs?"

"Wait for it," Slater grinned, "Just wait."

Of the two dozen or so tables that filled the lower dance floor of the Teen Center, all but a couple were full of game players, card players, puzzle makers, and kids working with construction paper, scissors, glitter and glue. There were at least a dozen juniors and seniors in the room playing cards, ping-pong, foosball, bumper pool, or just hanging out cutting up, cracking wise or playing grab ass. A typical Sunday, really. Three seniors from the varsity basketball team were there wearing their red and white lettermen's jackets and looking noble and studly. The last day of Christmas vacation was in full swing. Back in The World, the acknowledged babysitter had become television. In Royal Oaks, it was the Teen Center.

Then Sergio, the MP who picked up Murphy and I down the hill from Paracuellas, walked in the door and came over to Sgt. Slater. Slater was still grinning while the two men exchanged a 'soul' handshake.

"Man, are you sure about this?" Sergio asked Slater.

"Damn right I am," Slater said. "Go get them. Bring them in."

"Okay, okay," Sergio said. "It's your show. But just for the record, Sarge, I'm not totally onboard with this shit. Just so you know, okay?" Then Sergio looked over at me. "What the hell are *you* doing here?" I put my hands up to show I was as much in the dark as anyone.

"He works for me," Slater said. "Now, go get them."

Sergio shrugged and walked over to the entrance, stepped out, then waved to whoever was out there waiting to come in. Right then, the two Guardia Civil housing area patrol officers stepped inside the Teen Center.

Now, I've mentioned that the air base at Torrejon was pretty much a melting pot of just about every nationality on the planet—Blacks, Hispanics, Asians, Native Americans, South Americans, Europeans, whites—you name it—as multi-colored a population as there could ever have been in any one place. But, when the two Guardia Civil guys stepped into the Teen Center, you could actually see the different hues of skin color disappear with one instant draining and become one—stark pale. And the primary reason was this—while the Guardia Civil would patrol the High Road and Low Road twice a day, they *never* came down to the theatre area. Never. It's not that it was off limits to them or anything, but more because it was a long, steep slope down to the theatre area, which meant having to walk back up the steep slope to continue their rounds. I know. I walked it probably a half a million times, and there were already enough steep hills for them to walk up and down in Royal Oaks. The theatre area was pretty much the American MP's domain to swing through and look around from their pickups.

So, these two Guardia Civil guys came in—green shoulder capes, green uniforms, knee-high, shiny black boots with extra heel taps on the soles (at night you could hear these guys walking on the street from half a mile away...seriously), wide, black belts with shiny, black holsters and those bizarre shiny black hats they wore, of which the name, completely escaped me at the time. See, right along with everyone else, I was now completely drained of color and holding my breath. All activity came to a screeching halt—no giggling, no talking, no grab-assing, nothing.

The two Guardia Civil guys sauntered in. They actually *sauntered*, I tell you. It was apparent that they fully understood what their roles were in this charade— total intimidation. The two men split up and each went to the short, side staircases that led down to the dance floor area and slowly descended, heel taps clicking on the concrete steps like Clint Eastwood's spurs in a cobblestone cemetery, then began moving slowly from one stunned, heartbeat-less table of kids to the next, looking at what the American kids were doing but acting like they couldn't have really given a rat's ass. And, here's the kicker—beneath their green shoulder capes, both men were packing American M-16's—machine guns, mind you.

Now, I've gone into a little detail about Franco's Guardia Civil before, but it merits repeating. There were two main rules that were hammered into the heads of any and all newcomers to Spain: Don't ever drink Spanish tap water (Royal Oaks and the airbase had their own water treatment facilities) and never, *ever* mess with the Guardia Civil. There were green-coated Guardia Civil, like these two guys who, if not responded to, had the authority to shoot, but then there were the 'Gray-Coats' who were instant judge and jury and whose actions were always justified in the eyes of the Spanish courts. At least, that's what we were told. Both equally effective. I never saw a Gray Coat in Royal Oaks.

For instance, the confrontational bit of sassing that I did with the MP at the airbase flight line when the transport jet was off-loading the caskets would never have happened had the MP been a member of the Guardia Civil—no way, no how, hell no, no siree, Bob! I had already, by that time, seen the Guardia Civil in action for real—quick, precise, serious as shit, and not the least bit pretty.

~~~~

The Scarf
(A Short Story)

I'm no thief. That much I know. Well, once I took five dollars from my mother's purse when I was eight or nine, but that's all. It was stupid. She had a bunch of one-dollar bills, which, if I'd taken any of them, probably wouldn't have been missed. A bunch of ones and a five. I don't know what I was thinking. I took the five. I should have taken a couple of ones and been satisfied, but I took the five. I was just some dumb kid.

My mother was a waitress back then. My father worked for the government, civil service, which meant he did okay. My mother waitressed to help pay for my father's two kids from his first marriage and his former wife, who was shacking up with some slacker who counted the days until the child support checks arrived. You can see the dilemma. Back then dollar tips were normal. My mother got them all the time. Truck drivers and farmers would leave a dollar tip for a three dollar chicken fried steak platter with ranch fries, salad, hot rolls and coffee. It happened all the time. Sometimes they'd forget but then they'd come back the next day with the tip and not order anything but coffee and apologize for being so inconsiderate.

Everyone knew that if you were waitressing you needed the money and in that little eastern Oregon town where we lived there was nothing better, job-wise. Back then anyway. I'm talking about the '60's.

So, she's got a dozen or so singles in her pocketbook and what do I do? I take the five. A five dollar tip is something you don't forget easily. A three dollar meal and a five dollar tip? You remember stuff like that. But, that was then. Wheat was big. So was lumber. A lot of people in that town had money and nowhere to spend it. Good service was worth a good tip in these days. I'd seen my mother carry five plates of food without spilling a thing. Some nights during the summer, after the movie let out at the theatre across the street, I'd go into the restaurant and sit at the lunch counter with a cup of cocoa and a butterhorn and watch her until she got off shift. Truckers always winked at my mother. She made you feel good. They had to leave a tip. A five dollar tip was special. You don't forget a name or a face with a five dollar tip. I took her five, got caught, and received a severe tongue lashing from both my mother and my father. I was grounded but I don't remember for how long. In a few days the grounding was forgotten, I'm sure. It usually happened that way. But I was truly sorry. I even looked sorry. I could tell by the expressions on their faces as they were letting me have it that I was looking pretty sorry. It was a stupid thing to do. That was then. I'm no thief. But there was one other time that I did something. I did something, but I *didn't* do something.

It happened five or six years later, after my father had put in for a transfer. I was 14. We were living in Spain then, just outside of Madrid, in an American housing area called, 'El Encinar de los Reyes,' or 'Royal Oaks,' if you translate it. Royal Oaks was a beautiful, rolling hills housing project of huge, white, quad-plex homes that must have surely employed a few thousand locals when it was built back in the late '50's. It was spread across the hills just below 'La Moraleja,' a spacious estate area where many of the homes were owned by famous people. I'd heard stories about how John Wayne used to walk his dogs through Royal Oaks in the years before I lived there. The air base outside Madrid has been closed for some time now. Royal Oaks has been mostly torn down and rebuilt by developers. I doubt it resembles anything I remember, but it's still there.

The quad-plexes in Royal Oaks were three- and four-bedroom homes with four homes built together in one unit. I don't remember how many of them there were. Maybe a hundred. There was always a waiting list to move in. For a short time we lived in a duplex in Cannillejas, a suburb of Madrid, but my father pulled some strings and we jumped up the list. He may have been civil service, but he still had rank.

From the front gates of Royal Oaks, it was a ten-minute bus ride on the P-5 into Madrid to Plaza Castilla. From there you took the subway, the Metro as it was called, to go anywhere. The bus ride cost five pesetas, as did the Metro. About seven cents at the time. Then there were always taxis and tram cars. If it was winter, the Metro was best. The air underground may have been stuffy and smelled of lilac water, black tobacco and sweat, but it was warm and the trains were fast.

But, the incident I'm addressing took place at a large department store in downtown Madrid a few days before Christmas. I went into the city to find a gift for my sister. I remember it was a clear day, very cold and the wind felt like it cut right through my large winter coat. Don't try to look this incident up in any Spanish newspaper archive—you won't find it. It's as if it never happened. But it did happen. I was there.

The store was bright and large with many floors with

double escalators stretching up to each floor. I came into the city alone. Although I was only 14 years old, I could do this. As time passed, I came into the city more and more, mostly to bar hop. I knew the right forms of transit to get around. My Spanish was just fair at the time but I could get around okay, ask directions, prices. It was still a couple of weeks before Three Kings Day and the store was crowded with Saturday, pre-siesta shoppers.

Music was playing. Soft, orchestrated music drifted down from over our heads. This store, by volume and content, was not so unlike those I had wandered through in Portland or Salt Lake City. There were hundreds of counters and displays throughout every floor—cosmetics, clothing, soft goods, house wares, gourmet food, jewelry, toiletries, toys, shoes, linens, souvenirs, appliances, tools, music, china and glassware. China and glassware, the third floor. That's where the trouble began.

I was on the second floor looking through a large rack of records. I remember the Supremes and Elvis were pretty big in Spain back then. And the Beatles. I thought maybe I'd get my sister a record. But then I wandered over to an aisle that had a long row of tables set up, end to end, like at a flea market. The tables were heaped with discounted stuff like leather goods, stationary and bath accessories. One table had scarves in every color, size, shape and texture. The scarves with a fringe were silk and printed with traditional tourist scenes—flamenco dancers, matadors and bulls, castles, fountains. I decided to get my sister a scarf.

I was standing next to an old man who wore a black beret and a large brown overcoat that was much too large for his small frame. Together we examined the scarves, holding them out to see the detail of the artwork and feeling the softness of the fabric. I watched the old man take a scarf and rub it against his cheek to test its softness so I did the same. We held the scarves up to the light to check for flaws in the weave and the hemming. These scarves were easily worth the 175 pesetas they were marked down to. The old man would smell the scarves and I, too, would hold the bright fabric to my nose and breathe deeply the mixed aromas of dyed silk, ink and paint.

Then the old man selected four of the scarves, folded them neatly, and stuck them inside his overcoat. He stuffed them down into his sleeve like it was nothing. I was standing right there beside him. He was no taller than me. He paid me no mind and calmly continued to touch and smell the scarves. Then he stepped over to a table of discounted leather goods and began to examine those items, too, carefully, touching and smelling.

Right at that time, five Guardia Civil rushed up the escalator from the first floor, shoving people aside as they ascended. There were two 'gray coats' and three 'green-coats.' They arrived at our landing, looked about quickly, their automatic weapons at the ready, then continued up to the third floor.

Perhaps I should explain a couple of things. When American families, on an overseas transfer, first arrived in Spain, there was short indoctrination among the chaos of children, luggage and paperwork. We were told about some general customs, like 'siesta,' and other stuff such as the current money exchange rate, but then we were told about the Guardia Civil, the state-controlled Spanish police. The Guardia Civil were not to be messed with, whatsoever. We were guests in Spain. If, for any reason, a member of Guardia Civil shouted, "Espera!" then you'd better stop or risk taking a slug in the back. Two MP's conducted this part of the indoctrination. They were large, deeply tanned, muscular, unsmiling men. "No shit," one of them said And if a gray-coated member of the Guardia Civil shouted for you to stop, don't even think about breathing. Gray coats were judge and jury. It was all very legal.

Once, in the summer before my senior year of high school, I returned home late from a girlfriend's house (her parents were in Portugal) and was in the kitchen, in the dark, getting a snack and saw two green coats, the usual patrol for the housing area, walking slowly down our street, their calf-high, black boots polished to a high sheen, their capes draped neatly about their shoulders. They stopped for a cigarette beneath a street lamp just below our kitchen window. They conversed quietly then, suddenly, one of them got excited about something. He stood off to one side, his hands on his hips, and did a one-two-three-kick routine while the other man laughed and clapped in time. I remember thinking they must have felt quite alone down there in the street to cut loose like that. Any other time they would be cool and distant and reserved. All business. Then the two green coats finished their smokes and moved on at their slow pace through the housing area—all business, like the five men who rushed up to the third floor of the department store.

At first we heard the sounds of glass breaking. Lots of glass. Then there were screams and shouts. Shoppers came stumbling down the 'up' escalator scattering their packages and other bags of goods. A display stand of perfumes toppled. A larger, wooden display of winter caps, mufflers and gloves crashed hard with a loud, hollow sound. That's when we heard the gunfire—six or seven bursts of automatic weapons. Then it was quiet.

I just stood there by the table piled with scarves. All around me the other shoppers had hit the floor. I looked up toward the escalator but couldn't see anything. The music from the ceiling speakers continued to drift down. Then I felt someone tugging on my pant leg. It was the old man. He had hold of my pant leg and then my leg and began pulling me down to the floor. He was frantic and telling me to 'get down.' That much I figured out. I looked all around me and saw that dozens and dozens of shoppers were lying on the floor. Wherever they had been standing was now where they were lying. The old man pulled me down, practically knocking me off my feet, dragging me under the table of scarves with him. He was whispering and sputtering and speaking so fast that I couldn't make out a word he was saying. And he was shaking. The old man was shaking and muttering and he had such a tight grip on the collar of my coat that I couldn't move. Then there were two more gunshots from upstairs and more screams, more breaking glass.

A long minute passed. Everyone stayed put. Then the five Guardia Civil came down the escalator, slowly, first the three green coats, then the two gray coats. Even from beneath the table of scarves I could see them clearly. They walked slowly with their heads up and their shoulders straight. I could see blood splattered on the uniforms of the gray coats. They now carried their automatic weapons low, by their straps.

At our landing the five Guardia Civil stopped and looked around. One of the gray coats looked our direction. The gray coat looked at me huddled beneath the scarves with the old man crouched behind me. He looked me right in the eye. Then all five Guardia Civil proceeded slowly down to the first floor. Not thirty seconds later, six men in blue coats came running and shouting up the escalator from the first floor and carrying large canvas bags under their arms.

That's when the stampede began. People were standing up and looking for their bags and packages and making for the escalator. Some clerks were rushing among the patrons trying to calm them while others were trying to move the fallen displays out of the way. Everyone, it seemed, had determined it was time to go.

When I came out from under the table of scarves,

people were rushing past me, pushing and shoving each other. I didn't see the old man anywhere. He was gone like that. I was still holding a maroon scarf I had selected to give to my sister. It had a picture of the castle in Segovia printed on it. The scarf was beautiful and there were no flaws in the weave. The fringe was black, about a half inch long, and silky.

I took the scarf to three different checkout counters to pay for it. All the clerks I could see were busy with customers still shaken by the shooting. The older people especially. The older people needed the most attention. But, there was one clerk, a young man, who was curled up on the floor behind the third checkout counter I'd gone to. He was rocking back and forth and sobbing, his hands over his ears. I yelled at him to get his attention. The clerk looked up at me. I showed him my sister's scarf I had in one hand and the two, one hundred peseta notes in my other hand. The clerk just went back to his rocking and sobbing. I yelled at the clerk again. No use. I looked around the store. It was chaos. People were jamming onto the escalator and clearing out so I figured I'd better do the same. I could have left the money at the checkout counter, but, with all the confusion, who knows what would have happened to it? Someone could have stolen my money.

So, I took the scarf.

There, I said it. Like I said, I'm no thief, but I slipped the scarf inside my coat and stuffed it down into my sleeve like the old man had done. Then I made a beeline for the escalator and was literally carried down to the first floor and out through the front doors by the panicked throng of patrons.

Once outside I saw the five Guardia Civil standing off to the side along with a dozen or so soldiers next to a large flat-bed truck, smoking casually and watching all the people scattering as they exited the store. I turned away from the group of men and began walking very fast toward the stairs at the end of the block that led down to the subway, but fully expected a bullet in the back. Have you ever tried to hurry without looking like you're hurrying? I remember needing to get there as quickly as I could. I wanted to feel the warmth of the people crowded together on the platform waiting for their trains. I wanted to be under the city and out of the cold.

As I waited on the dock for my train, I took the scarf out of my sleeve. I folded it and stuffed it into my coat pocket. That's when I discovered my coat pocket was already full. I pulled my hand back out of my pocket bringing with it my own scarf and four more neatly folded scarves. The old man's scarves. I looked in my pocket again and found a gold-plated pen and pencil set in a nice, black, fake leather case, a small bottle of what I think was French perfume, and a silver bracelet with rhinestones. I quickly put everything back into my pocket. Then I checked my other coat pocket and discovered I was carrying two small packages of those traditional Spanish holiday candy-coated almonds, tied with elastic gold ribbon and a pair of men's soft leather wallets, a brown one and one that was dyed red. That old man must have been stealing gifts for his entire family. I kept the red wallet for myself. No one in my family ever asked me how I got their stuff and I never told them.

It was a very good Christmas.

~~~~~

So, the two Guardia Civil patrol officers moved slowly from table to table in the Teen Center. Not a single kid was even blinking. Three grade-schoolers came in and immediately froze in place. The juke box was still playing. One of the Guardia Civil guys glanced

angrily at it (these two guys really missed their calling—
Sergio Leone would have loved them both) and the kid
closest to it dove over and pulled the plug out of the
wall.

I looked over at Sergio standing by the door. He just
stood there, slowly shaking his head. I looked at Sgt.
Slater and he was no longer smiling but has put on the
'stern face' that all good sergeants employ. The other
Guardia Civil guy stopped at a table where some older
kids were playing a card game. He stood behind the
largest kid (a senior) and studied the cards the kid was
holding, then reached out and selected a card from the
kid's hand and laid it on top of a pile of cards in the
center of the table. Then he patted the large kid on the
shoulder and I'd swear everyone in the room flinched,
even Sgt. Slater.

Then the two Guardia Civil guys took a long look
around the Teen Center, adjusted the straps of their M-
16's beneath their capes, climbed the stairs and exited
through the door they came in that was being held open
for them by Sergio.

Now, *that* was royalty.

It was a good two minutes before the kids in the large
room began whispering, then, in no time, it was a full-
blown murmur. Someone plugged the juke box back in.
Things returned to normal. Sgt. Slater was smiling again.

"See you boys later," Slater said, "and thanks for
everything." Genius. Sometimes military life can be the
only kind of life there is. I've mentioned that there was
one time that I was never so happy to see an MP—well,
these two Guardia Civil guys were with the MP that one
time. Fortunately.

Chapter 11: Addendum

Alverez and I walked home after that. We had decided to come back down to the Teen Center again in the late afternoon. School started the next day so it only seemed right to see what might be shaking.

There were still a whole lot of kids hanging out for the last hurrah of Christmas vacation and the place was totally abuzz about what had taken place earlier. A sixth or seventh grader came up to us all breathless and goo-goo-eyed.

"Man, you guys missed it, man!" the kid said. "The Guardia Civil came in here and made everyone line up against the wall. They had their guns drawn and everything! They even attacked one of the big kids and sent him to the hospital!" I told the kid he needed to take a breath.

"Screw you guys! Man, you missed it, man!" the kid said again. I really loved Royal Oaks. I really did. Just for grins I went into the boys' bathroom and discovered that the booger someone had wiped on Sgt. Slater's smaller sign had now been cleaned off. I found out later that a couple of the kids' parents had come down to ask about the rumors that had started but when Slater told them what had really happened, and why, all was well again. Slater even got a couple of 'atta-boys' from the parents for his plan. Slater should have been in the CIA.

I don't think anyone ever collected a 1,000 peseta reward for turning someone in for *intentionally* messing up a bathroom, but it wasn't for lack of trying. If someone missed the trash can with a paper towel, they'd get reported. Alverez' and my janitorial obligations were much easier from that day forward. Sgt. Slater was, indeed, the *man*.

Chapter 12

One of the best things about being on a Madrid/Torrejon High School sports team (besides the uniforms) was going to away games. Another best thing about it was that all students on a team sport received a PE credit and were exempt from having to participate in the mandatory PE classes (you became an assistant to the teacher, refereeing, running errands, etc.). But, the best thing was definitely going to away games. Trips to Rota Naval Base (the Admirals—how original) could be two- to three-day trips for football, basketball and wrestling, and for track and field, they could be four-day trips. Trips to Zaragoza (the Toros) usually took no longer that 36 hours (I had only been there once for JV basketball). Another school in our league was at Kenitra Naval Base (the Sultans) located over the pond in Spanish Morocco, in North Africa, but they were a much smaller school and were usually only able to field basketball and wrestling teams as well as send some kids to track and field meets, but never football. There were two football squads in our league, for now—Rota and Madrid, but Zaragoza would finally having enough of a school population to field a football team for the first time in the upcoming fall (which I was unaware of at this time). Now there would be three teams. But things were in the works to change that.

Our varsity football team was named the overall #1 team in Europe last fall ('71) after the military sent Madrid to play the high school at the naval base in Naples (which the press figured was another contender for the best team in Europe) and we kicked the crap out of them. I didn't make the trip. Two guys from the JV football squad were selected to travel to Italy. I wasn't selected. I was pissed. So, for all sports but football there was a four-team league. There used to be a school in Seville (Army) and in Moron (Air Force, very small) but they shut down the year after I moved to Spain. Madrid was the largest school, by far, and there was no shortage of top-quality athletes. Parity was upon us, as I will note in the future. I'll say this much, what transpired was undoubtedly something no school in The World ever had to deal with. Truly unreal, considering what would happen, but more significantly, *when* it happened.

So, away games meant time away from going to classes. Bonus. The first week of school after Christmas vacation was when we'd have our first basketball games at Rota, way down on the southern tip of Spain, a nine to eleven-hour trip (usually, depending on what kind of driver we got), part highway, part winding back roads. Missing classes was cool by me because I always thought that high school would be my last educational stop anyway. I was a sophomore. Many of my classmates were already discussing going to college but I had no idea what I wanted to do after high school and wouldn't for nearly two more years.

Another thing I should mention, has to do with the buses we rode to school, to dances and on road trips over in Spain. When people back in The World think of a 'school bus' they conjure up the image of a standard, happy yellow bus. Our buses, for all activities, were like

Greyhound or Trailways buses—high back, adjustable seats, overhead racks, large storage compartments underneath—all the comforts of home, unless you were packed together, assholes to elbows, with the varsity and JV basketball teams, varsity and JV wrestling teams, all the coaches, assistant coaches and each team's manager. Packed, I tell you. Football and track and field road trips were just as crammed, which made for some interesting interactions, not to mention the ultimate disclosure of any teammate's personal hygiene habits.

Between the four or five Royal Oaks buses, the three or four Madrid and suburbs buses, the two buses for the Torrejon Apartments in the village just off base and the village of Alcala, a couple of more miles up the highway from Torrejon Village, back and forth, five days a week, not to mention the middle school buses, the after-school activities buses, air base teen dance buses, away game sports buses—the cost to the military must have been sizable—drivers, diesel fuel, maintenance. Sizable.

First week back from Christmas vacation—road trip. I had already made this trip twice before. The first time was my freshman year on the football team. I don't think my parents were ever more proud of me before this moment, in my entire life, than when I told them I was on the football 'travel squad' to Rota.

My high school had over 500 kids, our football team was overloaded, and we had no JV team. Anyone who tried out for the team, was *on* the team, providing they could pass the one physical requirement which earned them the right be issued their equipment—the mile run. Depending on your age, your weight and your position, you had to beat a particular time to be granted that privilege. The time I had to beat was seven minutes and thirty seconds. It took me three tries—only one try allowed per day—but I did it. I thought I was gonna faint dead away, but I did it.

We had more players than the school had equipment that year. My parents were very happy when I made the team, but they were ecstatic when I told them about going to Rota the first time. I didn't have the heart to tell them that I was the last player on the team that was allowed to go and that the seven players that weren't going couldn't go because they didn't have helmets of their own. I had gotten the last helmet, which was too big, but it was *mine*.

My second year of football was different—we had a JV team. So I went to Rota a second time last fall, played in the JV game on Saturday morning, then was told to stay suited up and got into the varsity game for a few plays that afternoon—enough plays to qualify for a varsity letter in football (12) but didn't actually, officially, receive a varsity letter. My coaches wanted to dangle that carrot in front of my face for just one more year. The only two JV players that received varsity letters were the two guys selected to go to Naples. Yeah, I was really pissed. No varsity letter meant no varsity letterman's jacket, which were very cool.

Getting off the bus in front of the school on Monday mornings, or any morning for that matter, forever burned an olfactory memory in my brain—even to this day— freshly baked bread. My high school buildings were converted, three-story military barracks, plus an auditorium/theatre building, a gym and locker rooms, a cafeteria and an auto-mechanics shop. Located just northeast of the high school was the base bakery. Strategically located, due to the fact that 75% of all early morning prevailing winds came southward, down from the northwest, the unreal aroma of baked bread would waft over the entire school and continue on toward the military barracks just southeast of the school. Heavenly, no doubt about it, and sometimes, a bit too irresistible, especially if your bus arrived early enough to give you time to beat feet the 200 yards or so to the bakery's entrance and back, and, if you had the extra 50 cents to buy a fresh baked loaf of Spanish *pan* (bread)—light and crispy on the outside, soft, fluffy and warm on the inside. More than a few times, I'd fall in with a pack of kids jogging to the bakery, get a fresh baked loaf, then make it back before the first bell rang. My bus arrived 15 minutes earlier than usual. I was a working man so I had the extra 50 cents. I got to the bakery and back, a two-foot long loaf of pan in hand, with five minutes to spare before the first bell rang and gave a very appreciative Alverez, whose bus arrived 10 minutes after mine, half my bounty.

One of the best things about road trips to Rota was the availability of Navy pants, Navy jeans, Navy dungarees (all the same thing). My entire school was nuts for Navy pants, especially the girls. But Tuesday, besides orders from my sister and three of her friends, I had four additional people to buy for, complete with their, 'don't-you-dare-tell-anyone-my-size' list. Navy pants were $12 a pair, no matter what size they were. One thing the Navy was, in all aspects, was consistent. All the trips I took to Rota, and all the Navy pants I bought for others, the price never changed.

I should mention that classes had started. I had classes in English, biology, history, bachelor of arts cooking, PE, where I mostly hung out in the teacher's office studying and handing out towels, and I spent the first hour each morning working in the school's main office. Big whoop—I was going to Rota!

The bus for Rota left Royal Oaks, from The Circle, on Wednesday night at 11:00 pm sharp. I got there at 10:40. I was just hoping for a newer bus. Newer buses smelled better. Newer buses meant happier bus drivers. Newer buses meant less diesel backwash and better shock absorbers. The first trip to Rota that I took was on a bus that must have surely been made during the Spanish Civil War and at some point its interior was used to butcher goats. On my second Rota trip, the bus was new and gorgeous—the windows worked, the engine was silent and the suspension made you feel like you were riding on soap suds.

By the time I got down to The Circle, I was *praying* for a newer bus and when it arrived, I realized my prayers were answered—big windows, extra cushioning in the butt pads, and this bus was so new that it had those adjustable footrests that popped out from underneath the seats. The worst thing about an 11-hour, packed bus ride was having your feet go to sleep. Pop-out foot rests underneath the seats on a long-haul passenger bus is Nobel-Prize-for-Physics-type-shit, in my book.

Alverez and I quickly stowed our gear and managed to grab a pair of seats near the back of the bus. The coaches always sat up in the front. Being in the back of the bus allowed a bit more freedom, being out of earshot of authority. Juniors and seniors hung out in the back of the bus. Alverez and I were sophomores, which meant we would be observers—comfortable observers.

The first hour of the trip to Rota was always spent getting adjusted and situated and snacking and cutting up and listening to guys playing 'The Dozens,' a form of creative insult exchange in which all subjects, religion, race, sex, family, intelligence, father's or mother's rank, were fair game, but usually it came back to sex, and usually with a homosexual angle. You put 50 high school guys on a bus for 11 hours, you're bound to get a little bit of lewd conduct, complete with belching, farting and grab-assing. I never knew what the term 'The Dozens' meant. I could only imagine that after about 12 well-crafted insults the enthusiasm would peter out. But, over the years I did experience a couple of classics:

~~~~

"Hey, you got a sister?"
"Yeah."
"Well, I got her, too!"

~~~~

"You were so ugly as a child, your parents tied a pork chop around your neck so the dog would play with you."

~~~~

"Hey, if you don't tell anyone about my wooden dick, I won't tell anyone about the splinters in your tongue."

~~~~

"You're so ugly, when you were born, the doctor slapped your parents."

~~~~

"Did you hear? Hedda likes you!"
"Hedda, who?"
"Hedda my dick."

~~~~

"Your girlfriend's so ugly, she has to sneak up on a glass of water."

~~~~

"Your mama's so ugly that when she walks by you, she wrinkles your clothes."

~~~~

"Your mama's so fat that when she wants to have sex, your Dad has to roll her in flour to find the wet spot."

~~~~

There were two others. An apartment complex was built rather quickly in the village of Torrejon de Ardoz, just off the base in the late sixties, to handle the excess of necessary military personnel because of the build-up in Vietnam, and always looked like it was never fully completed. It was called the 'Torrejon Apartments' (genius):

~~~~~

"Royal Oaks has the Guardia Civil. The airbase has the MP's. The Torrejon Apartments has the Rat Patrol."

~~~~~

But the most clever exchange went like this:

~~~~~

"Hey, if you don't tell anyone about my rubber dick, I won't tell anyone about the skid marks on your tongue."

~~~~~

"Yeah? Well, speaking of rubbers, give me one and I'll pack your lunch."

~~~~~

Classic.

Now, playing The Dozens could turn into a heated exchange from time to time, but I never witnessed a fight as a result (but I did *know* of one). The unspoken code was if you were bested by your opponent, you went down quietly without a fuss.

After about an hour into our road trip, coaches told the bus driver to cut the lights. Bedtime. It'd take a good 40 minutes for things to totally calm down but eventually they would calm down and the delicate sounds of teeth-grinding, farting, puppy dreams and snoring would fill the bus just beneath the rhythmic hum of the bus's diesel engine. All of the road trips to Rota were night trips. From inside the bus's dark interior, I saw villages and fields fly by, lit by the occasional street lamp or, with luck, some kind of a moon. Hypnotic—the perfect in-flight movie—conducive to solid, upright sleeping. If you were a coach or a star athlete or a team captain, or just plain studlier than everyone else, then you got to sleep in the aisle, a privilege only granted to the rightfully ordained. I didn't get to sleep in the aisle until I was a senior. But I only did it once. I liked looking out the window.

Someone always had a cassette player on these trips, usually two or three guys did. There was many a contemplative, reflective hour, usually the hour before sleep or the hour of waking up, when the entire bus would shut up and we'd listen to some Motown, Rolling Stones, the Doors, Lou Reed, the Moody Blues, Elton John or some other current, popular artist—Led Zeppelin, the Who, Al Green. We were worldly children of worldly parents, sent out to defend hotdogs, baseball and apple pie—there was a lot to think about, always. Music, any music, never sounded better anywhere else, ever, for me.

A year later, when I made the eight-man travel squad for varsity basketball to go down to Kenitra in Spanish Morocco (I vowed to never miss making a travel squad after Naples), we had to take a four-hour bus ride from the airport in Tangiers to get to the naval base. We left Madrid around midnight, got into Tangiers, then had to wait around for a couple of hours for our bus to arrive. Once on the bus, everyone zoned in and out of sleep, but just as the sun was coming up, we were driving alongside a long stretch of beach. There was a man out in the distance, dressed in the traditional robes and turban of the countryside natives, and he was exercising his string of four camels, all in a row. The man was out in front of his animals, holding their guide rope, his head held high, his arms pumping, his legs high-stepping, the camels loping gracefully, as if in slow motion, behind him, and the man was smiling. I had every reason to believe that this man was, without a doubt, the happiest person on the planet, and right at that moment, on someone's cassette player, playing softly, was 'I'm Your Captain/Closer to Home,' by Grand Funk. How is it possible to compete with that moment, that *witness* of the ultimate joy, the testament of exactly why we humans were put on this earth? Stuff like this affects me.

A person can search forever to find this kind of purity and wholeness, this kind of *whole-self,* and never find it. To be as one with oneself and to complement the world around you—the rising sun slowly illuminating the ocean behind this man and his camels—the only evidence necessary to prove that there is *some* greater power at work, burning its image right through my retinas.

And, in contrast to such pinnacle moments of clarity, were the bus rides home, late at night, after a dance at the Teen Center on the base. I think that, by law, the lights inside these activity buses (one for the Low Road, one for the High Road), were supposed to remain on for the 45-minute ride home, but within a minute after leaving the air base's front gate a chorus of, "¡Apagar la luz!" (turn off the light!) would ring out so that those couples who had hooked up at the dance could get down to some semi-private making out and the mutual search for 'Spanish moss' (that would be pubic hair)...the whole 'hello/goodbye' thing. I can't think of one time when the bus driver did *not* turn off the lights at our request.

Now, if a person calculated the time they spent on the bus from Royal Oaks to the airbase, and back, just for going to school, it's quite mind-boggling. For instance, I lived in Royal Oaks for four years, the daily to-and-from trip was about an hour and a half, five days a week, 20 days a month. With eight a half months (excluding Christmas and spring breaks) that meant it came out to roughly 255 hours spent on just the daily school bus, per year. Multiplied by four years made it 1,020 hours, divided by a 24-hour day, meant 42.5 days in four years spent riding a school bus. Factor in my first year of living in Cannillejas and it comes out to roughly 52.5 total days that I spent riding on a school bus—just to school and back. Unreal, really. So the types of buses that were employed to pack us back and forth on a daily basis *was* genius.

Our practices after school, Monday, Tuesday and Wednesday, before leaving for Rota Wednesday night, were spirited affairs. Coach was pleased with our fiery enthusiasm. I was challenged for my spot on the starting five six or seven times, but was able to keep the other glory hounds at bay. Keeping my position had everything to do with understanding the 'what' in regards to the concept and mechanics of Coach's offensive scheme, I'm sure of it, but grasping the 'why' of Coach's concept and mechanics easily remained a mystery to me because of the mathematical concepts that were employed for their success.

I'm no math person, never have been, never pretended to be. So much of what passes for algebra, geometry, calculus and all the rest, is just plain too elusive. In fact, I got caught cheating on a geometry test right after football season ended, but about a month before basketball tryouts were held. I paid $5 for the answers and believed my source to 'easy-street' was an honorable one—our varsity, all-conference quarterback, a senior. Now, the interesting thing about this was that I *knew* the answers I had received were incorrect once I started the test, but I used them anyway. Idiot mountain. So, our teacher, Mr. Johansen (greasy, thin hair, horn-rimmed glasses, short-sleeved, plaid shirt, clip-on tie with a picture of a trout leaping for a mayfly that he wore every goddam day) thought it best, because of my athletic status (favoritism?), that he keep my impropriety, as well as the improprieties of two other guys who spent five bucks for the same bogus answers, as *well* as the impropriety of the all-conference quarterback, 'in house,' and gave us each 21 zeroes accompanied by 21 makeup assignments to be completed before the fall term ended or receive a failing grade for his class. Not good. The best grade any of us could possibly hope to receive for the fall term was now a 'C.' I had three weeks to complete my assignments before JV basketball tryouts were to be held so I stayed after school every day for three weeks in Johansen's classroom to try and mitigate my crime and I did it. I got a 'C' for the class—a passing grade, still eligible for school team sports. In later years, I would receive an undergraduate degree and a master's degree, but the last math class I ever took was Mr. Johansen's. Note to self—never spend money to do something stupid and, never trust a quarterback.

Our coach's plays (he added three more at Monday's practice) were little more than living, moving geometry and somehow I *got* it (the what, never the why) and each challenge I thwarted hinged on my ability to *see* Coach's diagrams out on the court. Out of the two dozen or so overall challenges that were made, I don't think anyone challenged Alverez. Our current starting five remained intact according to Coach's specific requirements.

Somewhere, near the City of Cordoba, a little more than halfway through our road trip, the chant of "Nature break! Nature break," would erupt. You could set a clock by it. What greater visual could be imagined than the sight of 45 or 50 guys all lined up on the side of a Spanish back road, flicking their peters out in the early morning dawn to take a piss or at least to discard the once empty soda cans they'd already filled (the piddle panties)? Then there would be more sleeping or dozing as the sun began to rise and eventually, all of us delicate morning flowers were back to cutting up, cracking wise and grabbing ass—ball bouncers and ball-grabbers alike.

We pulled through the front gates of Rota Naval Base just before 9 am—just under 10 hours. Our driver must have been hauling ass because of the newness of his bus—it seemed like no time at all. God bless the U.S. Air Force and the USDESEA (United States Dependants School, European Area) for their deep pockets.

Chapter 13

Stork was a piece of work…a piece of work, I tell you. I'll get to him shortly, but I thought it best to put this observation out there before I continue.

The first thing that happened, once we arrived at Rota was the whole 'getting settled' thing—finding out which barracks we were bunking in, going to the first floor supply room of that barracks to be issued our sheets, blankets and pillow, locating which section of our designated floor we were supposed to be in (each squad stayed together), selecting our beds (three-tiered bunk beds) and lockers, stowing our crap, then without hesitation, hoofing it over to the Navy chow hall at the far end of the parade grounds that fronted our barracks.

Now, I don't mean to slam any Army post or Air Force base anywhere in the world, but I'm here to tell you that the best fucking chow halls on any military installation are Navy chow halls, and Rota's chow hall was unreal. The last 50 yards to the chow hall front doors were at a dead sprint.

Two things about Navy base food—first, it was prettier—a huge variety of fruits, salads, special diet plates, cheese, sandwiches, cans of soda pop and juice, cartons of milk and chocolate milk on ice, and prettiest of all—pastries. The Rota chow hall had the biggest, most beautiful platters of doughnuts (glazed, old-fashioned, cake, chocolate-frosted, strawberry-frosted, maple-frosted, vanilla-iced with sprinkles the colors of the Fourth of July), maple bars, éclairs, apple fritters, cream-filled, fruit-filled, butterhorns as big as your head, cupcakes, pies (apple, cherry, peach, apricot, strawberry, chocolate, banana and coconut cream), and cake (Devil's food, angel food, chocolate, German chocolate). Second thing was the quantity—this place was a dream come true for someone with an eating disorder and a diabetic's worst nightmare.

You'd grab a tray, a couple of plates, and the first stop was at the breakfast grill where you got your eggs-to-order, any style, including omelets, if you wanted, and in any quantity. Now, back in the '70's, the Navy had very relaxed appearance codes. The guy cooking your food might have a full beard, a Fu Man Chu, handlebar mustache, or mutton-chop sideburns that made him look like an American Civil War general and, compared to the bored looking, clean-shaven servers back at Torrejon, these guys *loved* to cook—they were artists with your food. And my being a Bachelor of Arts cooking student and a dependent of a civilian, and naturally full of questions about their magic, when I ordered a four-egg, ham and cheese omelet, I received the blue-ribbon treatment.

Next stop—breakfast meat. Ham, bacon, sausages, chorizo—as much as you wanted (three breakfast maple sausages, please). I skipped the next station—pancakes, waffles and French toast. Next was the fruit and salad bar—two cereal-bowl sized servings, one of fruit cocktail and one of canned, sliced peaches (naturally). Then, finally the pastry trays (two glazed, chocolate, old-fashioned doughnuts, thank you very much). Add a large mug of thick, Navy hot cocoa and I was good to go. All for $2.00.

If there was one unwritten rule about the Rota chow hall, it was that whatever you took, you'd best eat it all—wasting food was a serious no-no. Never let your eyes be bigger than your stomach which, for most newbies (me included, first time), considering the abundance of visual stimuli, was always a challenge.

The lunches and dinner meals were just as overwhelming. The Navy didn't have a changeable menu depending on what day of the week it was, though, depending on incoming transport jets or ships, from wherever they were from (Atlanta, New Jersey, Antarctica, etc.), they would do something special like roast a few turkeys, barbeque a couple of pigs or prepare 200 pounds of prime rib that was kissed on the lips by all the gods. But, you could always bank on dinner consisting of mountains of fried chicken, roast beef, lamb chops, steak (cooked to order) and all the fresh, available steamed vegetables and baked potatoes you could imagine.

The most pathetic part of all this delectable pornography was having to watch the members of the wrestling team who still had to weigh in before their matches began. If they were too close and needed to be cautious, you'd see them with their bowls of hot water with a couple of bullion cubes and a glass of ice water or cup of black coffee, which could totally kill the enjoyment of cramming a chocolate-filled éclair down your neck. I really felt for the wrestlers but that was probably why nearly all of them played football or went out for track—to eat at the Rota chow hall once or twice during the season. Of course, once the wrestlers had their weigh-ins, and *made* their weight, they'd become complete gluttons like the rest of us.

Our first game was scheduled for 3 pm—still plenty of time after stuffing our faces at the chow hall to hit the

Naval Exchange store and fill the orders for the Navy pants I had, then get back to my bunk in the barracks for some needed down time before the game. As luck would have it, I was able to find all the right sizes of Navy pants on my list. My work at the Exchange was done, but when I saw a bunch of JV and varsity basketball players making a mess of the shoe area while trying on sneakers, I decided to stick around for a bit.

The Exchange had just received a new shipment of Adidas and these guys were opening boxes and trying on shoes like it was Christmas morning at the orphanage. Frenzy. There was just one guy there to try and oversee all that was going on and apparently, working in retail really wasn't his thing. He was about to be ripped off left and right. I'd say of the 20 or so pairs of new shoes that left the Exchange, there were at least six pairs that walked out (literally), unpaid for. A guy would find his size, put them on, put his old shoes in the box, select another pair of the same size and then pay for that box of shoes—buy one, get one free. I'm no thief, but I'm no snitch either. I was a sophomore. I clammed up. All I could do was pity that Navy guy when he took his inventory down the road and discovered all the pairs of old shoes stuck inside the new boxes, and with no one to blame.

I walked back to my barracks, stowed my cache of Navy pants in my locker, then grabbed a two-hour nap, trying not to think about the whole 'starting five' thing. I laid in my bunk (bottom tier—I *was*, after all, on the starting five) thinking about what I'd seen at the Naval Exchange with the guys stealing shoes. I never really understood the shoplifting thing that I'd seen happen at the airbase, at Rota, back in The World in my hometown, or wherever. The airbase had MP's. They had guns. They had jails. Rota had SP's (Shore Patrol). They had guns. They had jails. Madrid had Franco's

Guardia Civil—they had automatic weapons (as I related earlier) that they wouldn't hesitate to use—and they had prison cells underneath the city (which I'll get to later). I mean, sure, I understand the desire for *things*. Everyone desires things. But the risk of getting caught always outweighed the potential pleasure from the things—plus it could have something to do with the experience of getting caught when I was a kid. I once saw a girl in my school steal nine record albums from the BX by hiding them underneath her poncho and acting like she was pregnant. Craziness, I tell you. Some of the guys I knew (officers' kids, no less) would steal stuff just for the thrill of it, just for the rush of potentially getting caught.

I never understood the attraction, the lure of it all, just like I could never wrap my brain around the whole drug thing that I became aware of a year later. I always made sure to never go into the BX with these kids. And, okay, that scarf thing, I claim it to be only *half* my fault—my intentions were pure. I wanted to do the right thing but circumstances dictated that I couldn't do the right thing. In retrospect, I should have left the scarf in the store—I wasn't thinking that clearly (gunfire...the old man), plus I knew I wouldn't have a chance to go back downtown into Madrid before Christmas. And, as for all the stuff that old man put into my coat pockets, yeah, I should've returned it, but I doubt any Guardia Civil would have believed my tale of how I acquired it. I guess I'm trying to talk myself out of any wrong-doing I may have done, on purpose or not. Everyone has ghosts they pack around. Hell, just being human can be one goddam guilt trip, all by itself.

Now, as I stated, Stork was a piece of work. Besides making the JV basketball squad (almost as much of a surprise as me making the team) he also fancied himself to be some kind of super-duper motocross motorcycle aficionado. Problem was, he rode a 50cc bike while all the other riders in our age group competed on 150 or 200cc bikes. The race categories were based on the engine size of the bike, not the age or the experience of the rider. So, naturally, Stork won every race he entered. Stork was King of the Nine Year-Olds. The helmet that Stork wore while racing had a picture of Woody Woodpecker on its sides so, not only was Stork the King of the Nine-Year-Olds, but the envy of them, as well.

Someone, a guy in my class who'd moved away about a year ago, once told me that he actually went to Stork's house and said that his bedroom and living room were wall to wall with trophies and framed photos. He'd been at Stork's house for barely half an hour and decided to make up an excuse to leave after Stork had taken him through page by agonizing page of two of his seven or eight scrapbooks. They got from the newspaper notice about Stork's birth, up through his fifth grade PTA newsletter and program regarding Stork's *brilliant* rendition of his role as one of the Three Wise Men in a Dover, Delaware grade school Christmas pageant, before saying, "Uh, hey, you know, I gotta go." This guy, who had a good sense of humor and a good eye for the obvious, also said that he figured as Stork was coming out of the birth canal he must have reached back and pulled his mother's ovaries out with him, to ensure he would be an only child (which he was).

Part of Coach's challenge system, besides seeing how well you knew the plays and how well you executed them with the other four players on the court, was your evaluation for one-on-one play. Stork challenged every starting five player. He challenged me twice. So we had to play our five minutes of one-on-one, with Coach sitting in the stands, looking on and writing notes, as usual. Both times we played, I beat him, but Stork always had some kind of something to say, like, "Man, I'd have had you, but I tripped on this stupid floor," or,

"I'd have made that shot but I got something in my eye."

One time, I made a move and blew right past him for a layup that I missed, got the rebound, missed again, and then made it the third time. Now, the fact that I blew right past him wasn't a miracle, really. I had *some* wheels as a sophomore, but the fact that I out-hustled Stork for the rebound—twice—was what sealed his fate. Sometimes desire outdoes skill. When I made the shot, finally, Stork said, "That was pure luck and you know it, man." Throughout high school no one from any team, my own included, ever figured out that the *best* way to defend me in basketball was to just let me *shoot* the ball and not try to defend the shot—just let me shoot, then set up for getting the rebound, many of which, it seemed, would always be there. It might take me two or three tries, but eventually, I would make the shot.

But, there's something to be said about perpetual optimism and those who employ it. I think Coach had a soft spot for Stork. Coach must have been an only child, too. Stork was in his own world and he lived in an exciting place, always. A few months later, at the end of the upcoming summer, after my family and I returned from our two-week home leave vacation back in The World, I went to the motocross races that were held just off the golf course out at the base, and watched Stork on his 50cc dirt bike clean the clock of every nine and ten year-old out there. So, after his final race, what does Stark do? He decides to take a *victory* lap around the course and revs his bike up for a final big jump off the last dirt hump, promptly miscalculates and plants himself, face first, at the bottom of the hump. Classic Stork.

About a month after school started, I saw Stork in the third floor hallway. The swelling from the two surgeries was gone but he still had a bit of yellow bruising around his eyes, all of which meant that any and all sports for him were out for a long time. Part of his 'face straightening' rehabilitation required him to get full braces on his teeth, top and bottom. Guess what he told me (go on, guess)? Stork said, "I was gonna get braces this year anyway." Seriously. And then he said, "Braces are cool, man, *you* just don't know it." Did I mention that while he now had braces that his jaw had also been wired shut to ensure that the plates of his skull that had been re-stapled together remained stable as they mended?

But, to be fair, I'm not going to go too overboard about this guy. I've only ridden a motorcycle once in my life, and once was enough.

But, you have to question a guy's internal synapses when, if he *could* have had a four-egg Denver omelet, four strips of smoky, molasses-cured bacon, prepared by one of the finest culinary artists in southern Spain, plus a steaming butterhorn smothered in real butter and a large mug of hot cocoa, but instead, opts for eight single-serving sized boxes of cereal and doesn't allow anyone else to sit at his table while he's eating. Yeah, classic Stork. There were some issues there. Yet, there was silver lining to this pain-in-our-asses and it became evident at halftime of our first game later that day.

Our JV game against Rota's JV was the first game of all the games that would be played. We were to play four games—two against the Rota JV and two against the Zaragoza JV. The varsity team had six games over our three-day stay (we left on Saturday night after the last varsity game)—two against Rota, two against Zaragoza and two against Kenitra. We had the second floor of the barracks—Zaragoza and Kenitra occupied the third floor.

Now, I don't want to be rude in regard to our fellow visiting emissaries from other bases, but the kids on the Zaragoza and Kenitra teams were fucking nuts. It's one thing to see someone's clothes or mattress go flying by your window from the floor above you, but it's entirely different when you see a team manager go screaming by, then landing in the thick hedges down below. Over the course of the next three days, I personally saw it happen twice. Both times, the team managers survived their falls, but I couldn't help wonder if at some point in their later lives, they weren't affected in some way. Falling from a third floor window is one thing, but being pitched from a third floor window is something entirely different. Nuts. It's no wonder that our own coaches insisted on making all team managers bunk in their cubicle areas.

The halftime score in our first game against the Rota JV was 53-7. I was the high scorer for our team. I had four points. Stork had the other three points. Unreal. As my father was prone to say, in situations such as these, we 'couldn't hit a bull in the ass with a bass fiddle.' Jesus (or whomever), did we *suck*. The plays were there, the shots were there, but nothing fell. And I mean, nothing, though I did manage to hit a jump shot that was tipped but went in anyway, and two free throws. But, first off, one of our starting five, a forward, turned his ankle and Coach put Stork in. Secondly, and I don't throw this out as some sort of an excuse, because they *were* in the same grade as we were, but three of Rota's starting five were *also* on their varsity team. That's the funny thing about high school—some kids develop earlier, physically and mentally, than others, and then there's that whole military, 'being held back' thing due to the constant moving around. I mean there were a couple of kids that graduated with me that had to have been at least 20 years-old. So there was no telling just how old these three Rota 'sophomores' really were, but they couldn't miss a shot while, despite Coach's perfectly diagrammed plays, we fired up one big fat-assed brick after another. 53-7 at halftime. Shit like this sticks with you. No doubt the total lopsidedness of the score was a severe disappointment to the 12 or 13 people sitting in the bleachers, too (it was a Thursday afternoon, a work day).

So, the three sophomores on Rota's varsity team played just the first half (totally allowed, by rules) then left the court and went home. Not only was it embarrassing, but totally 'bare-assing.' We got spanked. Now, *our* varsity team had a sophomore on it that we could have used, but he was *too* good of a player to waste a full half game on with the JV team. Too good. He was one of the Adidas-walking-out-of-the-Naval-Exchange guys and, in fact, in his new shoes, had 22 points in the first *quarter* of their first game, right after our game, against the Zaragoza varsity, which Coach made us stick around to watch.

But, I'm getting ahead of myself here, as usual. There were actually two things that happened during the 15-minute halftime break. To set the tone of the game, I got the opening tip-off, had a clear path to the basket, and promptly missed the easy layup by a mile. I was so excited when I approached the basket that my shot actually went *over* the top of the backboard. Perhaps I should have kicked up my heels. Nothing went right after that. But Stork put up an amazing shot.

On one of Coach's designed plays, Stork was supposed to come up to the free throw line as Alverez, who was playing center, screened Stork's defender, and I was to pass the ball to Stork who was supposed to immediately dish it off to Alverez when he rolled out of his screen for a one-on-one layup. The screen worked perfectly. I got the ball into Stork's hands but then Stork forgot what he was supposed to do next and he froze. He just stood there looking at me, his back to the basket. So, I told him to give the ball back to me, but instead, he threw the ball over his head, backwards, and sank a perfect bank shot off the backboard and got fouled in the process. Unreal shot. Then he sank his free throw and the half ended. 53-7.

In the locker room, we're all down in the mouth and down on ourselves, expecting some kind of philosophical half-time speech or new strategy from Coach. Then Coach came in, looked around the room at all of us and said, "Boys, get your shit together," then just left us sitting there. I, for one, had never heard Coach curse before this time nor would I ever again. So we're in the locker room being all serious and beating ourselves up, and then Stork came out of the john and said, "Damn! Did you guys see the shot I made? Was that cool or what?"

Okay. We're behind by 46 points as Stork goes on and on about his freak luck of a shot (simply because he forgot what to do during Coach's designed play). We'd gotten our asses handed to us royally on a silver platter with garnishes and hot towels and all Stork knew about was his 'shot.' Then someone told Stork to shut the fuck up, and then Stork said the most amazing thing. He said, "Well, don't *you* wish *you'd* made that shot?"

Silence. Totally true. We all wished we'd made that ridiculous shot. We were all wishing we'd made *any* shot (even though I'd made one that was total luck). So, Stork's bouncing off the walls, totally ignoring the fact that we were 46 points behind but totally jazzed about his own shot. Genius. Everyone on our team got the right idea from that moment forward—get the stats—run the plays, run the offense, run the defense, but bottom line, get the stats. It was full-on rat-ball, with some semblance of Coach's structured game plan. We were reborn.

By the end of the game, Alverez had scored 18 points just because he was pissed about not scoring any points in the first half. "Eighteen goddam points is a whole lot goddam better than no goddam points," he said, after the game. I managed to put in six more points myself. Stork didn't score any more points but was still ecstatic about his 'shot.' We still lost the game 77-58, but we scored 51 points in the second half to their 21 points—a marked improvement thanks to Coach and Stork.

Oh, and just so you know, those three sophomores on the Rota JV team that were also on their varsity team, *stayed* on their varsity team the rest of the year. Over the next two years, myself and many others met them many more times on the field of battle. It's still a mystery how some kids mature faster, mentally and physically, than other kids but the other kids eventually catch up. For the rest of the season, I was never the high scorer at half time, or any other time—not my role. I was out there to make sure all the other players 'kept up' with me, as Coach said. I'd do everything to get them the ball so *they* could score.

Our varsity team won all six of their games in their tournament. They beat Rota and their three sophomores by over 30 points in both of their games. We lost our second game to the Rota JV team, by only three points, but we beat the Zaragoza JV twice and were all in the bleachers cheering for the Zaragoza JV team when the Toros beat the Rota JV team on Friday afternoon. That Friday night the guys at the Navy chow hall had barbequed a couple of pigs. It was heaven.

Our JV team ended up with a record of six wins and six losses for the year. Rota won the league with a 10 and 2 record and Zaragoza had a 2 and 10 record (they beat us once on their home court). We beat Rota once when we were at home. Alverez went crazy and scored 30 points in that game. He just took charge, which is what Coach had wanted from us all along—it was up to us to win games. All Coach could do was give us the formula with which to begin. We also played an exhibition game against the base and Royal Oaks League All Stars, all sophomores and juniors. These were guys that either didn't try out for the JV team or (the juniors) didn't make the cut for the varsity team. Classmates. They called themselves the Brass Hunters. One thing about league play in any sport over in Spain, there was always a sizable budget for trophies. We won the exhibition game by nine points which certainly validated Coach's player selection at the JV tryouts back in December. I had 14 points in that game—my highest scoring game ever—every shot I threw up, dropped—7 for 7.

In one of the classrooms at school, there was a poster that was tacked to the back of a door of a monkey sitting at a typewriter that read—"If you give enough monkeys typewriters, you'll find a Shakespeare sooner or later." Somehow that phrase applied to our JV basketball team. We were all a bunch of monkeys learning to type, and some of us figured it out, some of us not so much, and due to another summer of massive rotation deployments, there would only be five of us from the JV team left to try out for the varsity team later in the year (Stork, having had to have his face reassembled, was not able to try out). We had officially graduated to the next level of competition where the game was faster, the elbows sharper and the trash talking much more creative.

Chapter 14

I've mentioned that sports in my high school was an 'equalizer.' Especially football. There were kids in my class that were stronger than a lot of us, more intimidating, who took it upon themselves to remind others how 'street-tough' they were—8th grade and 9th grade. But when these so-called street-tough guys chose to play football, the story changed. While in years past, it was humorous to them to be slapping the back of some unsuspecting kid's head, it became a little more dangerous in the late August heat in an environment of legalized assault.

Those that had brought their intimidation tactics to my attention the previous two years, were now on the receiving end of some extremely sound body slams or forearms firmly planted in their necks. I'd never forgotten their jerk-ness and did my best to make sure their fun and games were over. Many times, during a blocking drill or a tackling drill, once I had separated them from their helmets with a solid, legal hit, I'd whisper to them that they needed to remember what just happened and it was in their best interest to be nice, to everyone, from now on. All this began happening last fall. I'll admit...I enjoyed it. Now, a lot of our school's tough guys didn't even play football, but word got around about who the 'ass-kickers' were on the team. And there were many.

Now, there was one guy in my class who was definitely the toughest guy that I'd ever even *heard* about—a total non-bully, someone whose very aura said 'leave me be,' a walking poster child of chiseled, god-given (or whomever) perfection—a guy, it was rumored, that had kicked the living crap out of at least a dozen GI's on the air base and was on a first-name basis with every MP. He rode a big-ass motorcycle to school (no helmet), wore big-ass cowboy boots, had a sweet looking girlfriend who was as quiet and mysterious as he was, and he wore a big-ass, full-length white fur coat to school—a no-nonsense dude whom I only had the privilege of encountering one time, later in the fall of the upcoming football season—Montague.

But there was another kid, last fall, a white kid, a junior, who seemed to have a problem with just about everyone, except his immediate 'friends'—an angry kid with three older brothers (which probably explained why he was such a prick all the time). Now, for some unknown reason, this kid had given myself and my friends rations of shit for at least the previous year—right up until it was time for a tackling drill—one blocker, one ball-carrier, one tackler, and a confined space for the drill to take place in. He was the ball-carrier and I was the tackler. A coach blew the whistle, I hit the blocker, did a spin move around him to my right, squared up, then hit this angry kid for all I was worth, dead center in his chest and he went down like an office building janitor's large ring of keys pitched into a wishing well. I mean down, down, down and out.

I got off of him and leaned over him, his eyes

fluttering and rolling back in their sockets, and said loud enough for everyone to hear, that from now on he could just shut the fuck up. It was maybe five seconds before the coaches realized that the angry kid was out cold and grabbed some ammonia packets to wake his dumb ass up. It was over 90 degrees that day. Coaches made me run a mile for saying 'fuck,' and I was to think seriously about what I'd done (cursing) every step of the way then come back when I was ready to rejoin the team. And, boy, did I think. Sweet revenge. I'd have run *two* miles.

Now, naturally, being the bully that this angry kid was, he *didn't* shut up, but he did tone it way down...at least to me, and my friends, he did. Sports, especially football, were an equalizer when everyone is dressed in street clothes and wandering around the school hallways. This fact became important right after basketball season ended because it became evident that our school, like many schools back in The World, had a race problem— not an overall prejudice problem between whites, Blacks, Asians and Hispanics within the student body (though I'm sure there may have been a future KKK Grand Wizard floating about), no, but what would be determined as the *source* of the problem would be within the school's administration, a problem that had festered for far too long, due to complacency. Shit does roll downhill. Brilliant man, Murphy.

One of the courses I signed up for during winter team was a college-prep, pre-business class (I'm serious here) called, 'Advanced Office Management Skills,' which was nothing more than working in the school's main office with the principal, deputy principals, and secretaries—filing, memo typing, record keeping, etc.— the first period of the day. One of my responsibilities was to pass out hall pass slips to students who were late. If you live in Royal Oaks, and you miss your bus, and no cars come by to offer you a ride, what can you do? I never knew any records of any students' tardiness were being kept by our principal, Mr. Bolen (called Mr. Blow-Hole behind his back) who had a tendency to be too much of a disciplinarian for his own good. But Bolen *did* keep records. He had a secret squirrel clipboard with a secret list that he kept in his desk. If a student came in late old Bolen was always watching.

There were many students who were late at least once a week, it seemed, and I'd do my best to sneak them a hall pass slip without Bolen's knowledge because here's what I'd noticed—if a student was white, Bolen would tell them to 'run along to class.' If a student was white and their father was a ranking officer on the base or some kind of stationed dignitary or something, he'd tell them to run along to class, *with a smile.* But if a student was Black or Hispanic or Asian, he'd give them the third-degree about what their excuse was *this* time all while making notes on his clipboard then disappearing back into his office. If you were white you were summarily excused. If you were a student of color, your actions were tabulated. Bolen handed out one, and two-day suspensions plenty of times, but never to a white student. I, myself, was late four times during the fall term because the line at the base bakery was longer than I anticipated. Being tardy four times in one term was easily grounds for some kind of detention, but nothing happened.

Bolen's dressing down of the minority students was embarrassing to witness and being someone who worked in the office during first period, I witnessed it many times. The man had some serious personal issues that ran deeper than anyone knew—not the kind of person to be a principal of an overseas military base high school that had such a punch bowl of flavors as ours had and one had to wonder if his attitude might not be shared, however minutely, by other members of the faculty. One time (because I have a semi-problem with authority), I asked Bolen why he berated a student (a Hispanic girl) as much as he did just for being a few minutes late and he said, "Because you gotta know how to handle *their kind.*" So, naturally, I told a couple of people what he'd said and this only added more fuel to the fires of discontent (that whole 'rumor' thing). But, even before Bolen's comment had made it's way into everyone's conversation, there had been a shit-storm brewing, right around the corner, ever since he had become our school's principal at the beginning of my freshman year, and it started on this day, a Thursday, a couple of weeks before the end of winter term. In fact, it started a mere eight minutes after the final first bell had rung.

Sandy was a Black girl. Sandy was in my class. Sandy was my friend. We'd known each other for almost three years. She and her family arrived in Spain a week before me and mine did. For some reason, Sandy knew that I wasn't a typical military brat—she could tell. She could tell that this was my first transfer of any type, because I was so fucking lost about everything. She'd asked me where I lived and me, being the genius that I was, and having had yet to perfect my pronunciation of 'Cannijellas,' told her I didn't know. I think that, despite our color difference, she came to like me almost immediately. "Boy," she said, "looks like you need some kinda help." Now, from my first day of school, I knew I could use a friend of any type, color be damned. In my old home town, despite it having a military installation, my school had had only two Black kids that had ever attended the entire time I went there.

So, Sandy gave me the layout of the school and the air base and a general idea about being a military brat newbie. "Just ease your way in," she told me. "Listen...don't talk" Try as I may, and I did try, her advice, while helpful, didn't last long, and before long I was being my typical, idiot self and ensuring my lack of friends.

At the end of our 8th grade year, Sandy saw me in the main hallway and said, "So, I see you've been an idiot for the whole year, huh?" So, I told her that despite her good advice, I guess I just didn't listen very well. She gave me that laugh of hers, that perfect, heartfelt laugh that lets one know a genuine connection has been made—the kind of connection that was both familiar and distant, by way of the whole 'hello/goodbye' standard that was typical for dependents of military personnel—a connection that was there, then not there, but would always *be* there. The only person I knew for a longer period of time while in Spain was Alverez and we'd flown over to Spain on the same plane together.

Sandy was in Johansen's geometry class with me when I received the 21 zeroes for cheating on the test (though, I'm sure the whole school knew about it, even though Johansen said our punishment was 'in house'). A couple of times, while I was in Johansen's classroom after school working on my makeup assignments, she walked by and looked in and wagged her finger at me like a mother would do to her child, then she'd laugh that laugh of hers as she went down the stairs.

On *this* day, this Thursday, Sandy was late getting to school. She was with two other girls—all late by just barely eight minutes. She and her friends came into the main office, all smiling, because there's no one else around, just me, like what had happened a couple of times before, and said, "Sugar, can we get us some hall passes to get into class?" I was already filling their passes out. Now, I knew Sandy had been late a few times already this term. Her friends were a year ahead of us and I knew they'd been late a few times as well. They were being a little loud and boisterous, despite my attempts to get them to cool it, and not because they were Black, but because they were girls. But Bolen heard them and came out of his office with his clipboard and his list. The man was spitting all over himself trying to explain the purpose of responsibility, and all that, and how ashamed they should be, and the more he ripped on them the more angry Sandy and her friends got until, finally, one of Sandy's friends told Old Blow Hole that he could shut up and go fuck himself.

About time, was what I was thinking. Right then, Bolen expelled the girl who'd told him what he could do, then suspended Sandy and the other girl for a week. Here's the shit...and here's the fan. Sandy started crying. The other two girls were screaming and cursing. Teachers from their first-floor classrooms came out into the hallway followed by their students, and within ten minutes it seemed like the entire student body was down on the first floor—Blacks, Hispanics and Asians on one side and whites on the other with teachers milling about trying to figure out what was happening and why.

Once word got out about the suspensions and about the girl who got expelled for just being late a couple of times, all the students of color began comparing notes about their own experiences and it became obvious what was up—racism, favoritism, and any other 'ism' anyone could think of. Blow Hole finally got called out for his personal bias. In the beginning, the other teachers had a unified front in defense of the head administrator but that diminished within one day once the extent and the history of their boss' actions came to light. And, in their defense, it was true that you just don't know what you don't know, but that didn't mean there wasn't a whole lot of soul-searching going on.

The rest of this Thursday was pretty much shot and so many of the events that transpired were nothing more than misdirected anger at all the wrong people. Students of color were pissed and had every right to be—but, how

KERRY (PAUL) MAY

to vent anger at an illogical mind-set of one man? Misdirected, I say. The teachers did their best to gather any and all students back to their classrooms but there was little or no response from all students, whites included. Everyone was off to other parts of the school grounds to find out what else was happening. The deputy principal called the MP's, just in case, but they were told to stay just off the campus.

People were angry. They were angry because someone in charge, with personal issues, could be such a dick and no other faculty member ever said a word (again, in their defense, I doubt many of them ever knew) because the dick was their boss. Questioning authority has its merits from time to time. No one left the school grounds but no one really knew what to do next. This was a situation of *perception*—how each of us perceived each other. Mind-sets were in serious need of readjustment.

There were lots of shouting matches and scuffles throughout the day. While there may have been some undercurrents of prejudice from some students toward other students, this was never the crux of the problem— the problem was the *revelation* of a problem that resonated at the top. The complaint was legit. But it didn't stop students of color from speaking out and it didn't stop white students from responding defensively in kind. And, to be honest, like any school anywhere, there were some kids that just wanted to use this situation as an opportunity to raise some hell.

One interesting thing about all of this upheaval was that I never knew what Alverez may have been experiencing. He was a person of color—Puerto Rican— no doubt one of Blow Hole's 'their kind.' Alverez went through this mess along with everyone else. After it was over, the subject never came up—what he was thinking, how me might have felt at the time. We were as close as a couple of horn dogs could be, but we never broached the subject. Alverez always had an easy-going manner about him—probably his finest attribute. I could get mouthy and be a dick from time to time. Opposites attract, I suppose.

Before the day ended there were two incidents that took place that I can personally attest to. The first incident had to do with that whole 'sports as an equalizer' thing, and the second had to do with Montague.

My school locker was on the third floor. Our school building, being a converted barracks, was kind of divided into two sections with classrooms on both sides and a long narrow classroom in the middle with a hallway/breezeway alongside the narrow classroom that had a long row of windows that faced the cafeteria and annex building behind the main building. I had just returned from hanging out in the cafeteria with a 100 or so other students who, like me, were trying to figure out what to do next, and decided I was going to go to my next class, if indeed there was even going to *be* a class, which was on the opposite side of the building, on the second floor. That was when a kid in my grade, that I barely knew, came up to me. He was not an athlete, but more of the bookwormish type. I didn't know him, but he knew me, and he was pretty shaken up. He told me that a bunch of Black students had cut off access in the long hallways on the second and third floors and anyone who was white who tried to get through, was getting slapped around (anyone white who couldn't or wouldn't fight back, that is). The three Black students in the long hallway on the third floor had slapped this kid around pretty good before he was able to get away.

As I said, there were some kids that just wanted to raise some hell. In addition, while Black students were blocking access through the long hallways, white students had taken it upon themselves to block the entrances to the school building on the main floor. None of this was solving anything and, looking back, it was all pretty fucking silly.

So, this kid asks me if I could help him get to his classroom because there was nowhere else to go. I understood perfectly. This kid asked me if I had a weapon of some kind, a pipe or a knife or something, in my locker, because he was quite positive that the kids blocking the hallway had weapons. I told him I didn't but we should go check out what was going on. Personally, I was curious to see who would be blocking the hallway because the third floor lockers were used mainly by freshmen and sophomores.

Sure enough, when the shaken kid and I started down the hallway, I recognized all three of the Black students. The first kid was in my grade and was known as sort of a trouble-maker. He'd only been back from The World for a couple of months, having had to spend a six-month 'sentence' away from Torrejon with an aunt on the east coast for hitting a white kid in the face with a brick during a spirited game of 'The Dozens' (the only fight I ever knew of because of a spirited exchange). The Air Force did that as punishment sometimes—you screw up and your family had to send you back to The World to cool off. The second kid was a freshman—one of those mouthy short kids who wore a big hat and sunglasses down on the end of his nose and fancied himself to be some kind of a street-wise, tough guy when he was around his friends, but when he was alone, he was as humble as road kill.

The third guy in the group I knew the best. Bonner. Bonner was on my Royal Oaks League basketball team (Broncos!). He was an all-star player. Why he chose not to go out for the JV basketball team is anyone's guess— a brass hunter, I suppose. He was also one of the guys in my school, in the 8th and 9th grade, that would slap the back of my head for no reason other than to intimidate.

Yet, Bonner was *also* one of the guys on the football team last fall that I firmly planted on his backside during a blocking or tackling drill (legalized assault) and then told him to remember what just happened. Bonner knew I was no longer intimidated by him or his friends and he also knew I would no longer tolerate any of his pranks. We were friends as much as we could be friends—he had his space and I had mine—no need to trespass. What was happening in our school, right now, was solving nothing and somehow Bonner must have realized it as much as I.

So, I walked down the hallway with this shaken up kid and the brick-throwing deviant stepped forward to block our path.

"What the fuck, white boy?" he demanded. "Man, you must be some kind of dumb motherfucker to be walkin' down here." The shaken kid stayed behind me. So, I told this guy that I was just helping a fellow student to find his classroom and, what was wrong with that and, besides, he'd gotten it seriously all wrong with what he'd just said.

"What?" this genius replied. "What the hell you talkin' 'bout, Whitey?" So, I told him that 'dumb' wasn't the right word he should use and that the right word he was looking for was, 'crazy.'

We stood there, staring at each other for a few seconds, and then, with the shaken kid still behind me, we proceeded.

The short kid started to say something but I looked at him and he swallowed whatever it was that was on his mind. Then I looked at Bonner and I could see that the experiences of the previous football season were still fresh enough in his mind and that he hadn't forgotten what I'd whispered to him before I helped him up off the ground. Bonner's face was expressionless, but I understood his position and I think he understood mine as well. Once we passed by the three Black students, I told the shaken kid to run to his classroom, which he did. But, for some reason, I just had to turn back around. The deviant brick-thrower took a step toward me but Bonner cut him off and walked toward me.

"What now, man?" Bonner asked. "Man, you should be happy we let you pass by *once*." I *was*, sincerely, but I motioned for Bonner to come closer and then told him that this kind of shit he and his so-called *friends* were pulling, wasn't solving anything and that he should know one thing.

"And what's that?" Bonner asked. It was evident that he was already through with me. So, I told him that just about everyone in the school was on *their* side. Now, you'd think that I had just hit him in the face with a brick. Nothing quells a revolution better than the lack of an enemy or the presence of an agreeable adversary. Bonner looked at me and smiled. I held out my fist to Bonner and he tapped it with his own fist. "Damn that," Bonner said. Okay, now I could breathe again.

The second thing, the thing with Montague, happened about an hour later. Like the shaken kid, I went to what should have been my next scheduled class, in English, but when I got there the only person in the room was the teacher. So, I decided to leave again. When I left, the teacher told me, "Be careful."

She was not having a good day, as I suspected was the case with most of the teachers. No doubt many of them were searching their own personal histories to see if they had ever shown favoritism along color lines or not. Racism can be tricky. Many times it can be there with neither party aware that it's there, until an outside observer clarifies the situation. But, one thing I always noticed about our school's faculty, had to do with their own communication with each other. The school's yearbooks—there were always dozens and dozens of group photos of kids—sports teams, clubs, social gatherings, academic organizations, extra curricular activities, such as GAA (Girl's Athletic Association, which in my slovenly clan was known as Great American Asses), etc., but not once, not *once*, was there ever a group photo of any kind, of the faculty. No dinners, no socials, no banquets, nada. There was just the usual individual photos of each teacher with their name and subject taught beneath their photo. I'm sure some of them must have gotten together from time to time but you'd have never known it. Hell, you'd never have known that any of the teachers were even on a first-name basis. I was thinking that this 'wake up call' might be as good for the faculty as it could be for the student body—call it an 'awareness raising' or, at the very least, a 'gut check' of one's opinion of their fellow creatures. But, there was still a lot of nutso shit going on between different people back in The World—we'd see the half hour news reels every Friday and Saturday at the movies in Royal Oaks—so why should anything be any different over here in Spain?

So, I left the empty classroom and the English teacher and went downstairs to see what was shaking. My confrontation with Bonner and the other two guys seemed, to me anyway, to have resolved *something*, at least between Bonner and I, but now a sizable crowd had formed out in front of the school and I'd bet every MP on the entire base was now over in the bus parking lot— even Sergio.

There was a group of eight or nine students of color all yelling and posing and puffing up their feathers with a couple dozen white students nearby, looking on. Some of the running commentary from the group was directed at the school administrators, who were nowhere to be seen, and some was directed at the white students.

One of the Black students, a tallish, gangly kid with a large afro, seemed to be directing the chorus. He stood out in front cursing and gesturing, pointing and accusing, until he cursed and gestured at the wrong kid—a senior, a real country boy-type of kid, whom I knew of only because his little brother was in my grade. I knew that their mother had been sick. I was in the Teen Center in Royal Oaks when the two brothers came in, together, the day their mother passed away, to figure out how they were going to deal with it, together.

So, this kid with the afro singled out the country boy as the object of his ire and the country boy stepped forward. The Black student bobbed and weaved, took a few jabs at the air, then swung his fist at the senior who side-stepped the punch and, at the same time, brought his own round house haymaker and nailed the Black student in the temple. The Black student hit the ground, hard. He was on his back with his arms still extended out in front of him and began twitching terribly. Misdirected anger—nothing solved.

I looked over at the MP's and saw that they were beginning to move toward the school from the bus parking lot. I could see Sergio, and could also see the large Black MP from the front gate and the angry MP that was at the flight line when the caskets were being off loaded from the transport jet. But then something else happened.

In this group of minority students was a guy I knew pretty well, nicknamed T-Bone. This guy played football, wrestled and ran track for the school—an all-round athlete. I'd actually tackled him a couple of times during football scrimmages and had wrestled him once, just for grins, in the base gym because he needed a partner to practice some moves. T-Bone was livid after seeing his brother-in-arms get laid out and he stood in front of the crowd of white students and yelled, "I'll take on any one of you white motherfuckers!"

By now, the MP's had broken into a jog—this could have really gotten nasty. But then the crowd of white students parted like the Red Sea and Montague stepped forward in his big-ass cowboy boots and his big-ass fur coat and then, before saying anything to T-Bone, he held his hand up toward the group of jogging MP's, signaling for them to stop who, upon seeing that it was Montague, *did* stop. Then Montague turned to T-Bone and said, calmly, "I'll take you on, T-Bone."

Now, does the phrase 'shitting little green men' mean anything to you? I ask because T-Bone was doing exactly that, at that moment. His challenge had been met by the meanest, baddest, silver-backed fucking gorilla in the jungle and the end result would have just meant, 'the end.' T-Bone knew it—we all knew it. The MP's knew it because then they began to *walk* toward us all again and telling us to break it up, show's over. Sergio spotted me and came over to me.

"I figured you'd be here," Sergio said. I just shrugged.

That's how Thursday ended. I got on my bus a full half-hour before it was time to leave. I heard an engine fire up while sitting on my bus and saw Montague on his big-ass motorcycle, his girlfriend sitting behind him with her arms wrapped around his waist tightly, as he rode out of the school's parking lot, his long blonde curls flowing behind him, totally in his element, his work here done. Royalty.

Chapter 15

The next day, Friday, a large sign had been posted on the school's front door—'All Students! Auditorium! 9 am!' (which meant I had plenty of time to get over to the base bakery to grab a fresh loaf of 'pan'). Now, the students, for the most part, were still divided into their separate camps, but there were no confrontations, no shouting matches, no stand-offs. I heard laughter coming from many clusters of kids, Black and white. It looked to me that about a quarter of the students didn't come to school, judging by the quantity of students outside the front of the school's locked front doors. There were two MP trucks parked in the faculty parking lot and four MP's (none that I recognized) were just hanging out outside their pickups, looking official. I didn't see any teachers anywhere. The doors to the auditorium were locked. I found Alverez and gave him half of my fresh-backed loaf of pan.

"Man, this is goddam craziness, you know?" Alverez said, between bites of delectable morsels of Spanish goodness. "I'm supposed to have a goddam quiz this morning, you know?" Okay, that made me laugh and Alverez looked at me like I was loony.

Then Alverez said, "So, what do you think's gonna

happen?" I told him I had no clue. "Where do you suppose all the teachers are?" he asked. I told him that maybe they were all in the auditorium already. Twenty minutes later, when the auditorium doors opened, it was true. The faculty had had a pre-assembly meeting before the students were allowed entrance.

As soon as the auditorium doors opened at 9 am, about two dozen students of color climbed up on the stage and began setting up chairs while the rest of the minority student body hung out in front of the stage. There were three Black teachers employed at our school, as well as two Hispanic teachers, and one Asian teacher, who taught Spanish (no shit), who all made their way to the chairs on stage and sat down together on one side. The rest of the faculty that was present sat on the opposite side of the stage. Everyone else who entered the auditorium took their seats in the audience and even with about a quarter of the student body absent, the auditorium was jammed. Students were sitting in the aisles. What was apparent, immediately, was that there was a perfect division of faculty and students alike, based on race. This was definitely all wrong. All someone had to do to understand this was to open their eyes. Whatever had been brewing was not based on a single administrator's harbored, personal opinions, and it became apparent that it had been brewing for a long time.

The first person to address the student body, once everyone was settled, was Mrs. Neese, a Black woman who taught English and humanities classes. Apparently, she was selected to speak first because of her unique 'qualifications.' She was Black but she was married to a white man. In her humanities class, that I took in the fall, she had spoken at length about the necessity of self-empowerment, group-empowerment and then species-empowerment. Equal rights was always a running theme. She had a delightful delivery and a wealth of knowledge regarding oppressed peoples and societies going as far back as Egyptian times. Each student, on the first day of class, had to reveal what their nationality backgrounds were. When I told her and the class that I was not only Scottish and English, but also a quarter Navajo, Mrs. Neese found this quite humorous. "Boy," she said, "You're not only oppressed, but you're oppressed by your own self." No truer words. This brought quite a laugh from the class and established a bond I figured I'd never forget.

One time during one of her lengthy equal rights lectures, she caught me looking at her with my eyes crossed. She began to laugh and shake so much that she had to turn away from the class to dab at her eyes and compose herself.

~~~~

Reunion
(A Poem)

I know, and can tell you now,
Mrs. Neese, why I was looking
At you with my eyes crossed,
That morning in 1st period English,
Which halted your lecture,
And broke you up, until tears
Ran down the cheeks of your beautiful
Black face— For just that moment
I wanted to see what our world
Would be like with two of you in it.
How many more young, naive,
White boys could you reach
With your pledge of equality,
So that they, too, would carry it

With them for the rest of their lives,
As I believe I have tried, from that
Day forward, when you had to turn
Your face away from mine, to regain
Your composure, to dab your eyes,
And unknowingly be born into poem.

~~~~

One time, someone asked Mrs. Neese, if she was so full of herself about Black freedom and Black empowerment and all the rest, then why was she married to a white man? Her answer, classic—"Because, child, he *gets* me." Everyone looked around at everyone else for a few seconds. She couldn't be talking about sex, right?

Then, Mrs. Neese said, "That's what love is, you see. If you find someone who *gets* you, and you *get* them, it's love. Color doesn't matter." Her reasoning was becoming clear. Then she said, "Tell me, what color is love? Any kind of love. Anyone?" It was one of the deepest thought-provoking high school class periods of my four short years.

'Race relations' (never cared for that term—'people relations' is more to my liking, or maybe just 'relations') can be tricky, especially if one has had a formulated idea in their head from childhood, planted there by someone with an axe to grind, or just plain fearful or threatened. And then some people's ideas about *race* are just plain goddam goofy, if you know what I mean. For instance, during her senior year, my sister dated a guy, briefly, an officer's kid (some kind of colonel, not that it mattered), and one day this guy's parents decided that they wanted to meet this girl that their son (only child) was so gooey-eyed over and so my sister went over to their house (one of the six or seven single-unit homes), for some iced tea and pound cake. The niceties were all in place but then the guy's mother asked my sister about her/our family heritage. So my sister told her all about our 'white' side of the family and then she told her about how our grandfather was full-blood Navajo and her mother was half-Navajo and we kids were a quarter-Navajo—very proud-like, you know? This guy's mother looked at my sister, taking it all in, nodding politely, but then she said, "Well, that's all very lovely, I'm sure, but tell me, does your father know anything about all this?" Uh, pin-drop. Unreal.

Now, I can't say for certain what my sister's response to this inquiry was (when she told me, I almost peed my pants, I laughed so hard), but it was apparent that her boyfriend's mother was sincere. I can only imagine, out of respect, that my sister merely confirmed that our father was well aware of our mother's nationality and background. She may have rolled her eyes at her boyfriend a couple of times, but she was probably still nice.

Now, my sister could be as mouthy as me, on occasion—I know, I lived with her for 18 years. No doubt there were a lot of things she *wanted* to say to this idiot at that moment, but she probably felt like she'd been hit by a country boy roundhouse haymaker and was too stunned to say anything else. I mean, my sister had to have thought that this woman had just fallen off a passing asteroid or something because then this woman asked her, "And your father's okay with all this?" No shit. How can a person respond to someone like this?

Now, if it had been me (which I'm glad it wasn't) and if I had retained some semblance of wits about me, I might have said, "Of course, my father's okay with *all this*, you stupid cow—that's why he married my mother!" But, then again, my sister was dealing with a woman who, rumor had it, on the occasion of going into Madrid, to the Prado Museum, perhaps one of the top three galleries of artwork in the whole goddam world, could only complain about how dirty she thought the floors were.

Now, what Mrs. Neese spoke of on stage in the school's auditorium had to do with the responsibility of equal rights—those who ask for them and those who have them—the mind-set we all carry with us. Mrs. Neese lectured all of us—whites and students of color— but she also lectured those from the faculty who were present. "Complacency in changing times," she said, before sitting down again, "is a threat to all races." When Mrs. Neese took her chair the audience gave her a standing ovation.

Next to speak were a couple of coaches—varsity football and varsity basketball (both white men). They really didn't say a whole lot, other than they believed they always gave everyone on their teams a fair shake (which was true from what I witnessed), but they also acknowledged that what was happening here could set a precedent for better communication, a more free exchange of ideas and concepts and that they, along with the rest of the faculty, welcomed the possibilities. One thing was for certain, if there were ever any candidates for a 'group hug' it was the teachers present in the auditorium. Principal Bolen, the deputy principal and the vice-principal were not in attendance that morning. I always wondered if the faculty had excluded them from the pre-assembly meeting. I never did find out. The gears were turning.

The final person to speak was the minority students' 'appointed' student representative, Sam. Sam was a football player, a hard-nosed ball carrier who could not only be loud and boisterous, but silent and contemplative as well. Everyone (well, almost everyone—there *were* those KKK types, the idiots) liked Sam, so when Sam spoke, people were bound to listen. Sam began by announcing that a Black Student Union had been created, but that Hispanics, Asians and other minorities were welcome to join—and even (get this) whites could join. He said that there were some *needs* that were more pertinent to students of color than to white students, though he didn't elaborate on what those needs were. I heard a couple of groans from the crowd which silenced everyone. Then someone in the audience yelled out, "What about a White Student Union?" and Sam said, "There already *is* one—and it's the *only* one—and that's one of the problems." A murmur rippled through the auditorium like a tsunami. Some people felt accused of something they never believed they had done—being prejudicial against other students, and they were correct. Others, not so much. But, Mrs. Neese's statement about complacency being the enemy rang true.

Another voice from the audience spoke up, "Well then, what the hell do you *want*?" The crowd hushed.

Sam gathered himself and said, "We want to stop being looked upon as, and being treated as, second-class citizens." Then Sam tapped the side of his head lightly. "In here," he said, then put his hand over his heart, "and in here."

Okay, getting a little misty-eyed now, as were others around me. Then the same voice from the crowd called out, "Well, what the hell do you want from *us*?" And Sam said, "We want to know if you're *with* us." Within a heartbeat, kids began getting out of their seats and heading for the stage.

This was not only some heavy shit for a bunch of high school kids, but some kind of heavy *magic* as well. The largest group hug, perhaps the only group hug, in the history of my high school. When you get over 500 students, of all ages, all races, religions, experiences, from all parts of the world, not to mention a full load of faculty and staff, you're bound to get some disagreement. How could anyone expect anything different? One good thing to emerge was that those who just wanted to raise some hell were, from that point forward, summarily ignored…by everyone.

When the 1972 yearbooks arrived, there was a large group photograph of students that was taken on the football field, inside the front cover and on the first page. On that page was written, "This book is dedicated to the student body." Genius.

If you were there on that day then you knew that that day was remembered as 'Black Friday,' but the only color I remember seeing was love.

On Monday, we found out Principal Bolen was gone, the Vice-Principal had applied for a different job at a different overseas school and the Deputy-Principal was now in charge. Great, I remember thinking, because our new principal, Mr. Owens, lived in the quad-plex right next to mine. Lovely. There were a lot of parent/teacher conferences over the next week, mostly just to explain what had happened. To my knowledge, no kind of punishment was handed out to any student. Clean slate. I had access to the list of parents (being the noble main office assistant that I was) who came in to see the new principal. I never saw the names of Montague's parents on the list but I figured that cyborgs must not *have* parents.

All of this hearts and flowers, rainbows and unicorns, lovey-dovey stuff lasted through the rest of the school year and through the summer, but then the school board and USDESEA big wigs did something that put new divisions into place the following autumn that turned out to be both a good thing and a not so good thing.

Chapter 16: Part 1

I can't explain it, I really can't, try as I may. I've analyzed it a thousand times over the years and it still remains a mystery to me. But, I could now, for some reason, *see* the baseball, ultra clearly—the speed of the rotation, the directional spin of the seams, the potential future destination of the ball based on both speed and spin—as soon as it left the pitcher's hand, until a millisecond before crossing the home plate I was protecting. Very strange. What a difference a year made. I played baseball for two years while I was in Spain. The first year was in Little League, the 14-15 year-old division, and the second year was the Little League Big League Division, for 16-18 year-olds—the only year the air base had a Big League Division. The first year couldn't have been worse. The second year couldn't have been better. It's as if sometime after that first season my eyeballs had been baptized or something. It made no sense. Still doesn't.

But before I proceed with the baseball 'miracle,' there was one event that took place at Torrejon that warrants mentioning—it having taken place during the Vietnam war and all and Torrejon being such a strategic part of the war, not to mention we were told it might be televised back in The World—Bob Hope's traveling USO Road Show came to the base, on the way back from Vietnam. The show made two quick scheduled stops—one in Madrid and one in Rota. Quick stops, quick shows, jam-packed.

The show was set up in one of the two huge hangers on the flight line. Huge hangers. I think that everyone who had anything to do with the air base was there—it was like New Year's Eve in Puerta del Sol—assholes to elbows. The kids that I hung out with at school and at the teen dances scrambled to get to the front row of fold-out chairs as soon as side doors of the hanger were opened. Mr. Hope was in fine form. He came out on stage wearing a '98th Strategic Wing' baseball cap and carrying his usual golf club. The jokes were clean and Mr. Hope got in some good-natured ribbing of the new base commander which always brings the biggest laughs.

There were a couple of other celebrity types with the show, whose names escape me (no Playboy bunnies or Playmate of the Year, which would have been a nice touch) and a couple of camera crews on hand to document the stop, thus the rumor about it possibly being televised). But, the best part of the show was saved for last—'The Brothers,' a soul band made up of local servicemen.

The Brothers had played at teen dances on the base a few times—always a treat. Then they cut a record, a 45, with their two best songs, 'Brother's Groove' and 'Funky Paella.' Even before Mr. Hope could finish his introduction of The Brothers, the unreal electric guitar riffs from 'Brothers Groove' began blaring out of the amplifiers and the large dance area in front of the stage was crammed with kids doing their best to boogie down and show off for the camera crews. I was boogying (as best I knew how, having more than a few times been accused of dancing like a farmer). Alverez was doing his boogie-best—we all were.

The next day, I sent a letter to my friends back in my home town and told them to watch for Bob Hope's USO Tour show on TV because I was bound to be on it considering how many times I mugged for the camera guys. Two weeks later, I get a letter back calling 'bullshit'—yeah right, like I *really saw* Bob Hope, in person, in *Spain*. Now, this kind of response had happened twice before. The director of the air base's officers' club (of which my father was a member, based on his pay scale, even though he was technically a civilian) was able to book 'Herman's Hermits' for a one-night appearance. What kid from the 60's doesn't remember Peter Noone and Herman's Hermits? My parents and my sister and I not only went to the show, taking in their hit songs, Mrs. Brown (you've got a lovely daughter), Henry the Eighth, plus a spoof number in which the band became the Ink Spots or the Ink Blots or the Ink something-or-other. A fun show, to be sure. I wrote my friends immediately. They called 'bullshit.' But, to record the moment, my mother had had the presence of mind to ask Peter Noone if her son (me) could have his picture taken with him and Peter, and being the gracious man that he was, he said, "Absolutely, mum!" Now, getting a roll of Kodak film developed at the air base back in the early 70's could take 10 days to two weeks because all the dependents' film canisters were sent from the BX to a Kodak lab in downtown Madrid. I can only imagine (with sweet revenge, I might add) the surprised looks on the faces of my friends in my home town when they received my *next* letter which included a snapshot of Peter Noone and myself and then read what I had written on the back of the photo—"Eat shit." A classic 'corte tu bajo' if there ever was one. I love it when people call 'bullshit' on you and then you can actually *prove* that you were telling them the truth. I mean, how satisfying would it be if you were say, a magician on stage, and some heckler in the audience called 'bullshit' on you, and then you went down to where they were sitting and *abracadabra,* in front of god (or whomever) and everyone, you pulled a goddam, live pelican out of their ear?

A couple of weeks later Ricky Nelson, that good-looking guy from the Ozzie & Harriet TV show, played at the officers' club and my mother got a picture with him that included me, my sister and one of my sister's friends. This time I waited to send a letter back to The World until after the photos were developed. I wrote on the back of the picture, "Ricky Nelson and me." Two weeks later I get a letter from my friend, Darren, that read—"Good photo. Who's Ricky Nelson?"

So, Bob Hope shows up, The Brothers perform the A & B sides of their record, my friends and I dance our butts off for the TV cameras like we're on American Bandstand or something, fully expecting to be broadcast on every channel back in The World, and the entire time I'm inside that flight line hanger, I could only think about the forklifts moving the terrible cargo around like it was no big deal. I was 15 years old—I wasn't supposed to care—it was my job to *not* understand. I began to wonder why trying to make sense of shit was suddenly a crime.

But, I *do* know that some radio highlights of Bob Hope's USO show were carried on the Armed Forces radio. They replayed different portions of Mr. Hope's stand-up routine and The Brothers performance, at least a dozen times the following week. Now, the Armed Forces radio was a hoot and two thirds in my book—an aural window to everything that was good about The World. I never listened to the radio when I lived in eastern Oregon. Never. But the Armed Forces radio was on virtually every morning, afternoon and evening, not only in my house, but practically every house in Royal Oaks, as well as everywhere on the air base (could have been that lack of television thing). Who could go a whole week without hearing — "And now, another exciting episode in the life of the most fantastic crime-fighter the world has ever known...Bak-Bak-Bak-Bac-caaak... Chicken Man (He's everywhere! He's everywhere!) Ba-dada-da-DA!" Jim Runyon's two-minute narration of Dick Orkin's silly serial was as important a topic of conversation (that whole 'community' thing) as Kasey Kasem's Top 40 Countdown on Saturday afternoons ("Keep your feet on the ground, and keep reaching for the stars!"—good advice for a bunch of gooey-eyed pubescent pud-whackers like we were).

Now, the Armed Forces Radio Network was nothing if not fair, to all listeners—soul music, rock and roll, jazz, country/western, spiritual, easy listening, Appalachian hoe-down (no shit), informative interviews, an evangelical preacher or two, Paul Harvey, historical perspective tidbits ("George Washington Carver! Who was he? A Black man! What did he do?..."), the occasional Hudson & Landry comic routine, and of course, every hour, on the hour, the "Top of the Hour News."

In the mornings, for the first couple of hours, Monday through Friday, at the end of the news broadcast, would be the local weather report which was phoned in to the station by a Tech Sergeant whose son, whom I barely knew at the time, was on the JV basketball team with me. This kid's father's daily weather reports were a stitch and worth waiting for because of his delivery—total deadpan, total monotone. Example: "This is Tech Sergeant John Dye of the Eleven-Second Weather Wing with your forecast for today—today's high will be 93 degrees. That's 93 in the shade, people. Winds will be out of the northwest, as usual, with gusts 8-10 miles per hour. The skies today will be clear. No rain. Wear a hat. That's it."

But, if I were to pick a single radio moment that stood head and shoulders above the rest, it would be a time during one of the frequent local pledge drives to raise money for some local group or organization. Little League baseball had many such pledge drives. I know because I wore the new uniforms as a result of two such drives—for The Braves and the Orioles. Listeners would call in a pledge and say they'd donate it if such-and-such a person would do such-and-such a task. It was never anything crass or outlandish, but usually something innocent enough so that the person put into the spotlight could easily come through to ensure the needed pledge would be collected. All in good fun.

Torrejon Air Force Base had just appointed or transferred in a new base commander (being non-military, I never understood how that whole promotion thing worked) and someone called in and promised to pledge $100 if the new base commander would sing the United States Air Force Anthem on the air, via telephone. Innocent, simple, good fun. So, he agreed to sing and the moment of truth was at hand. Who was this guy? Outside of the typical rumors that would take flight at these times, it was important to understand the temperament and personality of a base commander (remember *it* rolls down hill) as well as their public/military service record, rank and accomplishments. He was the newbie on parade. A time for his debut was set. Word got around and everyone was listening in.

"Off we go, into the wild blue yonder..." the new commander sang, in a fine baritone voice, and then, nothing. He froze—dead air—three seconds, five seconds, eight seconds. Could it be that the man who was now in charge of so much, from laundry services to tactical jet fighter squadrons, had *forgotten* the words of the anthem of the very military branch that he had labored so hard for, in order to achieve such a lofty stature, at such a strategic post, during war time?

Ten seconds, twelve seconds, and then….."C'mon, boys. Give 'em hell!" The new commander nailed it— the best live radio recovery of all time, and one that was replayed again and again at nearly every military base radio station in Europe and southeast Asia. Classic. For the next couple of weeks, I'd hear my father, a man not prone to cursing, as I've said, humming the opening refrain of the Air Force Anthem and then, under his breath, singing lightly, "Come on boys, give 'em hell…" A couple of industrious souls started a petition to have the words of the Air Force Anthem permanently changed, but I never found out if the petition ever grew any real legs. And, of course, the immediate can of rumors that opened up was that the new base commander had had a stroke while on the air. But then, the next day, someone said that they saw him somewhere on the base and that he was limping so, naturally, the 'stroke' rumor was then downgraded to a broken leg. God (or whomever) bless the US Air Force.

Chapter 16: Part 2

In the spring of 1971, I signed up for Little League baseball (13-15 year-olds). As luck would have it, my baseball coach had also been my Royal Oaks basketball league coach, Sgt. Spencer, a firefighting squad leader on the base. He was the one who taught me that if you were playing basketball in a cold gym and your hands were cold, that you should reach inside your gym shorts and grab a handful in order to warm your fingers. Valuable advice that I utilized whenever the need arose, for decades to come. Coach also emphasized that when doing so (reaching into your shorts), to make sure they were your *own* gym shorts. Hilarious.

I signed up for baseball because all my friends in Royal Oaks were playing baseball—no other reason, really. I played a little baseball back in my home town, but not much. I did okay as a fielder (right field), but my abilities at batting sucked royal raspberries. The problem was my eyesight. I couldn't really pick up the ball until it was at least halfway from the pitcher to the catcher.

When I was eight years old, back in eastern Oregon in the summer time, I was riding a friend's bicycle and the handlebars didn't have any of those rubber handgrips on them. I was screwing around in the parking lot next to the Shoe String Drive-In when I hit a rock with my front tire and the handlebars whipped around promptly scooping my right eyeball out of my skull. I was fortunate because there happened to be a triage medic from the air base there at the same time and he knew what to do initially, which enabled me to keep my eyeball—I mean, it was just hanging down there, by its strands, on my cheek, and there was blood everywhere.

After I was all stitched up, I had to wear a patch on my eye for a couple of weeks while I healed up. And then, afterwards, I was supposed to wear the patch on my other eye for a couple more weeks to balance my eyesight out. That was the theory anyway. Yeah, right. Try telling an eight year-old kid he has to wear an eye patch over his perfectly good eye for two weeks in the summer time. Didn't happen. As a result, the sight in my left eye became fuzzy at a distance and my right eye was even fuzzier.

I'm right-handed so I bat with my left eye closest to the pitcher. Seeing a pitch happened a good second slower for me than most people. I never told my parents about needing glasses until my sophomore year because in my home town wearing glasses as a kid marked you as a definite target and I was already a target of the bigger kids in my neighborhood.

So, I signed up for baseball, got my league basketball coach as my baseball coach, and listened to him yell at me for swinging and missing big fat-ass pitches, right down the pipe, again and again.

I'm sure my coach must have assumed that I was *afraid* to bat. I wasn't (well, maybe sort of—the idea of possibly reacting a second too slow for a pitch coming right at my brain pan did cross my mind), but about halfway through the season Coach told me to meet him at a ball field on the base for some special tutelage. I didn't know it until I got out there that coach had also asked our best fast ball pitcher and our catcher to attend this special session as well.

The pitcher was in my grade but was one of those kids that just matured faster than the rest of us. He'd started, as a freshman, as receiver on the varsity football team the previous fall and could motor with the best of them—very fast. The catcher on our team, Deacon, was a grade ahead of me, but just made the age-cut to play in the league. Deacon was the finest all around athlete I ever saw at my high school. He was good at every sport. I always wondered why, when tryouts for varsity basketball were held my junior year (his senior year), Deacon wasn't chosen for the team and decided to wrestle instead. Some things which were perfectly logical totally escape me. This guy was far better at basketball than I was and was a far better athlete. If our school track team had had the decathlon as an event, this guy would have been the USDESEA European Champion four straight years.

So, it's the three of us and our coach. Our pitcher warms up with a few pitches and then Coach tells me to step into the batter's box, so I do. I let the first three pitches go by me without swinging—good pitches, playable pitches, and that infuriated Coach. The next pitch was a curve ball and, as usual, I caught the second half of the ball's flight when it was still coming right at me before breaking to the plate and I backed out of the batter's box to see the ball cross the plate dead center in the strike zone. My coach was livid.

"God damn it, you pansy!" Coach yelled. "That was a perfect pitch!"

Then Coach went over to our pitcher and spoke to him in whispers. Our pitcher listened, then stepped back and started to say something in return, but Coach says to him, "Just do it!" Then Coach yelled at me, "Now, get back in that batter's box and swing the goddam bat for a change! Jesus H. Christ, anyway!"

I don't know why, but I figured that the next pitch was going to be another curve ball and I decided I would hang in there no matter what. Wrong. The next pitch was a fast ball and it nailed me right on that little knot of meat just above my left elbow. My whole left arm went dead. I'd hung in there, looking for something over the plate, something I could swing at, like Coach told me to, and that son-of-a-bitch had told our pitcher to throw a fast ball *at* me. My arm was so numb I couldn't even hold the bat anymore.

"All right, let's go," Coach said. "Get back in there and let's try this again." No apologies, no inquiries about whether I was okay, nothing—just another life lesson from someone who believed they were in a position to dole out life lessons. I walked over to the backstop, picked up my baseball glove and left. This was Little League baseball, not life and death.

My coach told our pitcher to throw a fast ball *at* me and what could that kid do but do what the coach told him to do? I didn't blame *him*. For some reason that I'll never understand, this coach believed that all the players under his guidance were some kind of collective representation of his public persona and any glitches were a black mark on his inner being.

We were in first place at the time, no thanks to my abilities at the plate, though my fielding was adequate enough to continue playing in right field, and we had just four games left in the season—if we win two of the four then first place overall was ours and we'd get the trophies. I'm sure that after our little session, Coach figured I'd quit the team, but I didn't. The thought never crossed my mind. As it turned out, we won all four games. I got a couple of sacrifice flies in that span, but nothing more, except in the final game.

Our final game was the first one of the day at the big

field in Royal Oaks. We were playing the second-place team. We'd already won the league with our previous three wins. The second-place team had a pitcher who was probably the best infielder in the league other than Deacon—a short stop—easily the most fluid short stop I ever watched play. We were probably three runs ahead by the sixth inning and it was my turn to bat (I batted ninth, naturally). I don't think I'd said two words to my coach during our last four games, nor he to me, except when I'd get up to bat and I'd hear him yelling at me to "Just get a hit, for Chrissakes," but nothing other than that. I don't think I had looked the man in the eye, even one time, either.

So, sixth inning, three runs ahead, I'm up to bat. My father was at this game. He came to what games he could, depending on what kind of shift he was working. My mother wasn't at this game, though she'd usually attend them with my father. I told my sister to stop coming to my games after our second game, when I misjudged a hard grounder out in right field that ended up going underneath my glove and she made it her duty to yell out at the top of her lungs the same thing I'm sure my coach was thinking, "What in the hell are you doing out there?"

The first pitch was a called strike but the second pitch looked like it would be a little low and outside. I swung anyway and I connected, and the ball sailed high over the centerfield fence in a big-ass hurry. I could hear people in the stands behind the home plate backstop yelling, "Way to go!" and "Nice hit!" As I ran around the bases, my teammates met me at home plate. My coach was pounding his chest and yelling, "I knew it! I knew it! I knew it all along." Yeah, right. I never looked at my coach but went into the dugout and had a seat. A couple of innings later, the game ended and the season ended. I grabbed my glove and met my father outside the fence and we began walking to our car when my coach came up to us.

"You see? I told you you had it in you! I knew it! I knew it all along!" he yelled, standing there, so proud, so goddam full of himself, his public persona vindicated at last. Now, I never told my father what had happened at the little tutelage session Coach had set up for me—no sense in having it turn into some kind of pissing match between the adults (no telling if my father might have walloped this guy upside his head or not). I still had the stitching marks of the fast ball tattooed above my elbow. This was my problem, not my father's.

So Coach is just beaming his ass off about what I had finally done and without a doubt thinking that he was responsible for my little piece of glorified self-worth. But, I'd had it up to here. Did I mention that I had a problem with authority? Let me clarify—I have a *serious* problem with authority, especially if it's evident that the quest for authority is self-serving, like this was.

The season was over. I looked at my coach's sappy, self-serving, smiling face and told him, fuck him and the horse he rode in on. My father took a step back. My coach's face went totally blank, stunned, as dead as my arm went after getting hit by that pitch. I just said it, what was on my mind, what had been on my mind for over a month. I was seriously expecting a giant thunderbolt to come out of the gorgeous, blue, Spanish sky and drill me right down into the puke pits of hell for speaking my mind.

Then my father, who must have realized that I'd been keeping something bottled up for awhile and didn't want to share it with him because of some sort of code of manhood-pride or something, said to my coach, "Yeah, what he said, Coach."

Now, this coach wasn't a *total* dick (Got cold hands? Grab a handful.) He was very good at providing the proper fundamentals regarding all aspects of baseball. His only problem was his insistence on making a bunch of 13-15 year-olds function as an extension of his own psyche. A little too wound up for my taste. I had enough trouble just trying to figure out how to be myself without having to worry about someone *else's* needs regarding my performance.

A week later was our end-of-season Baseball Banquet. It was an outdoor, barbeque/picnic affair on the base with a small stage set up for awards presentations. My whole team got on stage to receive our First Place trophies and then got off, all except for our Deacon, who received a trophy for League MVP, and our coach, who received a plaque, for Coach of the Year. Then the League All Stars took the stage (Deacon stayed up there) to receive their All Star jackets. Four players on my team got jackets. Once I got my trophy, I went to grab a hamburger and a Coke.

The Awards Ceremony emcee then made an announcement about collecting donations for next season to form a Little League Big League Division for 16-18 year-olds. There would be a radio fundraising drive in the near future but people could donate right then if they wanted to. This new league was essential to keep the older teenage boys busy and out of any mischief and all parents were encouraged to sign up their kids. A good idea, really. Organized sports were vital to the well being of all parents in Royal Oaks and on the base. No doubt the MP's were grateful for the added help with hundreds of overly-creative dependent children, playing everything from Pee-Wee football to girls' softball. And to create a league for 16-18 year-old males would only make their jobs that much easier.

But, there was one more award that was handed out— 'The Most Amazing Game' Award. And it was amazing. I was there. Both days.

After our final game of the season there was a second one on the big field and then one more after that which would have been the very last game of the season for the league. And it was *that* game that would stand out…forever…in everyone's mind who was there.

The two last-place teams were playing and they had identical losing records—they were playing to see which team would *not* be the overall worst team of the year. Heavy stakes, to be sure. Now, one would expect the stands to only have maybe a few family members in attendance looking on, and it was true at the beginning, but word got out about what was happening and by the third inning, the outfield fence was surrounded by people. The stands behind home plate were packed as well.

I'd gone home with my father, a short ride of total silence, I might add, having told my coach what I'd told him. I took a shower and then, for lack of anything else to do, decided to go back down to the Teen Center to see what was shaking, because there was always something going on there during a summer Saturday afternoon. When I got down there someone told me about the two last-place teams squaring off and I figured it would be fun to see these guys going at it. Playing for a championship is one kind of pressure, but playing *not* to be the worst team of the season, is a whole other ball of snakes. There is something to be said for the 'spirit of competition' that it also applies to avoiding failure as much as achieving greatness.

Our games were nine innings. The second game had gone into extra innings and caused the third game to start later than scheduled. There was a kid named Curtis on one of the teams, the only player from either team to be selected to receive an All-Star jacket. Our catcher was leading the league in home runs—he had eight. Curtis had three home runs for the season at that time. He batted third on his team. After the first two guys in the line up struck out, Curtis came up to bat and jacked a long ball over the left field fence. At the bottom of the inning the other team tied the game up.

In the next inning, due to some fielding errors, walked batters and a batter hit by a pitch, Curtis got up to bat again and spanked a second homerun out of the park, this time over right-center field. At the bottom of the inning, the other team managed to tie the game up again.

The next time Curtis came up to bat was in the fourth inning. By now, the news had made its way up to the front gate of Royal Oaks and more and more people began to make their way down to the game. Curtis took an 3-0 pitch and sent it over the left field fence even farther than his first shot. Little kids were now scrambling to get the homerun balls as if they'd been swatted by the Babe himself. But, at the bottom of the inning, the other team managed to get a couple of runs and keep the score tied.

In the fifth inning, Curtis came to bat and fouled off four straight pitches before sending a slow curve ball over the fence just inside the right field foul line. Four at bats, four homeruns. Unreal. The people watching were going bananas—even the other team was applauding Curtis' feat. At the bottom of the fifth inning the other team got a run and kept the game tied.

That was when the home plate umpire called time and spoke with the two coaches. Dusk was setting in fast and a decision needed to be made. They could end the game in a tie, seeing's how five full innings had been played, enough to call it a 'complete' game, or they could schedule the final four innings for the next day, sometime right after church. It was their choice.

Was there ever any doubt? There were four innings to go. The game was called because of darkness and would resume on Sunday at 1:00 pm to give church-goers a chance to get out of their Sunday duds and get down to the ball field in time.

Now, in my opinion, the two coaches of the two lousiest teams in the league were the true 'Coaches of the Year,' not my coach. While there is something to be said about that whole 'winning is everything' thing, there's something *more* to be said about the 'spirit of play,' especially in regards to Little League baseball.

The next day, Sunday, after church, it was discovered that two of the players on Curtis' team had come down with the chicken pox and couldn't play, which left Curtis' team one guy short of fielding a full team. The perimeter of the field was jam-packed with people. Cars were lined up all around the outfield fence with kids sitting on the car hoods with their baseball gloves. The home plate umpire and the two coaches huddled up and made a decision. The opposing coach decided to *give* one of his own players to Curtis' team so the game could continue rather than be granted the victory by forfeiture. Seriously. Way cool. The 'donated' player would still wear his own team's uniform and was in total agreement with the plan after being told that out of all the players in the game, he was the only player guaranteed to *not* be on a losing team and he was to play a hard as he usually would, which he promised to do. Perfect.

At the top of the sixth, the score was tied 13-13. Curtis was scheduled to bat fourth. That's why everyone who showed up was there...Curtis. Only one of the first three batters had to get on base safely to allow Curtis to come to the plate to bat. And it happened. The first batter hit a pitch right to the second baseman. The second batter struck out. The third batter bunted the ball perfectly down the third baseline and then dove, head first, into first base safely. He *dove headfirst* into first base to beat the throw. I'm positive no one in the huge crowd, including me, had ever seen that before. Then Curtis came to bat and promptly sent the first pitch into the windshield of a ratty-assed looking, light green Ford Pinto parked outside the left-center field fence. That was five. Five at bats—five home runs. I'd almost bet that every living, breathing soul from Royal Oaks was down there at that ball field watching. Five home runs in one game? The most anyone had heard of before, in the annals of Madrid Little League baseball, was three, and there were still three innings to go. Have you ever watched a baseball game where everyone is hoping for errors, by both teams, not in a malicious way, but to allow the game to continue and for the batting orders for both teams to run through as many times as possible? This was unreal.

At the top of the seventh inning, Curtis was fifth to come to bat. The first two kids ahead of him got singles but had to stay on base when the next two kids struck out. Then Curtis came to bat. I'd bet that this huge group of people, all scrunched together around the entire field like pigs at a trough, were so quiet that we were all levitating as we breathed in unison. Curtis sent his sixth home run out of the park just barely missing some colonel's Mercedes by inches. Okay, by now I was sure I was witnessing some kind of divine intervention. Someone mentioned that one of the preachers at their church service had asked his flock to say a few silent words for Curtis and his bat. It had to be true. The score was now tied...again. 19-19.

The eighth inning came and went—three up, three down, then three up and three down.

In the ninth inning, Curtis would bat fourth. He would have a chance for a seventh trip to the plate if just one of the players ahead of him got on base. Fly ball—one out. Blooper to the short stop, throw to first base—two outs. Next up, the donated player from the other team.

What a position for this kid to be in! He could strike

out on purpose to help his own team (not likely, he'd played hard the whole time). He could get a hit, but be thrown out at first. The scenarios were endless. The home plate umpire called timeout and huddled with the two coaches, close together, whispering. I'd almost bet that a dozen people pulled a hernia trying to lean forward enough to hear what they were saying. Then the three men broke their huddle totally satisfied with this most unique set of circumstances and play resumed. What the three men had decided, so as to preserve the mental health of the donated player, was to intentionally walk him. They did this for the donated kid, not so Curtis could come up to bat once more, but for the spirit of play, the spirit of the game. Having Curtis come to bat was an added bonus. Yep, coaches of the year, in my book.

Top of the ninth inning, game tied 19-19, one man from the opposing team on base, two outs, Curtis comes to bat, and sends a 2-0 pitch over the left field fence that hits the top of Volkswagen station wagon that the driver had parked where he must have thought it would be safe. As soon as Curtis connected, the left fielder dropped his glove, followed the flight of the hit, then climbed over the fence to get the ball before anyone else could. The donated player crossed home plate and got a hug from his coach and when Curtis crossed home plate, he was mobbed by his teammates, as well as by all the players on the opposing team who'd run in from their positions to share in the moment.

Pandemonium, I tell you—the end of a rainbow hit the center of the field, a choir of angels began singing from the tops of the surrounding trees, golden pesetas rained down from the clear summer skies, babies were being born (okay, not really, but it was euphoria in it's purest sporting form). Seven at bats, seven home runs.

But, the game wasn't over. The score was now 21-19.

The home plate umpire cleared the field so the game could continue. The next batter on Curtis' team got thrown out at first base and there was just the bottom of the ninth inning to go.

The donated player was allowed to go back to his team and sit with them in their dugout. Their first player hit a line drive that was snagged with a leaping catch in mid-flight by the shortstop. The second batter hit a hard shot that cleared the right field fence and took out the headlight of a new maroon 'Seat' that looked just like Clancy Dunham's little car that I rode in a half-year later. But the home run was a foul ball, just foul, by about two feet. The second batter popped up the next pitch for an easy out. The third batter went down swinging, literally. He swung his bat so hard on his third strike that he ended up rolling on the ground halfway to the pitcher's mound. Game over. 21-19.

But wait, hold the phone. If there are rules in the official little League handbook about 'donated players' then no one knew what they were—no one at the game, neither of the coaches, nor the umpire—and no one had a rule book with them either (so they all said). The two coaches and the umpire huddled together, again, while all the people crowded onto the field. Curtis was hoisted on people's shoulders at least three times and paraded around. Car horns were honking, champagne was popping (poetic license here)—utter craziness. Then the umpire broke his huddle with the two coaches and in a deep and loud voice told everyone to shut up. He was the umpire, he was the head official, he was the final word, and he had something to say. Everyone quieted down to listen.

The umpire, tired, sweaty and drained, just like the rest of us, said that even though the donated player had played for the opposing team to allow the last four innings of the game to be played, and that he had scored

a run thanks to Curtis' final home run, and that because
he had only played *four* innings for the opposing team,
and not even a *half* a game (why this mattered, no one
knew, but it made sense at the time) and because he was
still wearing his own team's jersey when he scored after
Curtis' seventh home run, that the run he had scored
would be awarded to his *own* team and therefore the
final score was 20 to 20 and would be logged as an
official tie ball game.

Somebody break out the Kleenex. This was as perfect
an ending to any baseball game as there ever was. So
perfect, in fact, that not a single rumor ever sprang up
from this event. Not one.

Six years later, in October, during the World Series, in
a jam-packed bar just off my college campus, a couple of
friends and I watched Reggie Jackson hit three home
runs in one game. An amazing game to be sure, but he
didn't hit seven round-trippers, he hit three. After the
game ended I told these two friends (as much as guys
can be 'friends') the same story I just told you, and they
called 'bullshit' on me. Seven for seven and seven
homeruns? A guy couldn't even do that with one of
those T-ball stands set up at home plate. Three out of
seven, or maybe four out of seven, but not seven out of
seven. No way. Bullshit. So, I told them it was true and
that they could both bite me because I had been there.

Now, when the baseball banquet emcee called out the
winner of the 'Most amazing Game Award' everyone
expected Curtis to be brought up to the stage to accept it.
And Curtis did go up on the stage, along with all of his
teammates (including the two kids that had gotten the
chickenpox) and their coach, as well as all the players
from the opposing team including the donated player and
their coach. Each player was introduced individually and
each player received a medal on a ribbon that hung
around their necks. Both coaches received trophies that

were bigger than mine (deservedly so). The players and the coaches left the stage and then the emcee brought up the home plate umpire and presented him with a plaque shaped like a home plate for Distinguished Service in Fair Play.

Break out the Kleenex again. The poor guy was speechless, he was so choked up. Did I mention that the home plate umpire was Murphy? I kind of left that part for last, as a surprise. But, it was Murphy—the big, lovable dummy anyway. Now, had I known him at the time, and had I asked him about the tear or two he wiped away while getting his award, he'd have said, "It's allergies, kid." Needless to say, the donations for the new Little League Big League Division poured in after that. Everyone was writing checks and emptying their wallets. Stuff like this can stay with a person for a long time.

So, I'm getting a hamburger and a coke and my coach saunters over (not *quite* the saunter of the Guardia Civil at the Teen Center).

"Looks like the Big League Division is a go for next year," Coach says. "You gonna sign up?" I told him I had no idea, that it was a year away. Then he says, "Well, I've already been asked to coach one of the teams and, you know, if you change your attitude, I might consider picking you for my team."

Now, see, it was already projected that 1972 was to be a huge rotation year for the air base and no one knew, totally, who was leaving and who was staying—but Coach knew me and my family, because my father was a civilian, were going to remain in Spain for two more years. So I asked him why would he want me on his team, so *he* could have his pitchers practice throwing at my *head* this time?

"It was just one pitch! Get over it already," he yelled. Aha! No denial. He *did* tell my teammate to throw the ball at me on purpose.

"That pitch did you a world of good, son!" Coach said. So, I told him I wouldn't play for him again if he paid me—which was not entirely accurate—being *paid* to play baseball for this idiot would have been a hell of a lot better than cleaning up the Teen Center for Sgt. Slater twice a week. I showed Coach the baseball stitch marks just above my elbow so he could see that they were still there. Now, I'll admit, getting hit by that pitch *did* do me a world of good—I just wouldn't know it for another year. But, I was on a roll. I told him I didn't want to be the one to further destroy his already fragile ego (I'd taken an introductory psychology class at school during spring term).

"Now, you see?" Coach Spencer said, "That's what I'm talking about...your attitude." I held up my hand to him with my first three fingers up and told him to read between the lines. Right then my mother and father came up to me to tell me we were heading home. Coach looked at my parents.

"You know," Coach said to my parents, "Your son here is a real piece of work, you know that?"

"Really?" my mother said, "How wonderful." She turned and looked at my father. "Isn't that wonderful?"

My father looked at my mother, then at Coach Spencer, and with the smallest of smiles said, "Damn that." And then we went home.

Chapter 16: Part 3

I signed up for baseball—Little League, Big League Division, in March, right after JV basketball season ended. Why, I'm not sure. Everyone I knew signed up so I signed up, I guess. Did I know that a miracle of some sort of a physiological nature had taken place during the previous year? Short answer—no. But *something* had happened. A metamorphosis of sorts—some sort of testosterone/hormone imbalance or rebalance or realignment, but suddenly I could see better. I'd been wearing glasses for awhile, which helped in class, but I never wore them for playing sports because they were so fragile. Between JV basketball and baseball season I'd grown nearly two inches—two inches in three months. I must have been in some kind of overdrive reaction. It didn't last long, but it lasted long enough, and then things went back to normal, which really wasn't normal.

But, as is usual with my babbling ways, more information about recent current events tend to crop up at the oddest times, like now.

On Thursday night, the night before Black Friday at my school, something happened that's worth sharing, that I didn't know about until recently, involving two guys in my sophomore class—white kids—Toby Dodge and Evans Ball—DodgeBall as they were known, because usually when you'd see one of them, you'd see the other one as well.

Now, these two guys were two of the most studious guys you'd ever meet. Going to class was a game to them. They actually discussed whatever they'd learn in class *outside* of class. Smart. Both were taking the highest courses in pre-college math that our school offered, as sophomores. You'd see them in the cafeteria pounding down some lunch and pouring over their textbooks with slide rules and paper and pencils and from time to time, give a shout of, "Hah! Take that you son-of-a-bitch!" which meant they'd just cracked some sort of problem or theorem or some other damn thing. Dodge lifted weights when he wasn't knee-deep in some book or neck-deep in some bottle of cheap red wine (17 pesetas—about 30 cents) he'd picked up with his fake ID at a little store called the Fruiteria, on the High Road, a couple hundred yards down the road from my house. Ball played some football for the school but spent most of his time doing whatever Dodge was doing—math problems, lifting weights, drinking wine.

If you walked the High Road from the front gate toward the Teen Center and got to The Circle, then went left, just up over the short rise in the road, and looked down toward the Low Road, you'd see a dirt and gravel playground that had a huge steel pipe swing set as well as a sizable merry-go-round. The hill just above the playground was primarily weeds and a few short trees, but some genius must have thought that flowers and grass would eventually grow on the hillside (not while I was there, it didn't) because they had placed a couple of large, wooden picnic tables near the trees that, over the years, became more and more weather-beaten.

DodgeBall were camped on one of those tables on that Thursday night before Black Friday, no doubt having a bull session about calculus, Oppenheimer, Tesla, Einstein or some other crazy smart stuff, during which discussion a genius like myself would feel like they were falling over backwards and, naturally, they were consuming a couple of jugs of cheap Fruiteria wine. Then, here comes the brick-throwing deviant I had confronted earlier that day in the third-floor hallway, while trying to get that shaken up kid to his class, and with him was another Black kid, a junior, who was probably the best boogey dancer in school.

Sometimes a particular song would begin playing at a Teen Dance (say, 'Superstition' by Stevie Wonder) and some girl would ask him to dance just to get him out on the floor—then everyone would back away so they could watch his moves. Always a good show. He was the only guy in my school that I ever saw who could jump up while dancing and land on the floor in the splits.

Dodge was telling me this tale when we were at the back entrance of Royal Oaks on a Friday night when we three (Ball was off in the weeds selling a Buick) had all missed the activity bus to a dance at the Teen Center on the base. All through Dodge's story, he'd yell out to Ball up in the weeds selling his Buick, "Ain't that right, Evans?" and Ball would answer, "Damn that!" Ball stayed up in the weeds until a ride showed up.

Now, the brick-throwing deviant was carrying a half a brick (naturally) and the other kid, the dancer, was carrying a large stick. Brick and Stick. They came walking down the hill above the playground and see DodgeBall sitting at one of those picnic tables under a tree, and Brick says, "Mother fuckers, what do you mean by being here in my park?" This guy had issues.

DodgeBall didn't flinch. Dodge looked at one kid and then the other, then he said, as coolly as could be, "Now, Brick, you put down that brick and I'll kick *your* ass and, Stick, you put down that stick and Evans here will kick *your* ass." Standoff. Then Dodge said, "Or, you guys can come here, have a seat, help us with these two jugs of wine here, and we can all forget who we are for a spell." Classic. Dodge's father was stationed in Texas for three years before transferring to Spain, and Dodge, though he denied it, had picked up a slight Texas drawl. I'd asked him once what Texas was like and all he said was, "Hot." So, confrontation over. All four of them were giggling like seven year-olds high on Easter candy by the time the wine was gone.

Another interesting side-note that I had discovered about Black Friday was that while we students and teachers were all in the auditorium getting our shit together, Principal Bolen took advantage of our absence and had some MP's with their drug-sniffing and bomb-sniffing dogs search the school grounds, the buildings and the students' lockers—a last gasp attempt to vindicate himself against 'those kind of people.' No drugs or bombs were found (of course) and old Blow-Hole was sent packing before we all came out of the auditorium.

So, I signed up for baseball...again. I was beginning to believe that god (or whomever) hated me, or that the stars had set me up for some kind of earth-bound experiment in human torture, or I was being trained like a goddam circus bear to perform tricks that would somehow become valuable reference points for my forthcoming adulthood. It had to be something because when the rosters were printed out for the ten-team Little League, Big League Division, I was on the Orioles and the coach's name listed at the bottom of the page was Sgt. Spencer. Apparently, he had made a point of making sure I was on his team, but to tell you the truth, I was really getting sick of all this 'life lesson' crap and seriously thought about quitting before things even got underway. One thing that I knew for sure was better this year than last year, was how good of shape I was in—after about a quarter of a million goddam Turkey Trots during JV basketball season, I was feeling fit. Also, right as basketball season ended I started to experience that whole growth spurt thing. I figured if anyone could figure out why my vision suddenly improved, physiologically—the mathematical aspects, that is—it would be DodgeBall, but I never got around to asking them because this vision thing only lasted for 12 weeks—the length of our baseball season. But, see, I didn't *know* my vision had improved until the first time I took batting practice, at our first team practice, at the base, with Coach Spencer breathing down my neck.

"Now, you stand in that box, son, and I mean, you watch the ball!" Spencer said. "Any pitch that hits you only stings for a little while." Jesus, a whole season of *this*?

The guy pitching was the younger brother of Sam, the guy who spoke for the minority students on stage in the auditorium on Black Friday—Scooter. Scooter was a southpaw and his pitches were kind of sidewinder style—a hard thrower with a good mix of pitches and good control. I'd faced him the year before and pretty much struck out every time. A good athlete.

"Bring 'em over the plate, Scooter. Don't worry, he don't bite," Coach said.

First pitch, a curve ball—smack—deep left centerfield. Second pitch, another curve, little higher than the first pitch—smack—deep right center. Both pitches hit so hard they were past the outfielders before they could take a step. I looked over at Sgt. Spencer and he still had this grim, that's-nothing-show-me-some-more look on his face. Believe me, I was as surprised as he was. As soon as Scooter would whip his arm around I could see the angle of his wrist and could pick up the rotation of the ball instantly upon release. It was like looking through a telescope in slow motion.

One of the things I figured I'd try *this* season was changing up what size bat I'd use, based on what type of pitcher I'd face (a mind game, mind you, like I figured that anything at all would happen anyway...). I decided I'd use a 33-ounce bat if a pitcher was mostly a curve ball or knuckle ball pitcher, so I could delay my swing an instant longer and make contact, then use a 34-ounce bat if the pitcher was primarily a fast ball thrower and just swing like hell. In my mind, the plan was perfect and logical. Scooter threw both curves and fast balls. I was using a 33-ounce bat. The third pitch Scooter threw was low and away, out of the strike zone, but I reached for it, stepped into it, and sent it over the center fielder's head and hit the fence after one bounce—420 feet.

Then Coach yelled at me, "What the hells the matter with you? That pitch was way out of the strike zone!" Seriously?

"Get with the program, why don't ya?" Coach continued. I looked at Spencer and could see that he was just trying to be a coach rather than really being critical. I switched from the 33 to the 34-ounce bat.

Then Spencer yelled, "God damn it, Scooter! Is that the best you can do? Show this boy what pitching is!" Perfect—Scooter was going to fire a fast ball. He did. The pitch was dead center and it sailed over the left field fence. Batting practice for me was over. Damn...I could *see*. Coach called someone else in from the outfield to bat and I took their place all while he was giving Scooter an earful.

See, Scooter was another one of those kids that matured physically and athletically, sooner than the rest of us. His star status was already established. He was one of the two JV football players that was chosen to go to Italy over me. Scooter was not happy that he had been upstaged, and he was not happy to be yelled at by

Spencer. Scooter, I found out later, was the first player selected by Spencer for his team. I was picked next to last. After that first practice a bunch of us were walking to the hitchhiking stand. Scooter was with us, bitching the whole way.

"Man, you know what? You a lucky fucker, you know that?" Scooter said to me. I told them they were good pitches. I hid my smile.

"Yeah, but man, you hit my ass every time," he said. I repeated that the pitches were solid and not to worry—he hadn't lost his stuff.

"Well, man, what the hell happened then, man?" Scooter said. "I struck your ass out like 60 times last year and you was just standing there like the goofy bastard you are, you know?" Too true—Scooter's team finished third but he was an All Star.

Then Scooter said, "So, what the fuck, man? What'd you do, go get some new eyes or something?" So I told him that it was something like that, that I couldn't really explain it.

"Well, all's I can say is that if fucking Coach decides to go all Vince Lombardi on me again, he'd better watch it or I'll whip his ass," Scooter said. Scooter had a way about him. Having the 'hero' of Black Friday as an older brother had only elevated his status among the student body and Scooter could eat it up, big time. We had 11 players on our team. There were only a couple of guys I didn't know all that well, but Coach Spencer had chosen his players with a keen eye, except the last player he chose, right after me, who, in the rotation of selecting players was the last player taken overall. His name was Candy, and he insisted on being called that.

Candy was a piece of work. No doubt. He had to be the ugliest man alive. If he'd been born a girl he still would have been the ugliest man alive. I say 'man' because Candy was 6'3" and at least 225 pounds, and had to have been born two years too late. Candy must have been in kindergarten when he was eight years old. But, he *was* a sophomore in my class and no doubt had some documents falsified along the way. Shiny face, hair the color of the mop head I used at the Teen Center, teeth like a package of Chiclets spilled from a cup, narrow pale blue eyes and a nose that could steer the Lusitania—a mortician's nightmare. But, a nice kid/man—someone who needed to know everything about you—a born bullshitter if there ever was one—the perfect salesman. Candy was the only person I knew that could slap your face, while he was *facing* you, and then, within two minutes, not only convince you that he didn't do it but that it was your fault for getting slapped in the first place. An entertaining fellow, really, with a story for every situation, usually based on some adventure he'd had or one he'd made up.

It made perfect sense, when I found out years later, that he'd become a star air traffic controller somewhere on the east coast of The World, after trying his hand at cattle ranching and as a franchise salesman for strip clubs. Candy had a way with words—you couldn't help but like him, and as big as he was, it always made me wonder why he didn't try harder to apply himself in sports. I mean, I knew lots of kids that would have killed to be 6'3 and 225 pounds in high school—me included. He played football, then he quit. He played league basketball (never tried out for the high school team), then he quit. And now, for some reason, he signed up for Little League baseball and was on my team. We had 11 guys on our team, counting him, and if he quit and if just two other guys got sick or something, we were screwed. Candy wasn't at the first practice, or any practice for that matter. I almost didn't expect him to ever show up at any time, and he didn't, until the one time we really needed him. After our first practice, Coach Spencer gave us our uniforms (jersey and pants) and how Candy ever got his uniform is still a mystery.

Our season started the second week of April and ran through the second week of June, then the coaches and the league manager picked an All-Star team to play other military brat All-Star teams from Germany, Italy and England at Ramstein Air Force Base in Germany.

As it turned out, the three best hitters in the league were all on our team—myself, Scooter and a kid name Donnie Diana, who was a junior and had started at tailback for the varsity football team last fall. A tough kid (with a last name like 'Diana' you'd have to be) who had a tendency to spit just a bit if he got to really talking. One of the three of us led the league in batting average every week during the season. Our best competition was against each other. Coach Spencer was in pig heaven. Shortly after the season started, he never really yelled at anyone anymore (well, once he did), he just let us play our game. By the end of the season, Donnie, who was a classic contact hitter, had a batting average of .488. I ended up three hundredths of a point behind with a .485 average and Scooter had a .478 average. I led the league in home runs with ten. Scooter had the most RBI's. We only lost one game (which I'll get to in a bit) and we won the league with a record of 11-1. But there were four games that stood out that final season (considering I never played organized baseball ever again) and I'll address them in order of significance.

In our third or fourth game (they all sort of ran together, you understand), I smacked a fast ball into right-center field that caught both the right and center fielders flat-footed and the ball bounced all the way to the fence. An inside-the-park homerun. I beat out the final relay throw to the catcher by a good six or seven seconds (I had four inside-the-park homeruns overall). Then the guy playing shortstop, a tall kid named Fish, who would be the only returning varsity basketball player this coming season, called for the ball from the umpire and then stepped on second base and claimed I had missed it as I ran around the bases. This took place in the seventh or eighth inning. Between Donnie, Scooter and myself, the game had been a slugfest with all the pumpkins their pitchers had been throwing over the plate. In fact, Fish had pitched the first three innings and we had hammered him mercilessly. We were probably ahead by about a dozen runs by this time.

So the third base umpire goes over to Fish and Fish tells him that I didn't touch second base. Now, the third base umpire also happened to be the air base chaplain. So, the chaplain says to Fish, "Do you swear to God, son? Do you swear you're telling the truth?" Unreal. So Fish says he swears to God and the chaplain called me out.

Now, Fish didn't have an honest, holy bone in his entire body (remember the Rota Exchange and the Adidas shoes? Oh yeah, Fish got his 'buy-one-get-one-free' pair.). His favorite response was, "Eat shit, mutha-fucka." Oh yeah, a good Christian if there ever was one. And when the game ended I went up to the lying sack of snake bait and called him the liar that he was and he said, with a huge evil grin on his dumb-ass face, "Eat shit, motha-fucka."

Now, it's bad enough to cheat to win, but more worse by far to cheat when you've already had your lunch handed to you. Dork. That was the theft of the hit that dropped my batting average below Donnie's and for the rest of the season I couldn't ever catch up. And then there was the time that Fish hit me in the face with an orange (I'll get to it).

The next significant game was the only game that we lost all season. It was one of those classic struggles where hits were matched by hits and runs were matched by runs and it came down to the bottom of the ninth. We were ahead by one run, the other team was up to bat, there were two outs, a man on first base (a rare walk by Scooter), and a kid named Travers comes to bat. Travers was zero for 27 at bat. Twenty-seven at bats and no hits. I admit, I kind of felt for the guy—he was experiencing the same thing I'd gone through the year before. I knew the feeling.

So, we're playing at the largest field lot on the air base. The field is a huge square with a baseball diamond in each corner—no outfield fences. I mean, huge. Sometimes you could be out in center field and there would be a game going on in the opposite corner and you could have a meaningful chat with whoever was playing center field in the other game. It was kind of weird, but there was rarely any kind of interference between corners. I hit one of my inside-the-park homeruns in this game and the ball rolled almost all the way to the opposite corner field's second base. The second baseman and the shortstop in that game were totally confused when the ball rolled between their positions.

But this play with Travers involved Coach Spencer's three All-Star players—Scooter, Donnie and me. Scooter was pitching to Travers, Donnie was playing shortstop and I was in left field. Scooter hung a perfect curve ball on Travers and I'd bet a million bucks that, simply out of pure frustration, Travers did the same thing that I did the year before—he closed his eyes and swung his bat as hard as he could. I was playing shallow in left field—it's what Coach Spencer *told* me to do. After all, Travers *was* 0-27 at bat. One more out and we win. But Travers connected and sent one of the highest, longest fly balls that I'd ever seen, right over my head. Just as soon as he connected, I turned and began to beat feet after it on our fenceless field. Now, to get a home run you had to run the bases as fast as you could. So, I'm in a dead sprint and I hear the people sitting in the bleachers behind home plate let out a huge, collective gasp. Apparently, Travers had tripped over first base and done a couple of shoulder rolls before getting up again. There was still time.

When I got to the ball (hell of a hit—over 500 feet), I turned and saw Travers had just rounded second base. I was just about to throw the ball to our third baseman when Donnie, spitting all over himself out in shallow left field began yelling, "Throw it here! Throw it here!" So I did.

Donnie, despite being a good player, and having a better arm than I had, could be kind of a bitch about things once in awhile. Travers had just made it to third base when Donnie caught my throw and then Donnie turned and promptly threw the ball so hard and so high toward home plate that it went over the backstop fence and even over the street next to the field. 0-27 was now 1-28 with the game-winning hit and the game-winning run.

When Travers got to home plate, he was mobbed by his teammates. We lost, but I guess I didn't feel *too* bad about it. If you're going to end a batting slump you may as well do it big time and be the hero. And, of *course*, the reasons we lost the game were all *my* fault. Once I got back to the infield to get my stuff and leave, Coach Spencer asked me, "Why were you playing so shallow out there?" So, I reminded him it was because he had told me to. "That's no excuse," he said, and walked away, his ego in tatters. Then Donnie said, "Shit, man, why the hell did you throw it to me for?" So I told him it was because he *told* me to. "Yeah, well, thanks a lot, dick," he said, then walked away. Oh, and Scooter looked at me and said, "Nice catch, fucker," and I told him what a nice pitch that was. Holding oneself accountable for one's own actions has to be our species' most distinguishable and discernable non-existent asset. Idiot mountain gets taller by the day.

The third game of any significance has to do with a bit of sweet revenge—not great revenge—just sort of sweet. I won't address this or batting averages regarding this game. Most people forget that stuff unless it's some major league player, but also, it gets boring when whoever is speaking is always talking about their own stats. I'll just say that I went two for four—two sacrifice flies, a double and stand-up triple (I was motoring for an inside-the-park homerun, and I think I would have made it, but Coach Spencer had come racing out of the dugout yelling, "Hold up! Hold up!" like he didn't think I could have scored safely, but I think I could have—I still do).

The sweet revenge involves a girl, a girl who *had* been going out with the other team's starting pitcher, a kid named Alec, a kid who had hung out with Alverez and I from time to time for that past year or so. Alec had been going out with this girl for a couple of months and every time they'd had some kind of a make-out session he made a point of telling Alverez and I everything about it (not that we weren't curious, of course)—how big her bobbers were, what they tasted like, how much Spanish moss she had down between her legs whenever she'd let him touch her down there, and all that. He was just that way. He *had* to tell you, and to tell you the truth, he kind of rubbed it in that he was 'getting it on' with his girl, but he cheapened his exploits by going on and on about it.

So, anyway, he's dating this girl, and talking about it *all* the time, but then this *other* girl tells him he should date her and so he does it on the sly because she wants to go 'all the way' with him, which they do, and of course, now he has to go on and on all the time about this *second* girl and then dumps the first girl like lumpy

223

gravy so he can free up as much of his time to be with the second girl as he can and hang out in the baseball dugouts as much as possible and all that. Not a bad guy, just kind of a dick about girls.

A couple of weeks after Alec had dumped the first girl, I was out walking around Royal Oaks and saw her out in front of her quad-plex. We got to talking and I guess she was still sort of upset about being dumped, and then she asked me if I'd like to go to the movie with her that night so I figured it'd be okay because I wasn't doing anything that night anyway. So, we go to this movie and she held my hand all through the movie and then we walked back to her house and the next thing I know, we're in this sweatball of a make-out session and she let me put my hands up under her shirt and she let me put my hands down inside her jeans and she put her hand down inside *my* jeans and sort of rolls everything around down there (she had strong hands for a girl—she was a gymnast) until I was getting solidly worked up and then she said, "Okay, okay, that's enough," and we stopped (well, she did but I didn't—too late). We were in her driveway. It was dark. It was well after the second movie on a Saturday night. But by Sunday afternoon, you would have thought someone had filmed us privately and played the movie for everyone at church— both sermons.

It seemed *everyone* knew about us being together this *one* time. Now this guy that dumped her, Alec, the guy Alverez and I hung out with, the pitcher on the other team, knew his old girlfriend (or whatever) and I had been together and messed around this one time and he wasn't very happy because, if I was a true friend, then I wouldn't have betrayed our friendship like that. Okay, I just mentioned Idiot Mountain a little bit ago? This guy, Alec, dumps his steady girl to go banging on another girl because the other girl puts out and then he gets all pissy because someone he hangs out with, has *one* date with his dumped girlfriend. Brilliant.

So, at school, Alec comes up to me in the hallway and says, "You're an asshole, man. Friends don't do that stuff to friends." So, I asked him if he thought that the girl he dumped so he could go off to bang some other girl was some kind of piece of property of his or something.

"That's not the point," he said, though his expression indicated that he got my point. "The point is that you're my friend, and friends don't go out with other friends' girlfriends." So I reminded him that this 'girlfriend' was actually his 'ex-girlfriend' or had he forgotten that fact? Damn, you gotta love high school, you really do.

Alec decides to stay pissed at me and I guess I couldn't have cared less. I didn't feel much like hanging out with him anymore and the same went for him. It was over. We broke up.

So, in this third game of significance, Alec is pitching. He's a lefty, like Scooter, but not the same style of lefty. Alec was more of an over-the-top kind of lefty—a power pitcher. He used his first couple of pitches to brush me back from the plate and smiled at me after each pitch. Big deal. The next four pitches he threw, only four for the four times I came to bat, I spanked them all. When I got the stand-up-triple, Alec hid his hand with his baseball glove from the umpire and flipped me the bird. Right back at you, big guy, only I used both hands and didn't hide it. Coach Spencer was not pleased.

After the game ended, Alec's father, a Lt. Colonel, came up to me and slapped me on the back and called me 'slugger' right in front of his son. I guess I felt pretty good about that. While my family and I were back in The World for our home leave vacation (two weeks), a week after the season ended, Alec and his family got transferred to some base in Germany. Funny thing is, I never mentioned anything to anyone about the make-out session I had with Alec's old girlfriend after he'd dumped her—not even Alverez, who wouldn't let it go for awhile, then finally did when I told him maybe he should just go find out for himself. I didn't see the point in letting other people in on my intimate moments— what good would it do them? In some cases rumors (if any) can suffice just fine.

It was fun though, I have to admit, because, other than a private, soapy shower and an active imagination, I hadn't had a particular biological moment since New Year's Eve with the Junior. Anyway, I also kind of figured that Alec's dumped girlfriend did that with me just to get back at him for dumping her. It worked. Girls can be smart about shit like this. Believe me, they can. A girl can set two guys to practically killing each other without saying a word.

Now, Candy, more than anyone I ever knew all through high school, had to have had the absolute, full 'High School Experience.' Not that Candy was mixed up in all kinds of clubs, groups or extracurricular activities or anything, not like some students. Some students, when you check the index at the back of the yearbook have like 50 page numbers listed after their names with all the crap they were involved in, from Great American Asses to Future Accountants of America to year book staff to Vice President of the Officer's Wives' Club Annual Used Book Sale. Unreal.

But, I always admired those who tried to get the most out of their day, every day. That kind of motivation takes a special talent. I knew I couldn't do it. You could tell who these ultra-achievers were because, on the bus ride to Royal Oaks after school, their eyes would be rolled back in their sockets and their heads would be rolling around on their seatbacks like a freshly picadored bull in the ring at Plaza de Toros. Tired, I'm telling you. How they ever managed to do homework at night is beyond me. But, here's the kicker—these kids were usually at the top of their class, in every class.

Candy had his hand in everything at school, one way or another. Tell Candy something and the whole school knew it by lunch time—no need to post flyers or ever announce it over the school's PA system—just tell Candy. But, one thing Candy wasn't, was responsible. Well, sort of—he had initial good intentions but he lacked commitment to the execution of his good intentions. The game that Candy came through for us, the fourth game of significance regarding my final year of organized baseball, was one exception.

Our games were on Saturdays—all five games for all of the Big League Division on one day, starting at 9 am—two at the fenced, Torrejon Raiders Baseball Park (Torrejon Air Force Base, at one time, had teams for baseball, football and basketball that competed with other bases in Europe, thus the name of the baseball field), and three at the huge, unfenced, quadrangle field further up the road. The game I'm speaking of started at noon and because of one kid being gone with his parents for some reason, and another kid suffering from a hay fever attack, we were one player short from fielding an entire team—and then, here came Candy, walking down the road, wearing his Oriole's baseball jersey, blue jeans and cowboy boots, still about half drunk from staying up all night playing poker with a bunch of GI's over in their barracks.

This would be the only game Candy would play in, all season. No one on any league team in Royal Oaks or on the base, in any league sport, was ever kicked off a team—not officially, anyway. If a player signed up, but didn't want to play, then they just didn't show up. Simple. Which probably explained why so many uniforms or parts of uniforms came up missing.

Coach Spencer had just about forfeited our game when Candy was spotted walking aimlessly down the road, gawking at the other games already in progress and waving at people like he usually did. (I often wondered if there was *anyone* at Torrejon who *didn't* know Candy, or know *of* Candy, while he was there).

Coach Spencer told the home plate umpire to, "Hold the phone," then ran up the road and brought Candy over to our dugout with his big old head of wild-assed hair and big old nose and crooked teeth—now we had nine players. The game was still on. This would be the only game Candy would play in—well, so to speak.

When Candy got to our dugout with Coach, it was obvious that he could have used about 16 hours of sleep and a strong pot of coffee as well. I asked him how he just so happened to be wearing his baseball jersey (to be eligible to play, you *had* to have a team jersey, but not necessarily baseball uniform pants), and he said, "It's Saturday. I always wear my jersey on Saturdays. Just in case, you know?" So, I asked him, just in case of what, and he said, "How should I know, dumb-ass? Just in case is all. Like maybe….like *now*, maybe."

Outside the dugout, Coach Spencer, the other team's coach, and the home plate umpire were in conversation. As it happened, our home plate umpire for this game was Sgt. Murphy. They were discussing the league rules about the uniform code. There were two firm rules as I understood them—all players had to at least be wearing a team jersey and all players had to wear a hat with a bill or visor of some sort on it, to be able to shade their eyes—a safety clause. Candy wasn't wearing his team-issued hat (though I doubt he could have, with that hair he had) and Coach didn't have any extras, nor did the other coach. The search for a hat for Candy was on.

Just as their little conference broke up, Murphy said, "But, Jesus, Spencer, this kid is about half shit-faced!"

And Spencer replied, "Yeah, well, so were *you* about eight hours ago, Murph, and you're the head umpire here," which brought a laugh from the curious crowd in the stands behind home plate.

Murphy rubbed his chin. "Touché," he said. "But you gotta find that boy a hat. Rules are rules."

The stands behind home plate were about half full for the game. Nobody had an extra hat. Then Spencer spotted a couple of blue-haired, older officers' wives who must have played a couple of holes of golf or something before coming to our game. Both women had that great big, starched, poofed-up kind of hair. Their hair was so poofed up that their hats were bobby-pinned so they would stay on. Spencer took out his wallet and offered one of the women $10 for her hat and she took it. The hat was a very large, short-billed, fluorescent pink hat with a large pink and white yarn pompom on top. Perfect. The woman even gave Spencer her bobby pins, as well. Coach helped Candy stuff his hair into the hat and secured it in place with the bobby pins. Game on!

Now, there's a reason why baseball players don't wear cowboy boots while playing baseball, but that's what Candy was wearing. Coach told Candy he was playing right field—the other team only had one left-handed batter. Candy took Coach's glove and lumbered out into right field, weaving first to the left, then to the right, but eventually finding a mid-point somewhere near where he was supposed to be. I looked over at Coach Spencer—I think he was praying.

The game, for the most part, went along just fine. By the fourth inning we had an eight-run lead, thanks to one of my homeruns, one of Donnie's homeruns and an inside-the-park grand slam that ended up almost to the second base of the field directly opposite of us. We were cruising and Coach had stopped pacing around...somewhat. All the giggling about Candy's lovely hair had subsided. He'd batted twice and struck out both times.

When it was our turn to take the field next, the opposing coach had devised a new strategy to counter our hitting machine—he'd instructed all his right-handed batters to hit left-handed now. Now, whether any of these guys had ever batted left-handed before or not (except for the lone natural lefty), remained to be seen, but this new strategy got Coach Spencer to pacing around again. He yelled out to our center fielder, a gangly kid with bad acne, to cheat over into right field and yelled at me to cheat over into center field. Candy just stayed put.

Interesting thing was that the opposing team was now actually connecting with Scooter's pitches, getting blooper singles just out of the infield or slow rollers enabling them to beat the throw to first base. The bases were loaded with only one out when their natural left-handed batter came up to bat.

Out in left center field, I was on pins and needles, ready to go in any direction, with every pitch Scooter was throwing. I was concentrating on the batter's stance, the position of his feet, the angle of his bat, ready to focus on the dip of his shoulders once Scooter released his pitch—anything to try and get a jump in the direction the ball would go if he made contact. Intense concentration, light on my feet, total focus on the natural lefty in the batter's box. That's when it happened (a large meteor came down out of the pristine, crystal clear Spanish blue sky, hitting the middle of the field and blowing into a quadrillion pieces, leaving a 100-foot crater and killing everything and everyone within a two-mile radius… no, not really, but I thought it would be important to put all this intensity into some kind of perspective—we can get so wound up, we humans, about sports, you know).

Now, what *did* happen was, just before Scooter was about to fling one of his classic, side-winding curve balls to the natural lefty who was coiled up as tight as a double-trailer semi suspension spring, Murphy came out of his crouch behind our catcher, stepped off to the side, threw his mask off, raised his arms up high and in his deep, booming voice, yelled, "Time!"

All players, coaches and onlookers froze for a moment (Murphy had that kind of affect on people). I think everyone over at the game on the opposite field froze as well. The whole world stopped. Everyone was looking at Murphy. He pointed out to right field—so all eyes followed the imaginary line from Murphy's pointing finger, which ended at Candy who had his back turned away from the stands, had Coach's glove tucked up under his arm pit and was quietly taking a piss. For a few seconds you could have heard a cleat drop. Candy was taking in the sights, as he stood out there with his peter in his hand and relieved himself. Then a murmur started in the stands behind home plate as Candy began to shake it off. Then came the laughter. Now, whatever shame or smear I had ever imposed on Coach Spencer's fragile psyche, by any failed performance of mine in the past, had to have been totally eradicated in comparison to this.

Candy tucked his member back safely into his jeans, put Coach's glove back on and turned around. People were still laughing—all eyes were on Candy.

"Are you ready now?" Murphy yelled at Candy. Candy motioned with Coach's glove to "Bring it on." Then everyone, myself included, broke into applause. Candy grinned his big, troglodyte grin and took a deep bow.

The natural left-handed batter struck out. The next batter struck out. A couple of innings later we won the game. I don't remember a single play from Candy's performance on. I don't remember seeing Coach Spencer anywhere from that moment on either. I could only assume that he had crawled into the backseat of his car, curled up in a fetal position, and began gently rocking himself. I never saw Candy leave the field. I couldn't tell you if he kept his pretty hat on or not. But, what I do remember, is Murphy.

I came out of our dugout with my junk stashed in my new gym bag as Murphy was stuffing his own junk into a burlap sack. He spotted me and motioned for me to come over, so I did.

"Tell me," Murphy said, with that little grin of his, "Why is it that whenever there's some kind of weird shit going on, you're always around?" So I told him I guessed I was just lucky that way. "New gym bag?" he asked, so I asked him if that wasn't obvious. Then he said, "By the way, you'll be happy to know that I got myself another car." I told him good for him and asked what kind (OK, so I was curious). "Ford Pinto," he said. He puffed up a little like a proud father with a newborn. A Ford Pinto. So I told him he had to be kidding and he said, "What? It's a good car. The GI's on this base here have been using it since it was new and I got it for next to nothing. That's her over there."

Murphy pointed to a light green Pinto parked on the side of the road behind the backstop that had a completely different colored passenger side door (red) and the rear window covered with plastic secured by duct tape. I recognized the car. It was the same ratty-assed car Curtis had hit with his fifth home run the year before. So, I told Murphy that she was, indeed , a real beauty all right and he must be very happy. Then I asked him how she ran.

"The engine's fine," Murphy said. "Only has about 150,000 miles on her, give or take." So I asked what else, because it sounded like there was a 'what else' in there somewhere.

Murphy said, "Well, to be honest, her brakes could use some work and her suspension could use a little bit of an upgrade." So I asked, what else, again.

"Okay," Murphy said, "the steering column has a tendency to stick from time to time, but other than that, she's a gamer." So I told him I was glad he got himself a 'new' car and good luck to him.

Then Murphy said, "You going out to the Oaks? You wanna ride?"

Quick...........think of something!

Neither of my parents had made it out to this game. They were busy preparing for our two-week home leave vacation back in The World and I indeed would need to hitchhike back to Royal Oaks. So, instead I told Murphy I was going over to the Service Club to grab something to eat, but thanks for the offer anyway.

Murphy said, "Great. I'll join you. In fact, I'll buy. C'mon, kid." Trapped, I had to agree, but I was thinking about an automobile's steering column that had a 'tendency to stick, from time to time' and just exactly what the hell that meant.

Murphy and I went to the Service Club and I had my usual chili on rice and Murphy said that sounded good so he had the same. We talked about Candy taking a whiz out in right field in the middle of the game, and we both had a good laugh.

At one point, while we were eating, Murphy said, with a dead serious expression on his face (which meant, 'pay attention, kid'), "You know, by the time you leave this place, you're gonna really have some stories to tell." I told him I doubted it, but boy, he wasn't just whistling sixty.

We left for Royal Oaks after that but we didn't go through Paracuellas this time. "She doesn't do hills very well, kid," was all Murphy said. He kept his speed at 75 miles an hour on the highway and with his sticky steering column, we only ran onto the shoulder of the back road twice, with Murphy screaming, "I said left, bitch, left!" and he was able to wrestle his car back on to the road safely. A calm ride.

By the time I got home, showered and made my way down to the Teen Center, the rumor of Candy's exploits had turned into the fact that some kid playing baseball out at the air base had stepped on an old undetected German land mine from the Spanish Civil War and had been blown completely to shit. Unreal.

After the season ended, a couple of weeks after school let out for the summer, there was no awards banquet for the Big League Division teams—no trophies, no barbeque, nothing. The only thing that happened was that an All-Star team was selected and the leftover funds for the Big League Division were used for the sweet, red, embroidered, silk All-Star player jackets that were ordered for when they went up to Germany for the European tournament the last week of June. Scooter and the kid with the acne that played center field for us were the only ones picked from our team. Donnie wasn't picked because everyone knew his family was scheduled to rotate back to The World the last week of June and I wasn't picked because everyone knew my family and I were going back to The World for our two-week home leave at the same time. A total bitch of military politics, I tell you.

As pissed off as I was, my father was even more pissed off. Apparently, he totally dressed down our league manager, a staff sergeant that lived on the base, out in front of the BX the Friday before we left for our home leave. My mother was with him and no doubt gave this sergeant an earful as well. A crowd had gathered to listen in but surprisingly no rumors sprang from the exchange. My father told this guy that Donnie and I should have been named as All Stars because we deserved to be recognized as such and then alternates named to take our places. 'Recognition' was the key here. But the sergeant, to his credit, cited protocol in regard to some sort of pre-determined mandate set by the league rules, that if it was known at the beginning of the season that a player would not make the All-Star traveling squad, they would not be considered for selection to the All Star team. Donnie's and my replacements got the sweet All-Star jackets because they needed them to ensure the overall continuity of the team's appearance while representing Torrejon Air Force Base.

"Bullshit," my father said. Then my father got up close to the sergeant's face and let him know that he knew which unit the sergeant and his family lived in, and which building on the base he worked in and that he, my father, was one of three of the power plant foremen and that, just in case the sergeant had forgotten, winter was coming. The next day, Saturday, there were at least 100 flyers posted all around the air base—on bulletin boards, on breezeway poles, underneath windshield wipers on cars, everywhere—of the Little League, Big League Division All-Star team that included my name and Donnie's name on them, with an asterisk next to them, and our alternates' names at the bottom of the list. Classic.

Chapter 17: 'Home Leave,' Part 1

Now, here's a good rule of thumb—never listen to a person telling you about a place you've never been to, but are going to, if they've never been there themselves.

My family's home leave vacation back to The World was for two weeks. We'd stop in Kansas City for a couple of days to see my grandfather, my mother's father, the full-blood Navajo, and some of his third wife's family, then on to Salt Lake City for a couple more days to see my parents' other family members and friends, then on to my hometown, Condon, Oregon, in time for the Fabulous Fourth of July Celebration. I'd saved $50 of my janitor money to spend in Condon for the week we'd be there.

When we landed in Dover, Delaware to catch our connecting flight, the pseudo-commercial jet all us military folks flew on (Crystal Airlines—'Your Glass Eye in the Sky') had to park about 100 yards away from the back entrance of the terminal annex. The ground temperature was about 97 degrees and the humidity level was about 187. By the time everyone hit the doors to the 60-degree air conditioned annex building, we were all soaking wet, and then freezing our asses off while waiting for some bored Air Force airman to process our paperwork and keep us all moving.

The terminal annex was a goddam mess with people running all over the place, little kids bawling, luggage being located and everyone trying to keep track of everyone else. Once paperwork was cleared, everybody would then run into the interior of the regular terminal to find the gate for their connecting flight. We made it to our gate with five minutes to spare. It may not have been the most efficient system of travel, but we *did* make our flight. Next stop, Kansas City.

To tell you the truth, I don't remember a whole lot about Kansas City—a few cousins by marriage I'd never met before and who really didn't want much to do with me (there's a reason why the term, 'distant relatives' was created, which I get now), hot, humid weather with every person in the entire city walking around with some kind of fan in their hand, all flapping away. I was on a city street somewhere and they looked like a large field of butterflies or something.

Seeing my grandfather was good. Before we left for Spain in 1969, he'd said to me, "Go have an adventure, boy." Smart man. He'd lived in my hometown for a few years back when I was much younger. His little house was just down the block from ours. He'd been the janitor at the hotel and bar on Main Street. A big man, but a quiet man. I did get to watch some color TV while I was in Kansas City. Color TV was still new to me. There was a kid in my neighborhood, when I was growing up, whose parents got the first color TV I'd ever seen. The shows were either blue and green or red and yellow. On Sundays, this kid would always announce that he was going to watch 'The Wonderful World of Disney' in *color*. Our family's TV was a black and white that worked most of the time (a couple of good whacks on the cabinet always seemed to do the trick). I never thought it was such a big deal. The difference between color TV and black and white—not much. Up on a plateau, like where my hometown was, we'd still only get two channels regularly. I don't know if Dark Shadows was broadcast in color or not, but it looked good and creepy in black and white.

So, in Kansas City, I watched some color TV and found I was bored within two hours (although I did catch a rerun of the Doris Day Show, which was okay, but not the same as seeing her on a theatre screen). I spent a lot of time reading from the book my best friend's (Darren) parents had given me to read when we left for Spain in 1969—'Instant Replay,' by Jerry Kramer. I'd already read it maybe six or seven times and thought it would be a good thing (for some reason) if I had it with me when I returned for a visit three years later.

In Condon, I'd read a lot of books about pro football and pro football players. I once had the complete, 'Punt, Pass & Kick' library. 'Instant Repay' was easily one of the best. I also read every book or magazine I could get my hands on about Johnny Unitas. As much as I loved watching Doris Day at the movies, I loved watching Johnny Unitas and the Baltimore Colts on our black and white TV more—something to do with his dedication and that whole throwing a football through a swinging tire for endless hours a day thing. Old school. But I *like* old school. The book store down the sidewalk from the BX always had lots of books and magazines about sports. Weekly and monthly sports magazines were just one of the windows back to The World.

In Salt Lake City, it was hotter than blue blazes, but not so humid. I got dragged around from one relative's house to the other, doing all the howdy-do crap and what not. One thing that was becoming evident about my family going to Spain—people really didn't want to talk about it. They were more interested in wanting to inform you about what *they* had been doing while we were out of the country. It was kind of evident that our going to Spain was being held against us—that going off to live in a foreign country for five years was not such a 'big shot' thing in their opinions—a defensive stance to which no offensive stance was ever mounted or expressed. People are funny that way. Something good can happen to you and, in their minds, they're suddenly in some kind of a pissing match.

Not all the relatives were this way. My grandmother on my mother's side (she and my Navajo grandfather had been divorced a long time) was genuinely interested in where her daughter had been and what she had seen. She clung to every detail and asked a lot of questions (always a good sign). Mostly, it was uncles, aunts and cousins that figured we must have returned with a chip on our shoulders about living abroad. I saw my cousins for about five second each, which is about what I expected. I remember one of my uncles telling my father that he needed to come back to The World and get a *real* job. No shit.

I made no bones about letting people know how much I loved living in Spain—I could have cared less if they thought I was bragging or if they thought I was comparing my life to theirs (I wasn't...not really). People are funny. If you win a lottery of some kind, don't tell your friends because there's that chance they'll resent you and probably begin thinking that *you* think you're some kind of big shot now and then you won't have anyone to talk to. But then again, if you were a dirt bag *before* you won the lottery, then there's a pretty good chance you'll be a real shit bag afterwards.

Our move to Spain was voluntary, a request for a transfer. No one on either side of our family ever truly understood the need to just 'get out' for awhile, even if the getting out was what was necessary to save my parents' marriage, which it was.

The only real highlight about being in Salt Lake City (other than the couple of days spent at my grandfather's cabin, which I'd just as soon forget) were the two days I spent with my grandfather (my father's father), and his second wife, at his property somewhere just outside the city limits. I slept on a cot in a sleeping bag on their screened back porch and both mornings was awakened by him shooting at gophers in his large garden plot with his 20-gauge shotgun, then screaming, "Take that, ya little bastards!" At noon, both days, I went with him to the post office which was about a mile down the road. We'd get into his big, fat-ass Ford and go at least 75 miles an hour. My grandfather was as much a maniac behind the wheel as Murphy was. The only thing *this* grandfather said to me when we left for Spain in 1969 was, "I'll be dead before you get back."

The time we spent at my grandfather's cabin was a time best forgotten, as I said, but my father was in pig-heaven—he'd spent his childhood summers there and knew every inch of the property. He'd spend the day fishing and come home with nothing and it was a very good day. Note to self: more people should feel this way.

I tried to ride their 50cc motorcycle, got my hand-foot coordination mixed up and ended up going ass-over-teacups over the handlebars and having the motorcycle run right over my face...with both tires. I went over the front of the motorcycle like 'a strip-ed-ass ape,' according to my grandfather. I believe I gave that man a good 15 more years of solid living with the 'ass-over-teacups' visual he got from my screw-up. The man could not stop talking about it and I encouraged him to keep telling the story. I loved my grandfathers, both of them, very much—two ends of the spectrum, for sure.

The Fourth of July was on Tuesday. We arrived from our two-hour drive from the Portland airport on the Friday afternoon before.

I'll say this much about growing up in my home town, up to the age of 13 anyway—it was perfect, despite all the crap I had to take from older kids in my neighborhood—that, and the couple of years before we transferred to Spain when my parents were at each other's throats so much. So, it wasn't Norman Rockwell, by a long shot, but it was still good. There were distinct seasons—snow sledding in the winter, swimming in the summer, 4-H club, cub scouts, dirt roads everywhere for bike riding, camping, hunting, fishing, baseball (sort of)—mowing lawns, washing cars, pulling rye out of wheat fields (ways to make extra cash)—birthday parties, 4th of July, Halloween, Christmas and always enough kids around to field two teams for a game of football or enough for a 'work-up' game of baseball. Magic.

I was a townie, even though my father was 'stationed' at the small air base radar outpost on top of a large hill seven miles outside of town. There were other civilians from town that worked out at the radar base, but not many were stationed there. Base housing was only for military personnel and their families (a few Air Force employees lived in town, but only a few) and all the civil servants lived in town. My father was stationed there for nearly 14 years. My sister was still a drooling toddler when my mother and father came to Condon—I wasn't even born yet. Thirteen years in one place, even for civil servants, was virtually unheard of. The hunting and fishing and all the other outdoor crap was just too good for my father to put in for a transfer to anywhere else and every year when my mother (a city girl who was bored out of her mind in a little town in the middle of nowhere) would inquire about open positions for my father, with his specific qualifications, elsewhere in the world, he'd tell her there was nothing available.

He lied, of course, but to his credit, he was the one

who initiated the move at the eleventh hour of my parents' marriage and kept us all together. Now, to be clear, for 14 years, my father told my mother that there were no positions for his specific qualifications out there, somewhere else in the world, because *he* loved being in Oregon—but when he finally realized his world was about to crash and burn, he said 'adios' to his personal desires in order to preserve his family (one divorce already under his belt, you know).

We left in 1969. The radar base closed in 1970. Everyone in town thought my father had inside information about the base closing, but he didn't. A small town can kill you if you're not careful. Back in the '60's, wheat was big, and with so many ranchers and farmers with so much money and nowhere to spend it except in one of the three bars on Main Street well...things happen. There were stories upon stories, I tell you.

Of all the many things that stood out while growing up in that small town, there were two that stood head and shoulders above the rest, besides my nearly losing my eye, or the time the very first snowfall (3') of the season came on Christmas Eve after my sister and I had already gone to bed, or the time I fell out of the hayloft of a barn (another story).

In 1966 our City Council decided it was time to build a golf course, the edge of which was two and a half blocks from my house. Now, what was out there, on those acres and acres of land, besides some old anchored machinery, were thousands upon thousands of wooden boards, one-by-two's, two-by-two's and two-by-four's— thousands and thousands of six foot-long pieces of lumber just waiting to be terra-formed—once off limits, now free game, restricted only by the extent of the collective imagination of a town filled with kids ages 7-17, with far too much time on their hands that final week of summer vacation before school started up again.

The weathered boards had gone gray from all the years they'd been stacked out in the field next to where the buildings that once housed the anchored machinery used to be. At some point in the past, before the mill closed, the mountains of lumber were once covered with huge tarps that were tied down by railroad spikes hammered into the ground. Then the mill closed, the large saw blades removed from the machinery, the buildings taken apart and hauled away and the tarps removed, leaving the wood to the extreme shifts in eastern Oregon weather. Only the boards on the outer edges of the piles had warped and twisted—the interior boards remained straight and true, under their own stacked weight.

We built a fort—the biggest goddam fort in the history of anyone's childhood. This structure covered at least three quarters of an acre, complete with three 12' towers of three floor levels each and double floor passageways that led from one tower to the next, and all surrounded by an 8' fence, complete with a moveable gate. In the center of the fort was a courtyard that was long enough and wide enough for two high school kids to throw a football around. It took three days to build, then for the rest of the last week of summer vacation, there were organized battles of Cowboys and Indians. Older kids picked the two sides. I was an Indian. I was picked last, as usual.

After the first day of school a couple of friends and I went out to the fort and it was gone. All the wood had been hauled off and a large earthmover had already begun scraping away the sage brush and rocks for a wide fairway. Change is supposed to be a *good* thing, but when you're a kid, it can sometimes happen too fast.

They built a new high school which meant the old high school had to be torn down. The new high school was way on the other side of town—the old high school was a couple of blocks from my house. It was a huge, 3-story brick and mortar structure that was falling apart. The old high school gym was being converted into an assisted living facility for the elderly and it wouldn't be long before my hometown would have a lot of elderly people in it. Progressive thinkers, the City Council. The summer after the whole fort thing, when the new golf course was being created, was when crews began knocking down the walls of the top two floors of the old high school, which meant bricks, salvageable bricks—thousand and thousands of them—needed to be stacked up so skip-loaders could haul them away easily. For every brick you stacked, you'd get half a cent—you were on an honor system. I got up to 60 cents before I realized the futility of the task. I figured if they had machines that could pick up and haul away a million goddam boards without them being stacked, then they must certainly have machines that could pick up a couple hundred thousand bricks just as easily. I quit, took my 60 cents and went to the ShoeString Drive-In for a hot fudge sundae. By the end of summer, all that was left of the old high school was the floor of the first floor and the basement. That's where the other thing I spoke of took place.

A girl in my class, whose father was regular Air Force, took me and three of my friends into the old high school basement, then took off her pants and her underwear. She not only showed us everything but she let us play with her 'everything,' too. She even let one of my friends *kiss* her 'everything.' Her father's transfer had come though and they were supposed to leave in two days. Some things can leave an impression on you, if you know what I mean. That was the first time I remember ever seeing 'it' even though my sister and I were tub mates until I was four years old.

So, on Friday afternoon, my family and I rolled into town. We'd been gone for nearly three years. I was 16 now. Friday afternoon and evening I would spend my time with my three closest childhood friends. On Saturday, the annual Elks Lodge picnic was being held at the usual spot somewhere out in the woods near town. Lots of woods near my town. Lots.

Here's the primary difference between 16 year-old kids in Royal Oaks and 16 year-old kids in my hometown—cars. At least half of the kids in my old class were driving cars. Some were driving their parents' car (unless it was a station wagon) and some had their own cars.

My best friend, Darren, who lived up the street from me, had his own car that he'd purchased six months ago and then fixed up a bit. In fact, of my three closest friends in my neighborhood, Darren was the only one with his own car. I sort of found myself sitting back and observing when all of us got together that first afternoon, and watching to see who the Alpha Dog was, and it was quickly apparent that it was Darren. He was one of those guys that had developed physically more quickly than the rest of us, then sort of dominated while everyone else caught up. He'd been varsity football since his freshman year and was the starting tailback the previous autumn. He also ran on the track team. Now, he didn't play basketball or baseball, because his eye-hand coordination wasn't up to snuff—to not be *great* would have diminished him in the eyes of those who granted him his Alpha Dog status. He'd also become somewhat of a ladies' man, having spent many a time with many an upper class girl.

Darren may not have been the most popular guy in the high school, being just a sophomore, but he was certainly the most liked and respected. He'd beaten up a few of the usual bullies every school has. He'd even pounded a few bullies that went to high schools elsewhere in the county. The whole county knew who Darren was—a tough running back who preferred to go *through* a tackler, rather than around him.

The summer before his freshman year, he worked on his grandfather's property digging about a mile's worth of fencepost holes with a hand-held, old-fashioned post-hole digger. The boy had an impressive set of guns for sure, and the first thing he said to me when he drove up in his car was, "You should go dig some holes—get yourself some muscles." Yeah, one of those guys that matures more quickly than the rest of us. Now, he was no *Montague*, not by a long shot, but then, only Montague was Montague.

When Darren drove up in his car the other two friends from my neighborhood were sitting in the front seat with him.

"Get 'n the back seat," Jason said. He was sitting in the middle. Jason was the same age as Darren and me. The other childhood friend was Mickey. Mickey was a year younger.

"Yeah, get 'n the back seat," Mickey said, "You can ride nigger. Better you than me." Mickey, being a year younger, was a stout kid, not fat like I was as a child, just stout. Whenever we played any backyard football, Mickey was the 'designated center,' for both teams. "Hike it, sick of it," he'd say, more than once, during any pick-up game.

Now, all through high school, I played center. I touched the ball first on nearly every offensive play. It's a common misconception that the most important player on a football team, on offense, is the quarterback. I'm here to tell you that whoever believes this myth is dead wrong. It's also believed that the second most important offensive position is the quarterback's blind side tackle. Again...wrong. The shortest distance between two points is a straight line—which means that if a quarterback gets under the center's butt, and there happens to be a defensive player right in front of the center, on the line, then the quarterback better hope like hell that the center can keep *that* guy out of his face. Shortest distance. Ask any quarterback, after he comes out of his coma, which player is the *most* important on a football team's offense. Mickey also played center all through high school.

Now, the whole concept of 'riding nigger' pretty much set me back. My hometown, all the time I was growing up, had maybe one Black family living there that was *not* connected somehow to the radar base or the Air Force. The people in my hometown weren't prejudiced, per se, just ill-informed about the depth of the hatred attached to the euphemisms some of them bandied about so freely. You can't know what you don't know. When the comment about 'riding nigger,' was put out into the universe, I just told them that they should try saying something like that in my high school and then see what happens, to which Jason said, "Oh, boy, here it comes... 'Mister Worldly' is gonna set us straight about the Negroes." I let it go. What they didn't know, they didn't know, just like I once didn't know. There are a lot of people on this earth and the biggest percentage of people aren't anything like who these guys know. Somehow, thinking this thought, as I was sitting in the back seat of Darren's car, made sense. I filed it away.

Then Jason said, because I hadn't responded to his 'Mister Worldly' comment, "You're not some kind of *lover* now, are you?" He turned around and looked at me sternly from the front seat. He studied my face. I gave him nothing. Then he smiled and said, "I mean, you're not one of *those*, are you?" I just put my hands behind my head, leaned back in my seat, and told him that I was just another nigger on the magic carpet of life. For some reason, this brought the house down with these guys.

One and all had a good laugh at that one. Darren pounded on his steering wheel.

"Man, you haven't changed a bit, you know that? Not one bit!" Darren said, which got me to thinking just who the hell I was when I left, and just who the hell I was now, now that I was back. These were my friends, people I grew up with. It had to be some kind of transformation—there's no way it couldn't be—for all of us.

That's when Darren said, "You know, 'riding nigger' is just a saying." He laughed. "I mean, we could have said you'd be 'riding queer.'" So I told them that that was a genuine relief, and thanked him

"Darren's right. You haven't changed a bit," Jason said. "Tell us about Spain, man."

Mickey turned around. "Yeah, tell us about Spain. Tell us some Spanish cuss words," he said. All was well.

Then Darren said, "Pony up boys. Let's see if we can score some beer." I let them know that I had fifty bucks on me. You should have seen their faces.

Around 5:00, having secured a case of Olympia beer for the four of us, we hit Main Street...to drive. We drove up to one end of Main Street, to the gas station, turned around, then drove down to the ShoeString Drive-In at the other end, turned around and headed back—back and forth, back and forth. There must have been at least 25 other cars doing the same thing. Every time we'd pass another car slowly going the opposite direction, Darren would give the driver of the other car a finger-wave or a nod and they'd return the gesture in kind. People who were in the bar, halfway down Main Street, would come out onto the sidewalk, some of them already about half-hammered, and watch the cars going back and forth, back and forth. I could only handle this for about six runs and then had to ask just what in the fuck we were doing. You'd think that I had just taken away their Christmas stockings. Jason turned around with a classic 'confused dog' expression.

"What's it look like we're doing?" he asked. I guess my response wasn't up to snuff when I told him it looked like we were wasting time.

Mickey turned around. "We're cruising, man," he said. So, I inquired as to what it was we were cruising *for*?

Darren held his hand up, indicating, 'Silence.' He nodded at a passing driver. "We're cruising to see what's gonna happen," he said. I mentioned that the beer in the trunk was getting warm.

"Just hang on, man," Darren said, "Someone will think of something. It won't be long now." Then he said, "Don't you guys cruise over there in that housing area, or whatever, that *you* live in?" I told him that the legal age to drive in Spain was 21, unless you already had your license in the States before you got there.

"Man, that would just suck not to be able to drive," Mickey said. "Spain's kinda stupid, you know?" So I reminded him that I could drink beer legally, anywhere in the country (okay, I'd lied to them, in letters, about how I could purchase alcohol, legally, in Royal Oaks— shoot me) and that I didn't have to come up with some goddam secret squirrel plan to get some 21 year-old to 'score some beers,' and just how stupid was that?

Darren gripped his steering wheel and squared his shoulders. "Okay, smart ass, if you guys over there don't cruise, then what *do* you do?" I told him we walked.

"You walk?" Jason said. "What the fuck, man? Walking's boring, man." So I told him not if you were drinking beer, it wasn't. Priceless.

All three of the front seat sitters clammed up for a good minute mulling over the trade-off between drinking beer legally and cruising up and down Main Street for an hour, wasting time. I couldn't be sure, but it seemed like they were communicating telepathically while their 'nigger' friend sat, oblivious to local tradition, in the back seat. My inner smile was as wide as it could be.

A driver in an approaching pickup motioned for Darren to stop. I recognized the kid as someone in the class ahead of me, a cowboy-type guy who played baseball. He leaned out of his window. "Party at Burton's, 6:00. Admission's a case of beer. His parents are in Portland for the weekend," the guy said.

Darren turned around and looked at me. "See? Told ya." He turned to face the pickup driver again. "Got it," he said. The pickup driver nodded in my direction.

"Who's the fag in the back seat?" he asked. Darren told him it was me and that I was back for a visit. The pickup driver rubbed his chin, obviously remembering who I was. Then he said, "Well, I guess he can come, but you'd better keep an eye on him." I leaned over to my window and told the pickup driver he could blow me. The pickup driver laughed. "See ya there, fag," he said, then drove on.

There must have been 50 people at Burton's—people in high school, people who'd graduated, and everyone with a can or bottle of beer in their hand. Darren, Jason and Mickey paraded me around like I was a Grand Marshall of some kind. I was wearing my Converse All-Stars basketball shoes (white, low-tops) and all those that were wearing sneakers were wearing Adidas. One guy looked at my shoes and said, "Man, Converse are for old-timers, you geezer. You need some Adidas—get with the program." I told him that Converse suited me fine and besides, I was an 'old soul.' The guy just looked at me, totally confused, shook his head and wandered off.

When you leave a childhood place, and then return, knowing it's only for a visit, there's no real need to have to jockey for some kind of position in the social pecking order. You just stand back and watch the dynamics of what has unfolded while you were gone. Darren had certainly risen to the top of the heap, even among those who had already graduated. One thing was for certain and that was that the girls in my class were happy to see me...well, some of them. Only a few were a bit standoffish about my return, automatically assuming I'd come back to rub their noses in my 'Mister Worldliness' while they had only grown three years older in a little town in the middle of nowhere. Not true. Well, one girl did come up to me, full of attitude (she was dating a senior so that seemed to give her the green light to speak freely) and said, "Why the hell did you come back? I thought we were rid of you." So I asked her how her Daddy's pigs were doing. No, I wasn't here to try and pick up where I left off (whatever *that* entailed). I was here to reacquaint *myself*.

But, the girls that *were* happy to see me were genuine, even though they were pretty much paired up with a steady boyfriend. One girl, who'd succeeded in becoming completely shit-faced, kept telling everyone, "I feel so crazy!" I figured it had to be because of the wind, which blew steadily for 300 days a year through here.

All things regarding this large gathering were clicking along well for a party atmosphere, but there were two things that took place that could give a 16 year-old pause. The first happened when I excused myself from an invigorating conversation regarding one of Darren's touchdown runs to relieve my bladder in one of the Burton's two bathrooms. No sooner had I set myself to piss when the bathroom door opened and the driver of the pickup walked in. I glanced over at him and said I'd be done in a minute. Silence. I finished my task, zipped up, turned around and saw him leaning up against the clothes hamper. It's not that he looked confused that concerned me, but what did concern me was that he was kind of smiling and kind of not, if that were ever possible. I went to the sink to wash my hands and told him that the toilet was all his and to have at it. When I finished washing my hands he was still leaning against the clothes hamper. His arms were crossed. So I asked him if something was wrong.

"Were you serious?" he said. So, I asked him about what.

"About what you said, you know, on the street, when you were in Darren's car," he said. Okay…awkward. So I told him it was a figure of speech.

"Because no one has ever said that to me before, you know?" he said. He looked down at his boots for a moment, then looked at me again. His face was clouded with what I could only believe was fear. So I repeated that it was only a figure of speech. His face lightened just a bit and I caught the hint that his secret was still a secret and that he believed I didn't know his secret. Moments like this can stamp a person permanently in the eyes of all who know them. Diversion time. So I asked him if he could answer a question for me.

"Sure thing," the pickup driver said. So I asked if a large group of sheep is called a *flock* then why aren't sheepherders called *sheep-flockers* even though a lot of folks consider a large group of sheep a herd.

The guy looked at me, totally dumbfounded. I gave him a light punch on the arm and told him he should think on it and left him leaning against the clothes hamper in the Burton's bathroom.

The second thing that happened at this party happened when this one kid from my old hometown class showed up, a kid who used to be a nagging thorn in my butt for as long as I could remember—at least since the second grade. Purvis.

Purvis was a piece of work—a farm boy who, for

some reason, in the nearly three years I'd been gone, hadn't grown an inch. Purvis' dad raised cows, horses, sheep and pigs, and it was a well-known fact that Purvis liked to be at the slaughterhouse, front and center, whenever the animals were to be killed and butchered. If I didn't know better, which I didn't, I'd say Purvis was seriously disturbed in the head. Once, while waiting for my parents who were attending a PTA meeting, Purvis and I were on the playground going down the slide. Purvis got up to the top of the ladder, turned around, and spit a huge loogie at me that landed right in my eye. I was busy wiping the spit off when he knocked me down and screamed as loud as he could in my ear. I was rolling on the gravel, holding my ear when Purvis' parents came out of the school and they all left. I'll admit, I was perplexed as to just what Purvis' problem, or psychosis, mind you, was, and those perplexities resurfaced when he spotted me from across the yard at Burton's place and made a beeline for me.

"What the fuck are you doing here, fag?" Purvis asked. Gee, not even a "Hello, how are ya?" Now, Purvis wasn't just my own personal thorn in the butt in grade school— he was a pecker-head to lots of people. It was nothing for him to trip you in the cafeteria when you were carrying your hot lunch on a tray or sneak up on you in the hallway and smack you in the jewels. He'd pull girls' dresses up to show everyone their underwear. Why Purvis was never thrown from the top of the school building long ago was anybody's guess. He was at least two inches shorter than me now. So I told him I was just visiting and what was it to him, anyway?

"Well, you ain't welcome, so you best leave," Purvis said. I found humor in his attempted verbal assault and told him he could go suck a fart. Okay, his face got red and a few other guys began to gather around us.

"I hear you like to ride nigger," Purvis continued.

Unreal. So I called him an idiot. I turned to go look for someone else to *talk* to, but Purvis grabbed my arm and came around in front of me. He just wouldn't let it go, whatever *it* was in his mind. Then he said, "Okay here's a joke for you, fag. What do you get when you cross a pig with a nigger?" And before I could say anything, he said, "Nothing. A pig won't fuck a nigger." There were chuckles all around within our curious ring of on-lookers. Then I told Purvis that wasn't necessarily true and that I knew for a fact that the union in question had at least spawned one offspring and that I was looking at him. No, he was not very happy with that comeback, at all.

Now, it was a well-known fact that Purvis had a special 'it' in for me long before I went to Spain—why, I never knew. For some reason, some people just have it in for some other people with no need for explanation. So, Purvis did what I expected him to do. He pushed me in my chest like a playground seven year-old. So I pushed him back, and when he stepped forward once again, I punched him, straight on. A solid connection, right dead center in his face. The 'pop' his nose made turned all 50 heads in Burton's backyard and the volume of blood that gushed from his nose showed up real well on the mostly white polka-dotted Western-style shirt he was wearing. Instantly, Purvis was a mess. Now, I've never been one to pick a fight of any kind and hitting people with the intention of incapacitation, legally, was pretty much confined to the football field, but I had to admit splattering Purvis' nose did give me a certain amount of justified satisfaction.

Darren stepped between Purvis and me. Purvis was now holding his nose gingerly. "I think it's time for you to go," Darren said. "You finally got your answer."

Purvis nodded and left the party. But he was back within a minute, now holding a 12-gauge shotgun, his nose still dripping blood on his shirt and even more enraged than before. He walked into the Burton's yard, the group of kids making way as he came, and started to level the gun at me, when Darren grabbed it away from him, then pushed him down.

"I thought I told you to leave? What are you, deaf or something?" Darren asked.

Purvis looked up from where he was now sitting on the ground. "So, now you're a nigger-lover, too?"

Darren shook his head. "Whether I'm a nigger-lover or whether I'm not, makes no difference to you, Purvis, ya dickhead! This is a party, stupid!" Darren said. He reached out his hand and helped Purvis to his feet. "Now, take a walk. Go cool off or something. I'll give your gun back to you later," Darren said.

Purvis looked around at everyone staring at him and slouched away. Darren looked at me and smiled. "Happy now?" he asked. So I told him, just so he knew, that I *really* had a problem with the word 'nigger,' and would appreciate it if he'd refrain from using it.

Darren smiled again. "Whatever you say, queer." Okay, *that* was funny. Then Darren pointed Purvis' shotgun skyward and pulled the trigger. The shotgun fired off a thundering blast causing everyone at the party to duck briefly, then to look at Darren. Darren looked at the shotgun, then at me. "Shit," was all he said. High school, I determined, right then, no matter where you're at, can be a goddam dangerous place to live. I spent the rest of the evening getting quietly blitzed and trying to teach my semi-inebriated childhood friends how to cuss in colloquial Spanish.

Chapter 17: 'Home Leave,' Part 2

Now, the difference between attending the Elks Lodge Annual Family Picnic when you're nine years old, or eleven, or even thirteen years old, compared to when you're sixteen years old, is immense—barbequed burgers, deep-fried corn dogs, Dixie Cups of ice cream and endless cans of soda pop, no longer held the same interest as sneaking cans of beer out of the adults' horse trough of ice water and taking risks climbing on the lava cliffs at the far edge of the expansive field where the picnic was held each year. Sack races, egg-and-spoon races, arts and crafts—they no longer held the same appeal. Beer and girls, on the other hand, did hold my interest. Unfortunately, the pickings of girls in my old class, because most of them were already dating someone, were slim. There were a few girls from the class behind mine and the year before that, but despite being nice and semi-interested and all, they were more interested in getting Darren's attention. Darren played the game with great skill—just aloof enough, but his well-placed comment or glance gave him never-a-dull-moment summer evening, if he chose.

At Burton's party, the night before, Jason mentioned that hanging with Darren had its perks—that on more than a few occasions, he had picked up where old 'love 'em and leave 'em' left off and had a fine time himself. Darren kidded Jason about 'sloppy seconds' but Jason said he didn't care—"Action is action, the way I see it," Jason said. Mickey, on the other hand, being a year younger, never followed suit and was too busy trying to build up his own flock of 'fillies,' as he called them, from his own class and the two classes behind him— girls far too young for Darren or Jason. Mickey said he had a list but I never saw it.

What was most interesting at the picnic was the interaction Darren had with the adults. Being a star football player and wearing a T-shirt with the sleeves cut off to show off his amply-muscled arms and bronzed upper torso, garnered much attention from the men and women alike. The men would inquire about the upcoming season or comment on one of his touchdown runs from the year before and the women would just give him the long look-see, up and down the length of his body, then whisper among themselves. While Jason or myself would play sly at picking ice cold cans of beer out of the horse trough (one side was soda pop, the other was beer), though we weren't really fooling anyone, Darren would brazenly pick what he wanted, as many as he wanted, in front of anyone who was watching. One adult man, Del Campo, a thinning-haired late 40's Elks Lodge Assistant Manager, tried to intervene in Darren's beer selection once and Darren gave Del Campo a look—just a *look* and Del Campo turned and walked away. Royalty...well, sort of. Darren could have run for mayor and been unopposed. Or even a local judgeship. It was a lesson in the most primal of human interactions— a wonder to behold.

One of the things that took place to determine the order of boldness in our merry band of sophomores- soon-to-be-juniors was the ultimate dare of passage.

About 200 yards away from the picnic site, across a wide field of lava rock, was a high shelf of jutting rock, with a wide, 12' half-circle ledge, some 30' above a solidified base of ancient magma. The idea was to traverse the shelf, hand over hand, from one side of the ledge, around to the other side, safely. Twelve terrible feet in total.

Now, a lot of kids, over the years, during many picnics, had accomplished this feat. Only a couple that had tried had failed—which was where my focus was. Result: broken elbow and shoulder for one kid, broken leg and tailbone for the other. Darren swung himself around the rock shelf easily, as did Jason, though not so easily. Me, I never even tried. I watched these guys go around this rock shelf from down below. Mickey was standing beside me. I'd had my fill of heights when I was eleven and fell out of that barn I spoke of earlier and Mickey had had his fill of heights when he *saw* me fall out of that barn. But, actually, I didn't *fall* so much as I was the victim of idiocy—my own.

When the new golf course in my hometown was being plowed and planted, the city council had put a short, metal fence around the whole thing A dirt road ran around the golf course, just outside the fence. There was an old barn next to the dirt road that hadn't been used for years. High school kids would sneak into the barn to smoke and drink and mess around. We'd found a few weathered Playboy magazines in the barn as well as a couple of pairs of girl's underwear. For high school kids the barn was a well-known secret. So this one afternoon, Darren, Jason, Mickey and I were snooping around up in the hayloft of this barn and found a large coil of rope. We also found a piece of rope that had been tied into a loop that had a large metal hook attached to it. What we did was secure one end of the coiled rope to a large rafter above the hayloft's large door then strung the rope down to the golf course fence just across the dirt road, some 60' away, pulled the rope as tight as we could and then Darren and Jason tied that end of the rope to the fence.

Next we put the loop of rope with the metal hook around us, under our butts, put the hook on the tight rope then slid on the rope all the way down to the fence from the hayloft, which was some 12' above the ground. Brilliant. Darren went first, then Jason, then Mickey. I was last. I put the rope loop under my butt, put the metal hook on the taut rope, pushed off from the hayloft opening, got two or three feet into my rapid descent, watched in horror as the rope-knot on the fence instantly unraveled, then went straight down and landed on my back. Oh, sure, the rope couldn't unravel when one of the three skinny kids got on it...no, it had to unravel when the fat kid got on it.

I laid on the hard ground for a good minute before the blackness went away (the first of four concussions I'd receive in my lifetime, thus far, which no doubt explains a lot). My three childhood friends all thought for sure I was dead. When I came to, Mickey was crying and Jason and Darren were arguing about whose fault it was for tying the rope so poorly to the fence and about whether to call the Sherriff, the fire department or the town doctor. There are very few things to compare to the pain I felt in my entire body (except for 'Bull in the Ring' which I'll get to later). God (or whomever) was pretty smart to give humans the inability to recall physical pain lest we all go crazy. Yeah...'lest.'

When I finally woke up you'd never seen three happier boys than these guys. They let me lay there, having a brief cry, until I thought I was ready to get up. Once I stood up, they brushed me off and we decided to forget about the barn and spent the rest of the day hanging about at the city swimming pool.

It was just after we left the Elks picnic that I began to realize what a difference three years of absence and three years of aging can make. I became convinced that my boyhood friends had indeed gone over the edge in their efforts to stave off their middle-of-nowhere doldrums.

The access road to the picnic area, was a 12-mile winding stretch of loose gravel barely two lanes wide. This road, for much of the distance, ran adjacent to a series of extremely steep, and deep, drop-off canyons on one side and nowhere to go but virtually straight up, on the other side. Jason, Mickey and I rode out to the picnic in Darren's car. There were also at least a dozen other cars, driven by high school kids, all full, at the picnic. On the access road it was all fun and thrills for two cars to drive side by side as fast as they could make their car go until the outside driver lost their nerve and backed off. And of course, Darren, being Darren, had to choose the outside lane when another car pulled up behind him. As usual, I was in the back seat, by myself. The car that pulled up had eight kids in it.

What happened next, as I should have expected, was that two of the kids from the other car decided they wanted to be in our car with us. In a sane world, the drivers would stop. Not here. The plan was to pass from their car to our car while bombing along, side by side, on the narrow, gravelly road with the puke pits of hell at arms' length on one side and nowhere to go on the other, at about 50 or so miles per hour. Lovely. I could already envision next week's headline in my old hometown's weekly newspaper, *The Globe Times*: 'Three Idiots and a Backseat Fag Found Dead at the Bottom of Puke-Pit Canyon.' Now, because the front seat of Darren's car had three people in it, it only made sense that the two boarders from the other car would have to come in through the backseat window. The two cars got side by side, as close as they could without touching, and I rolled down the window.

The first kid was a soon-to-be freshman with wild-ass eyes that kind of reminded me of that kid named Nickel in Cannillejas. He was light and wiry and made the transfer easily, but the second kid was a hefty-tote, soon-to-be senior, an offensive lineman who had opened many a hole on the line of scrimmage for Darren. It didn't help that this kid was shit-faced, either. He got halfway across, had his big-ass arm locked around my head, when one of the wide, winding turns appeared ahead.

"Hang on, boys! It's a big one," Darren yelled. Halfway into the wide turn this big, dumb-ass lineman launched a projectile stream of vomit, complete with beer and half-digested corn dogs, half of which came through my window onto my shirt and pants, while the other half ended up all over Darren's rear window and splattered all across his freshly Simonized trunk. The lineman still had a locked arm around the back of my neck as I was trying to push on the door to pull his fat ass inside the car, when the wild-eyed kid grabbed me around the front of my neck and began to pull on us both. It was fortunate that I waited to black out for a few seconds until *after* the lineman made it into the backseat. I came to with him laying on my chest and breathing his gastric juice-corndog-beer breath in my face, with an expression of supreme bliss which was due, not only to the expression of his mortality but, as we all found out in a matter of seconds, but to the fact that he'd released his bowels into his Wranglers.

"Hey, man, aren't you the guy that punched old Purvis in the puss?" the lineman asked, all gastric-juicy into my face. I nodded, yes, as I was trying to get out from underneath him. He continued. "Just want ya to know that that was great, man. I've always hated that sick little psycho." So I told him that was lovely, and thanks, and to get the fuck off of me.

Darren dropped the lineman and the wild-eyed kid off, once we reached the edge of town and made them walk the rest of the way to their homes. "Fucker ought to know better than to puke in my car," Daren said. He was livid. Having kicked fat-ass and the wild-eyed kid out of his car, Darren calmed down...somewhat.

A minute of silence passed. Then Jason said, "That was fun."

"I thought last year's picnic was better," Darren said. I, having already thrown my barf-covered shirt out the car window, was convinced that had I not moved to Spain when I was 13, I would have ended up in the town cemetery before I was 17.

On Sunday and Monday nothing happened. Everyone else said they had stuff to do, so I was on my own. I went by my old house and checked it out. My hand prints and my sister's hand prints were still there in the patio concrete my father had poured when we were little kids. The two large elm trees in front of the house had begun to rot and had had to be cut down, then uprooted. The field across the street was just as overgrown as usual. I spoke with what close neighbors were still there from when I left in '69. But, mostly, I just did a lot of wandering on foot around my old home town trying to figure out if what I'd left behind was what I actually missed. It was kind of confusing, to be from somewhere, then create a myth around it, then come back to the myth and see it firsthand, for a *second* time, and to see that so little of the myth was true—what was once familiar and reliable, what I somehow expected, after a mere three-year absence.

At the book and magazine store at Torrejon, there were deep wire racks on the walls that held paperbacks of all genres—romances, sports, detective fiction, biographies, jokes, popular comics, and all the current best sellers—an ever-changing and rotating wealth of new information and entertainment. But there was one book that came in that was *always* there since it came out in paperback—'The Godfather,' by Mario Puzo. This paperback was well-thumbed, the cover bent and cracked, the spine taped together again and again, dozens of pages dog-eared, and someone who worked in the book store had written with a dark marker, on pieces of masking tape, on both the cover and the back, 'Not For Sale.' If you happened to drop the paperback on the floor, the book would fall open to the same pages every time—22 and 23—the scene where Sonny bangs the bride's maid...the closest thing to legal porn there was on the air base. Despite all the faces on the air base and at school, that you'd see one month, and then the next month not, some genius who worked inventory at the book and magazine store had realized that there should be at least *one thing* that should never change—the lure and appeal of a well-written sex scene, the availability of a quick-fix peek into this book and the fact that this book would remain on the rack *forever*—yes, familiarity and reliability—the continuity of 'place.'

I found so many glimpses of my past as I walked the streets of my old hometown, yet every glimpse was offset by the new growth of a familiar tree, the appearance of a circle of flowers where no circle had been, a new fence, or the now weathered peeling of paint on a signpost or a garage wall whose shade I had lounged in on many a hot summer afternoon. I found that I now had a hunger that could never be fed, that the myth had been starved by its own changing history, a history I'd had no part in, but was there at every turn on every road I walked down. The stasis of memory had been broken, though somehow I knew I could visit it at any time. Then I remembered a kid from my childhood, a 17 year-old box boy who worked in one of the two grocery stores on Main Street—a kid with freckles, floppy hair and an easy smile for anyone, who'd lost control of his little sports car on a wide curve, just outside of town, and was thrown against the rocks and died instantly. I wondered if he'd ever felt lucky to have had it end right then, that because he'd never had to go away and then come back, years later, to find that he would have had the same hunger, that somehow he was *complete* and that his passing made his completeness easy, and that being complete, when you pass, had to be the hardest thing in the world to do.

I walked a lot during those two days. I looked at things as hard as I could. I tried to memorize things as they *were right then,* rather than as they were before. I remember, even though I was only a little kid, maybe eight years old, how after that teenage boy's car accident and the remains of his car had been brought back into town on a flatbed truck, how the entire town spoke in whispers for the next few days because a *change* had been forced upon the entire community and there needed to be a period of adjustment, a period of filling-in-the-gap that was necessary to restore the wholeness. I never really knew the kid, but I remember how deeply I could feel the vacancy his sudden absence had created. Hello/goodbye.

Part of my walking took me out by the train tracks next to the huge grain elevators that loomed over the town. How many times had I walked these rails or set the clock in my head by the daily arrival of the trains? I walked through the loose grains that had spilled from the cars and then, two rails over, walked through the spilled coal dust until my white Converse low tops were nearly black, sparkling in the noon sunlight, just as the daily, single, noon whistle from the fire station on Main Street sounded, and then wondered how many times I had set my internal clock by that familiar friend while I was growing up?

Some conclusions needed to be rendered—some kind of closure needed to be made. I was thinking too much. I was pushing two hard against the natural order of change. I left The World and came back to find that the gap in the wholeness I had created, however small, had not been restored on my return and would somehow, for the rest of my life, remain open. And now I had to convince myself that I was okay with this, that it was okay to have such an absence, such a vacancy, and how now, I had become merely a sequin that was sewn into a bright red Christmas sweater and was bobbing along, gently, on a bumpy, winding, Spanish back road. And it was all okay, and maybe The World wasn't where you were from, but The World was where you were. Oh, yeah, thinking way too much for being barely 16 years old. I needed to go score myself some beers. Boy, howdy.

Chapter 17: 'Home Leave,' Part 3

"Shit, yeah, you think too much!" Darren said, sitting behind the wheel in the front seat of his car. "Man you were *always* thinking too much! It took us an hour driving around town just to find your fag-ass!" It was late in the afternoon—a perfect, warm, eastern Oregon summer afternoon, when my three friends found me wandering up by my old grade school.

"And talking, too," Jason said. "You were always yakking your yap. You'd read something in some goddam book and then have to tell us all about it."

"Lectures," Darren said, "You were always going on and on about some shit or another." So I asked if it bored them.

"No, not really," Darren said, "But it was hard to get used to the quiet when your ass left. Especially, when we'd walk to school." So I asked what about now and Mickey turned around.

"For crying out loud, you may not talk as much, but that doesn't mean we can't still hear you thinking. You should hear yourself from up here."

"Yeah, tone it down a bit, ya noisy fuck," Jason said.

Darren laughed. "No, you ain't changed a bit, man. Trust me on that," he said.

We cruised up and down Main Street for nearly an hour, our case of Olympia beer getting warm in Darren's trunk. Nothing was shaking, despite the fact that my old hometown's population had literally doubled overnight for the Fourth of July celebration tomorrow. Darren headed back down Main Street to the city park. The four of us took the case of beer and sat in our old favorite spot, hidden from the street, behind two large trees surrounded by thick shrubbery, and laid back on the cool grass and drank it, then proceeded to relieve our bladders into the bushes. We spent a couple of hours going over all that we could remember, together, from before I left for Spain. It was a good and spirited time, almost like before, but not quite...but close enough. I didn't find out until after I got back to Spain, in a letter from Darren, that my three friends had decided, together, to make themselves scarce and to give me those couple of days to myself, because, no doubt, I needed some time to work shit out in my head. Darren's letter also said that, for some reason, if I ever decided to write a book about all this that I'd better be sure to change their names, otherwise they'd call 'bullshit!' to *my* bullshit and sue my ass off. After that Darren wrote, "Corte tu bajo, yourself, fag! Ha-ha!"

In the content of Darren's letter was a phrase that I was certain would never make it into the ticker-tape in my brain—"If I ever decided to write a book..." Authors of books were supposed to be smart people. Me, not so much. Not like that. I'll never know where the hell Darren got *that* idea. He included a postscript with his letter—"Good luck in football this year. Hope you kick as much ass as I intend to. Really good to see you again, man." And then, "PPS: Hope you found what you were looking for. XXX"

When I was eleven years old, the uncle of a kid in my class, named Lindon, drove all the way from Tennessee up to Oregon for our hometown's Fabulous Fourth celebration—and he brought fireworks—all of the most glorious, big-booming, sparkly, dangerous, hand-held, explosive-type, incendiary devices ever created that, due to the seasonal, expansive dryness our massive plateau experienced every summer, were dutifully outlawed and fantastically wonderful. Lindon gave Darren, Jason, Mickey and myself one package each of Black Cat firecrackers—100 firecrackers per pack. Oh, what a summer! "What to blow up next," was our daily quandary for nearly two months. My personal favorite was launching tuna fish cans and burrowing a firecracker into a crabapple from the Maynard's backyard tree then watching it go off like a hand grenade.

Lindon's family owned a farm about ten miles outside of town. Near their house was an ancient lava flow that Lindon and I explored the couple of times that I spent a weekend out there. Out in the middle of this lava flow, nearly hidden by chunks of large rocks that had broken free and tumbled about, god (or whomever) knows how many thousands or millions of years ago, was a perfectly preserved foot print of a small dinosaur. No shit. The impression was at least three inches deep and about a foot wide and must have been made when the magma was almost cool. There was just the one footprint hidden among the rocks. Lindon's father had discovered it a long time ago and, when word got out, turned down all museum offers to have it removed and put on display. Lindon told me about it, then took me up the craggy hill of rocks to see it. Then Lindon and I did what we believed needed to be done—we pissed in the foot print. There aren't many kids that can say they've done *that*.

On that Fourth of July when Lindon's uncle came to town, Lindon and I bummed around together for part of the day. We picked a prime spot in the city park to watch where the parade came to an end. Lindon had a paper sack full of smoke bombs and he had this look in his eye. Something was about to happen. Now, these smoke bombs weren't the little marble-sized kind you may have seen before—these were from Tennessee and were the size of a golf ball and would smoke for a good three or four minutes before burning out. The thing about smoke bombs is that once the fuse burned down inside the ball, flames would shoot out of the hole for a couple of seconds as the smoke powder inside the ball was igniting and then the ball would just shoot out smoke. Flames, then smoke—a handy piece of sequential information that is.

On the Fourth, the air base had entered a float in the annual parade—'Washington Crossing the Delaware'—a very pretty, professionally-made float completely covered with blue and white crepe paper florets to represent water and a large crepe paper American flag on both sides of the huge flat trailer the float was built around. There was a large row boat in the middle with about a half dozen GI's all dressed in Colonial-style costumes, complete with powdered wigs and tri-corner hats. It was one sweet looking float—easily the hands down grand prize entry for the year, in my opinion. The air base's float came all the way down Main Street to continuous applause and was about to make its turn right across from the park next to the ShoeString Drive-In and head back up Main Street for its final run when Lindon lit the fuse to a smoke bomb.

Flames, then smoke—Lindon forgot that part and threw the smoke bomb as soon as he lit it. It took less than 15 seconds for the entire float to be totally engulfed in flames (oh, and the smoke was pink). The GI's on the float leaped out of their boat and down to the ground just as all the flaming pieces of crepe paper went airborne and began scattering in all directions, causing all the appreciative onlookers to scatter in all directions. It was something to see. Pandemonium, I tell you. Someone thought to hook up a garden hose to a spigot at the drive-in and began spraying the float which only scattered the flaming bits of crepe paper even further.

Did I mention that the wind in my old hometown would blow about 300 days out of the year? This was one of those days. People were running around trying to stomp out the bits of burning crepe paper all while making sure their own hair or clothes didn't catch fire. Lindon boogied, big time. I hung around for a bit but thought it best I should make tracks as well. Nobody knew where the smoke bomb came from. Lindon had pitched a perfect strike, concealed behind a tall clump of hedges, and hit the air base's entry dead center— *floosh*…instant bonfire. The air base's float won First Prize but there were some who grumbled that they got the sympathy vote. Sour grapes, I say. The Fourth of July parades were usually orderly affairs, but something else happened a couple of years before this. Right in the middle of the first run, the town got absolutely hammered by a hail storm and nearly every float in the parade was destroyed.

~~~~

Mid-Summer
(A Poem)

The Grand Marshall's Stetson takes a beating.
He abandons his vintage Model-T
To be inside the dark tavern
As hailstones, sharp as dimes, shred
The Junior Leagues' commemorative float
To honor our Constitution. The street
Bleeds with runnels of dye

As crepe florets choke the storm grates.
The rodeo queen and her court,
Still astride their mounts, huddle beneath
The Liberty Theater marquee until
The curtain of stones passes and everyone
Emerges from cover to examine
The ice balls before they melt— larger
Than musket shot but not so large
As a Jefferson nickel. The wheat fields
In the swath will be lost. A good
Indian summer might save the rest.

The Model-T needs a new windshield.
The queen and her court have shed their gloves
And modified their salute to complete
Their route down Main Street, along
With the Blue Devil's High School Marching Band,
The Den #6 Cub Scout troop, and what remains
Of the Columbia Basin Utility Board's entry
In praise of John Glenn. The soles of the shoes
Of the watchers are permanently stained.

Later, after the Buckaroo Breakfast,
Inside the dark tavern once more,
The Grand Marshall will proclaim
That when the storm first hit ,the air
Felt electric and he could feel it
All the way down to his rings, but that
He was happy for this opportunity,
To be in such fine community,
To share in such good emergency.

~~~~

Later on, after the parade and the fire, there was a
bandstand that had been set up in the park and the local

talent took the stage. What was a Fourth of July celebration without a banjo-banging rendition of 'Old Rattler,' I ask you? People had parked their lawn chairs all around, sneaking mixed drinks in their soda pop cans and watched an impromptu, old-fashioned square dance demonstration put on for the city folks from out of town.

Midway through the show, the Grand Marshal, whose name escapes me now, some politician or other, announced the winner of the person or persons who had traveled the furthest to partake in the day's festivities. Lindon's uncle from Tennessee was the winner and went up to the stage to collect his prize—his and hers matching chaise lounge chairs (blue and pink—no shit) and a Styrofoam ice chest filled with ice cold Olympia beer. Unreal.

When I was a little kid, most of the stuff surrounding my hometown's Fourth of July celebrations held little interest for me. The parade was okay. The rodeo was okay. The early morning Buckaroo Breakfast was always over by the time I got out of bed. All of the adult highlights were on-the-edge boring. Back then, that is. The things that did hold my interest were the kids' games down by the football field, the swim party at the city swimming pool after the sun went down, because it was the only time air mattresses and inner tubes were allowed in the pool and because the water in the pool was actually heated, and then there was the fireworks display which was always huge and watching them going off overhead while lying on the grass at the football field was a sight to behold. So this time I decided I'd do it up right and try to take in a bit of everything.

I'd been rotating between Darren, Jason and Mickey's houses to sleep. I stayed at Mickey's house on the eve of the Fourth. His family and he woke early to go to some park for a family reunion something-or-other and I was out the door by 6:45 am. The Buckaroo Breakfast started at 7:00 am so I thought I'd go check it out, for the first time. Darren and Jason got a 'hot tip,' as they called it, on a couple of 'hot-to-go chicks,' as they put it, in a neighboring town and we wouldn't meet up until later in the afternoon. I could bum around by myself for most of the day.

Now, first off, there's nothing quite like a couple of flapjacks with butter and syrup, a couple of sausage links and scrambled eggs, all on a paper plate and washed down with a carton of orange juice while outdoors on a typical eastern Oregon high plateau, freezy-ass, dewy-ass, early July morning. Nothing. Good–tasting and chock full of old-fashioned nutrition. Seriously. I ate two of the breakfasts, then wandered up Main Street with all of its light poles covered with red, white and blue ribbons and waited for the parade to begin.

When I was younger, I actually rode in the parade once, in the back of a pickup as a Den #6 Cub Scout. Our job was to toss candy to the kids lining the street, but we actually threw more candy *at* the kids than tossed it *to* the kids. Nothing like nailing a kid in the head with a nougat chunk or a sour ball. The parade had some nice floats and plenty of antique cars that were sweet and, of course, the Rodeo Queen and her Court, all on horseback, were very nice on the eyes (there's always been something about tight, form-fitting, western-style clothing that gets me—especially if the pant legs and jacket sleeves have some kind of fringe on them—go figure). There were a couple of guys dressed up like clowns, carrying shovels and pulling a wagon, following along behind the horse riders. They'd scoop a fresh, steaming pile of horse droppings, then take a deep, animated bow for the onlookers.

After that the parade people made their way down to the park for the kids' games and an outdoor art show. I saw my parents at the park for the first time since we'd arrived in town. They said they'd been having a good time. They asked about my sister and I told them I hadn't seen her at all. Then they reminded me that we were leaving bright and early the next morning for Portland to catch our flight, one of many, for our trip back to Spain. Then my father snuck a twenty dollar bill to me and whispered that I probably needed it seeing as how I'd bought so much beer for my friends. So, I'm thinking, unreal, how does he know this shit, anyway?

I watched the kids' games with fondness. My favorite game when I was a kid was called 'The Penny Scramble,' which became known as, 'The Pig Scramble.' Take a couple of bales of hay, break them up and scatter the hay around, then have four or five adults tear open rolls of pennies, nickels, dimes, quarters and half dollars and begin spreading the coins around, underneath the hay, right in front of all the kids who were being held back by a rope. Over the years I learned that the trick was to closely watch the adult with the half-dollar rolls and memorize every clump of hay they put their hand into. For a couple dozen kids, or more, this would become a veritable free-for-all—kicking, pushing, grabbing, tackling—the works. More than a few bloody noses emerged from the pile over the years. I always had a sneaking suspicion that the adults got kind of a charge out of watching the 10-minute melee. This Pig Scramble I watched brought back old times—these kids were certainly as nuts as we were. Walking away with a few bruises and a pocketful of coins for doing absolutely nothing, except for being a *kid* is something that can enrich a person's dreams for a lifetime.

After the kids' games, I hitched a ride in the back of someone's pickup to the fairgrounds to watch some of the rodeo. I shared my ride with a pair of sheep, who took a great interest in the scent of my hair. The rodeo didn't start for another half hour, which gave me time to wander the grounds and the huge sheds where I had spent many a winter evening with my 4-H archery group.

Now, whatever possessed me to think, with my eyesight, that I could shoot a bow and arrow, with any kind of accuracy, is anybody's guess. At one end, inside a large shed, would be an eight-foot high, triple-deep, wall of hay bales with targets mounted on them. The first 15 minutes was always spent going over proper technique and the rules of safety. The next hour was spent on self-competition from various distances. Each archer was allowed to use only six arrows during each session we met. There were maybe only two sessions during the entire ten weeks of each of the three years I participated, that I was able to leave with any arrows at all—most of them either having sailed high over into the dark nether regions beyond the mountain of bales or slid underneath the two or three tons of musky bales or wedged in between the bales, where there were no targets at all. As hard as I tried, I came to loathe the term 'goose-egg,' which meant 'zero targets hit.'

Our local Coast to Coast store kept an ample supply of cheap arrows (three for a dollar) on hand for my weekly visits before archery class. At the end of the 10-week sessions each year, there was an outdoor tournament in some forest area outside of Portland for all Oregon 4-H archery groups. The course was about a mile in length, on hillsides, down in deep gullies and through dense foliage with target distances that ranged between 10 and 40 yards. Again, six arrows per competitor. The first target was down in a gully, just across a dried creek bed, some 30 yards away. The first year, I lost all my arrows shooting at the first target and spent the rest of the tournament following my fellow 4-H chums from target to target.

By the end of my third year of archery, I had actually managed to make it to the fifth target before losing my final arrow. Progress. The best thing about these tournaments were the boxed lunches everyone got at the midway point of the tournament—Underwood deviled ham sandwiches, a cup of potato salad, a bag of Fritos, two Oreo cookies and a soda pop. Worth the trip. I took 4-H archery class for three winters in a row, when I was eight to ten years old. At these tournaments, there was an individual score and a 'club score.' No doubt my contribution did little to put my local affiliate on anyone's leader board. I guess that it's a wonder none of my wayward shots killed anyone.

Now, not all of the 'good times' that I spent at the local fairgrounds were as good as this—some good times were better. During the County Fair days, there were always all kinds of competitions, from various arts and crafts to floral displays to baked goods to sewing to quilting to canned fruits and jellies to canned vegetables. I usually entered a couple of things in the Arts and Crafts categories for my age group in hopes of scoring a little walking around money. Back then plastic models were pretty popular—cars, planes, ships—and plastic models of movie monsters were *very* popular—Dracula, the Mummy, the Wolfman, Frankenstein, the Creature From the Black Lagoon, the Phantom of the Opera, the Hunchback of Notre Dame, King Kong. I bought a Frankenstein model and bottles of paint with my birthday cash and set to work for a couple of weeks for what I knew would surely be the first-place winner. After gluing all the pieces together, I spent hours painstakingly painting my gift to the most critical of judge's eyes. I was about two-thirds done with my masterpiece when the typical summer distractions kicked in and I let the model sit untouched on my dresser for two months. Three days before the entry deadline, I discovered that I had not properly sealed my bottles of paint and they had all dried up. I was screwed. None of my friends had any model paint. I was broke. I had no hope. But, I entered my model into the fair anyway. Every item entered into any competition had a tag attached to it with the artist's name, age group and the title of the work written on it. I filled out the tag and titled my masterpiece, 'Frankenstein, Unfinished.' I won first prize. Apparently, the judges were delighted and impressed by my 'artistic vision.' Thank you Andy Warhol (or whomever). I won six bucks.

Before the rodeo started, I bought a couple of hamburgers at a booth behind the grandstands. In my lifetime, there have been two places that served the best burgers in the world—the fairgrounds in my home town and the snack bar at the Royal Oaks swimming pool—not because of their flavor, but more because of what they represented to me—good memories.

A rodeo is the most unique of all sporting events—Man vs. Animal or Man (or Woman) working *with* Animal. The rodeo on the Fourth of July in my home town was always quite sizable. Riders from all over the northwest would come, not for the nominally-sized purses, but more as one of the preliminary events leading up to the premiere event in the state—the Pendleton Roundup, which commenced in early September. I always liked the variety of events equally well—Saddle Bronc Riding, Bull Riding, the Cow-Milking Competition (one guy ropes and the other guy tries to get a squirt or two of milk into an old-fashioned milk bottle from a usually, *very* uncooperative cow—I always thought that whoever it was that dreamed up this event had to have spent time in some big city opium den way back when—totally nuts), Calf-Roping, Steer-Wrestling—and for the women, Barrel Racing.

There were events for kids of all ages, as well (future

circuit contenders, no doubt)—Calf-Riding and Calf-Roping for the older kids and Sheep-Riding for the younger set. If you've never witnessed a sheep-riding competition for younger kids, you should—you'd never forget it. Personally, with all the rodeos I've ever been to that have this event on their docket, I've never seen a kid stay on the sheep until the bell. Never. High entertainment, to be sure—not that I could ever stay on a sheep for eight seconds, at *any* age.

I remember exactly when my appreciation for rodeo performers was heightened to the level of true admiration. During the summer I was nine, I spent a weekend at a farm that was just outside of town (not Lindon's, another farm). Two of the kids in this family were in my grade (one had been held back a year) and my parents always believed that a weekend or two spent in the atmosphere of good old country living was good for the soul. This family raised cattle, sheep, chickens, geese and had quite a sizable wheat crop. They had maybe six or seven horses as well. So, naturally, one of the highlights of any good old country experience was horseback- riding.

Being a total newbie at this venture relegated me to riding the oldest and slowest horse in the bunch—Freckles. Freckles had a touch of Appaloosa somewhere in his blood that put specks of different colors across his big flanks. Thus the name. Freckles, while a tame horse, was not ridden very much anymore. Most of his day was spent eating or rolling around in the dirt in the corral and farting. All horses fart, but Freckles could really rip them. So, everyone has a saddled horse and I'm partnered with Freckles. While Freckles was the oldest and the slowest of all the horses, he also happened to be the biggest and the tallest of all the horses. "Don't worry, he's safe," the other kids told me. "He's really gentle." Oh, sure, except when it comes to fat little, half-blind, nine year-olds who don't know dick about riding a horse. Everyone else got on their horses and I got on Freckles.

Now, in the grand scheme of things, regarding the animal kingdom of which we humans are a part (don't kid yourself, I know...I'm a janitor), the human end of the scale may have been blessed with a heightened sense of cognitive reasoning for the most part, but in exchange the standard five senses were then minimized, while animals, such as horses, had developed the ability to sense human emotions. Emotions such as, *fear*. Freckles, in this regard, was no different than any other large cat or wild canine—the fat kid on his back was terrified. I was on this horse's back, holding tight, for all of three seconds before Freckles bolted for the barn.

Now, the way I understand it, the best method for stopping a horse while you're on it, is to pull on the reins and to tell the horse, firmly, to "Whoa." Pulling the reins, screaming at the top of your lungs, and kicking the horse's ribs with your heels is *not* recommended. The opening to the barn was about a foot and a half higher than Freckles' back. The logical reaction for a rider is to duck down below the top of the barn door in order to enter safely, but Freckles and I arrived at this juncture far too quickly for me to have this logical reaction and I was promptly face-planted against the barn, above the door, which knocked me backwards into a pair of perfect Charlie Brown somersaults once I hit the ground. End of lesson. Watch a rodeo, watch the riders on horses and ask yourself if you could do what they do. There's a lot more beauty in rodeo than most of us will ever know.

Now, the most anticipated event at my home town's Fourth of July Rodeo was always the Bull Riding—even better if it was Brahma Bull Riding—the biggest, most ridiculously schizoid (flank straps) bovine on the planet. Just getting a Brahma bull out of the chute safely was a challenge. The men that rode these beasts were in a club all their own. An exclusive club to be sure—almost as exclusive a club as the one for astronauts. (Surely there *must* be a private club for astronauts.) Most of these Brahma bull riders (or any bull rider, I suppose) could document their careers by the quantity of teeth they were missing, the quantity of screws that held their limbs together, the number of fingers they were missing, or the size of the metal plate that held their skull together. I'd always thought there was a special place in heaven (or wherever) for these 4-Star whackos. But I always admired their guts—these guys actually paid (entry fee) to ride 2,000 pounds of flesh with a large hump between its shoulders that wants only one thing (until the agitating flank strap is removed) and that is to stomp the shit out of the human on its back. Unreal. At least a matador, in the ring at Plaza de Toros, in Madrid, during a bullfight, is on the ground and has a sword. The only real protection a thrown bull rider has is his wits (providing he isn't pitched on his head) and the rodeo clowns. And, as it turned out, the two rodeo clowns were the same two guys with the wagon and shovel collecting the horse droppings in the parade.

If a bull rider somehow gets thrown, but his hand somehow remains caught in his hand strap, then the rodeo clown has to get to the bull to release the flank strap before the bull rider has his arm or hand yanked off, all while avoiding horns, hooves and fury. If a bull rider is thrown clear, then he becomes the prime target for the bull's rage and the rodeo clown has to distract the bull long enough for the rider to get out of the way or be carried out of the way. Now, there are horseback riders who also work in the arena—they're the ones who usually pluck the rider from the bull if the rider stays on for the full eight seconds, and they also remove the bull's flank strap. But, for the first seven seconds of a bull ride, the angels of the arena are the rodeo clowns, and they are not without their own protection, should an animal go berserk.

During bull riding and bronc riding events, there are usually a couple of padded barrels in the arena for the rodeo clowns to jump in to if they need to—a sure prescription for a concussion should a bull draw a bead and unload. More than a few times over the years, I saw a rodeo clown get his cookies tossed, but bounce right back up to complete his task. Bar none, these guys were either superior athletes with above-average speed, agility, vision and strength, not to mention a keen understanding of the brain-workings of an enraged bull or supremely pissed off horse, or they were card-carrying members of that small minority of psychotic patients whose medical records are stored in a locked filing cabinet under the letter 'C,' which stands for 'crazier than a shit-house rat.'

As luck would have it, nearly every rider either completed his eight-second ride and then leaped to safety, or were assisted from their mounts by other horse riders, or were thrown without injury. Only once did one of the rodeo clowns have to release a bull's flank strap in the midst of a collectively held breath by all in attendance and garnered an appreciate round of applause and a manly slap on the back from the grateful rider. Yeah, these guys had cornered the market on courageous lunacy.

After nearly three hours, I left the fairgrounds and began walking toward Main Street. Darren, Jason and Mickey pulled up beside me.

"Get in, fag," Mickey called. "Man, you gotta hear what happened." So I got into the open back seat, as usual, and was met by the delightful aroma of Lysol. Once in Darren's car, he and Mickey began giggling while Jason, sitting in the middle, up front, was slowly shaking his head.

"It's not that funny, you guys," Jason said.

"The hell it isn't!" Darren said. "Tell him."

Jason nudged Mickey with his elbow to get him to stop giggling, but it only raised the pitch of Mickey's merriment.

"C'mon, guys," Jason pleaded. Darren threw Jason a look and Jason was all in. Alpha Dog. So I told them that perhaps they should start from the beginning. Darren started.

"Well, while Mickey here was hanging out with every geriatric in his family tree, Jason and I drove over to Arrington," Darren said. So, I asked him what was in Arrington. Arrington was just across the county line about 20 or so miles away.

"Pussy. Whaddaya think?" Jason replied, turning around. This took Mickey's giggling to yet another level and Darren started to giggle again in between sentences.

"We met these two girls that I told you about, at our last track meet, and got their numbers so I called them and we drove over there," Darren said.

"Yeah, they asked us *both* to come over," Jason said.

"Anyway," Darren continued, "they were hot, you know? I mean, they were all tuned up by the time we got there."

"Yeah, they'd snuck some bourbon or something from somewhere and we met them at that little park there when you first get into town," Jason said. "You know the one." I told him I remembered that it was the park where, after a baseball game we played against Arrington (I never got to actually play), the first year I'd ever played organized baseball (I was ten, then), when the coaches had stopped the bus to get our victorious team some snacks, a couple of the older kids took my baseball pants and shoes from me and wouldn't give them back, even after the bus got back to Condon, and I had to walk home from the grade school wearing only my jersey, my underwear and my socks. Sure, how could I forget *that* park?

"Yeah, so anyway, they gave us some of their booze, you know, and a couple of Cokes, and told us we needed to catch up," Darren said. I asked if they were sisters or something. Mickey turned around.

"Nah, just two chicks, ya know? Keep going, Darren," Mickey said.

We got to Main Street, then slowly drove down to the end and turned around at the ShoeString Drive-In and started back up the street. It was after 4:00 and there were still lots of people milling about. My old hometown usually doubles in population for the Fourth of July, as I've said. Most everyone was beginning to make their way down to the city park for the outdoor music at 5:00 and to partake in some good old, old-fashioned, eastern Oregon barbeque.

"Right. So Jason and I pound down some of their booze and then we paired up," Darren said. So I asked if they were nice.

"Not the best-*looking*, ya know? But nice bodies," Jason said.

"Yeah, nice enough tits and all. And they were both pretty drunk, too," Darren said. Mickey started giggling again. Jason elbowed him.

"Shut up, man," Jason said, to Mickey. "What kind of action did you get today, virgin boy?"

Mickey caught his breath. He actually had tears in his eyes. "Yeah, right, if you call what you got *action*." Jason slumped down a bit in the front seat again.

"So, we're in that park and we start, you know, making out and all," Darren said. We got to the top end of Main Street and Darren turned around and started back. "So, I decide to take my girl into the back seat first, and all, and Jason's outside at a picnic table doing his schmoozing thing."

"Yeah, right. *My* schmoozing thing. Shit, this girl was all over me, man," Jason said.

"Tell him what happened next, Dare," Mickey said.

"Shut up, man, I'm getting to it," Darren said, "So, yeah, I'm in the back seat there with *my* girl and she tells me her daddy is the Arrington Chief of Police." Darren turns around and looks at me, briefly. "I mean, you believe this shit? This girl is totally swacked, you know, and I'm thinking I'm gonna jump her bones and then she throws this shit up at me."

"Tell him the other part," Mickey said, as he really starts giggling. Mickey could get you going. He had one of those laughs that when you heard it, you wished it was yours.

"Then the other thing this girl tells me is that her fucking uncle is the goddam *mortician* in town!" Okay, *that* got me going. Mickey was rolling. Jason was wiping his own tears now and Darren was pounding on his dashboard. If anyone on Main Street were looking at us driving slowly by they'd have figured we'd been sucking the nitrous gas out of the Reddi-Wip Cans in the grocery store. Mickey catches his breath.

"Old Dare would have been bagged and tagged, man! Bagged and tagged!" Mickey said. He disappeared below the top of the front seat momentarily. I caught my own breath, then asked what happened next. Darren put his hand up to signal quiet to Jason and Mickey. I shut up as well. Yeah, Alpha Dog.

"What happened next was this—she let me play with her tits, then told me that she only gave hand jobs," Darren said. "We drive all the way over to Arrington and all I'm gonna get is a goddam hand job?"

"You could have done that yourself and saved the gas," Jason said.

"No shit!" Darren said. "I mean, how do you deal with

a police chief and a mortician? It's a wonder my buffalo soldier even got hard, you know?" So I asked if he thought this girl was telling the truth.

"Who the fuck cares, man? Like I was gonna risk my ass to test this girl, you know?" Darren said. "Anyway, I at least got my rocks off." Darren turned around. "In fact, you're probably sitting in it." To say I jumped, quick as a cat, and moved, would be an understatement—I'd already been puked on by the fat-ass lineman after the Elks picnic. Jason started pounding Mickey on his back who'd gone into a fit of coughing.

"She emptied the sperm bank, I'm here to tell you," Darren said. Okay, I'm looking everywhere and feeling my butt to see if it's wet. Darren turned around briefly. "Just fuckin' with you, man. She wiped it off on the floor mat," to which I raised my feet.

Mickey, his coughing fit subsided, turned around and said, "Now, ask Jason what happened to *him*." So I did.

"I don't want to talk about it," Jason said.

"Fuck that noise, man. Tell him," Darren said. He looked in the rearview mirror at me. "This is good," he said.

"She was wearing a skirt, man!" Jason said. "How the hell was I to know?" So I asked what her wearing a skirt had to do with it, as if I didn't know myself. By now, Mickey was practically upside down in his seat.

"Tell him, man," Darren said. He was wiping his eyes with the back of his wrists.

"All right! All right, already! Shit, you guys!" Jason said. He took a keep breath. "All right, after Darren's girl yanked his crank, they came out to the picnic table and me and my girl go into the back seat here." So, I asked if this girl's daddy was a priest or the mayor or someone.

"No," Jason said, "Nothing like that. Now shut up."

Mickey popped his head up, looked at Jason, then

looked at me. "It's better than that," he said, then started giggling again. Jason elbowed Mickey again, which had no effect at all.

Jason took another deep breath. "Okay, so we're in the back seat, like I said, and she's undone my pants and pulled them down to my knees, you know, and I got my hand up her skirt and all, and this girl is wet, you know, I mean she was really foaming," Jason said. "I mean, she was really ready and so was I. So I ask her if she's on the pill or something, because I ain't got any rubbers on me or anything, you know, and she says not to worry about it and then she hikes up her skirt and just hops on."

Mickey was in hysterics. Darren pulled his car over in front of the drug store on Main Street and was shaking. His whole body was quaking. So, I asked what was so wrong with that, and Jason spilled, "She put me up the other hole, man! She put my dick up her ass!"

"Butt sex!" Mickey said, then fell out through his door and on to the sidewalk, rolling back and forth, hugging himself and gasping for air. Darren got out of his car and laid across the hood and lost it. Cue the opening theme music from 'Dark Shadows.' Poor Jason had his knees pulled up under his chin. I couldn't tell if he was laughing or crying or both.

Jason turned around in the front seat, looked at me, and with total sincerity said, "Butt sex is still *sex* isn't it?" I told him I had no clue and got out of the car and sat next to Mickey, just to get some air, just to take all of this in. As tempted as I was to let these old friends of mine in on what I had experienced with the Junior on New Year's Eve, I felt it best to just clam up and to let them deal with their own memory. From the sidewalk, I asked Jason how he was so sure about what had happened.

Jason got out of the car and came over to the sidewalk

and just sort of stood there. Mickey propped himself up on his elbow. "Tell him the rest," Mickey said, who'd managed to catch his breath.

Jason slumped totally. He had no choice but to finish his tale. Darren stood up and came around and sat down on the sidewalk next to Mickey and I. Jason stood still, in front of us, then quite slowly, raised his pant legs. Jason was missing a sock.

"Her, her...stuff was all over my, you know...my thing," Jason said slowly.

"Poopy-doops!" Mickey said, and fell back again into another fit of laughter as did Darren.

"Yeah, her poop was on my dick, so I used one of my socks to wipe myself off, then I threw it out the window," Jason said. Then he added, "My goddam sock! I threw my goddam sock out the window!"

Darren looked at Jason. "You mom is gonna be pissed!" he said, then he fell back again, too.

Mickey was spent. Darren was shaking all over. My ribcage hurt from laughing. Evening was setting in. Evening on the plateau, in early July, meant a small bit of chill factor. Down in the city park, I could hear the local talent begin to play. Jason leaned back against Darren's car.

"Well," Jason said, folding his arms, "what are we gonna do now?"

Darren spoke first. "First, we need to get you another sock. Second, we should get some sweatshirts or something if we want to watch the fireworks. And third, everybody needs to pony up so we can score some beers."

"I'm broke," Jason said.

"Me, too," said Mickey.

I told them I still had 13 bucks.

"Boys, we're good to go," Darren said.

"Wait, nothing's open now," Mickey said.

"Don't worry," Darren said. "I'll get it from Del Campo out the back door of the Elks Lodge. He'll give it to me. He likes me." So I told him that Del Campo was probably afraid of him.

"Same thing, man, same thing," Darren said.

We got our beer from Del Campo who grumbled all the way through the transaction until Darren gave him *all* of my $13, which meant a five dollar tip for Del Campo, for which we received a smile and a "Have a good evening, boys!" We hung out in the city park, drinking our beers and listening to the local talent twang their best, then walked over to the football field and watched the fireworks display which was on a grand scale as usual.

I spent the night at Darren's house and got up around 5:30 am. I left Darren sleeping soundly in his sister's bed and walked the five blocks to the house where my parents had been staying. My sister was already asleep in the back seat of the car we were riding to Portland in, to catch our flight to the east coast and then back to Spain. My father had already loaded all our luggage into the car. My mother asked me if I'd had a good time being back and I told her that maybe sometime I'd tell her everything, but yeah, it was a good time. I fell asleep in the back seat almost as soon as we started our two-hour drive. When I woke just outside of Portland, I realized that not only had I been using my sister's big boobs as a pillow, but that I had also drooled, big time, on her shirt. Okay, that was weird.

The return trip to Spain was entirely uneventful except for one thing that took place in Dover, Delaware. A military baggage guy put luggage tags on our suitcases that had the initials, MUN. So I told my father to check with him—that I thought the guy had screwed up. He did and he had. Our suit cases would have gone to Munich instead of Madrid. The guy apologized and switched the tags to MAD. Home leave vacation saved. We flew over the Atlantic on another converted transport jet, but this time the seats had actually been installed facing forward.

People are always leaving you, or you are always leaving them. That's the nature of people, the nature of change, and it's even more so if you happen to be a military brat, as I was now aware of. Things can happen overnight, or in the blink of an eye. Your stability is based on the instability of your history. I thought about my old friends in my hometown a lot on my flight over the Atlantic and realized I'd never see them again—not like it was before I first left for Spain, nor even after this second departure. Those friends were gone. These were new people and I was just as much of a stranger to them as they were to me. Hello/goodbye. But I loved them anyway. The boy never really left Oregon—Oregon had just let the boy go. The World remained as it was, as it always had been, but for the second time, in as many weeks, I was going *home*.

End of Book One

The following pages are an introduction to:

The World
(Book Two)

Chapter 1: 'Home' Again, Part 1

When we landed at Torrejon Air Force Base, once the converted transport jet had powered down and everyone on board (a totally filled flight with some people having to use the seats that folded down from the fuselage sidewalls—assholes to elbows, seriously) had gathered up all their crap, we were instructed by one of the flight crew to exit through the plane's back loading ramp, instead of through a side door and down a mobile staircase. Yeah, out the back door and down a ramp like a goddam flock of sheep off a train into a stockyard. The primary reason for the change in our exit was so that the MP's on the tarmac could get a much quicker head count in order to assist the medical personnel that were standing by. Before going anywhere, from this point forward, everyone was to receive a cholera shot. Uh, excuse me?

No sooner were we off the plane than two MP's were instructing us to form two lines and then to walk over to a pair of large tents that were pitched on the edge of the tarmac, about a 100 yards or so from where the baggage carts had been parked. I say that the MP's were 'instructing,' which was not entirely accurate. One MP was making sure that two lines were formed while the other MP was yelling at anything that moved. Aw, geez...*him* again—the same guy I'd had my exchange with back in December when I'd witnessed the caskets being off-loaded. Lovely. The other MP was calmly going about his job and assisting those parents with kids while the angry MP was walking up and down the lines, barking orders and screaming about 'mandatory this' and 'mandatory that' and how 'nobody gets their luggage until they've gotten their shot' and how 'we seriously didn't want to find out what would happen if anyone refused to cooperate' and blah, blah, blah. There were over 100 tired, sticky, stinky (and now pissed off) civilian-dressed travelers on this plane who all probably wanted nothing more than a warm shower, a cold beer and a piece of shade somewhere out of the already 85 degree heat waves rising off the flight line concrete in which to take a 17 or 18-hour nap. Me included. But this MP was on some kind of a power trip or something. I mean, the guy was even more overboard now than he was with me that day he threatened to shoot me in the neck. Now, I have no doubt that this guy was effective with his chosen *modus operandi* with say, drunk and disorderly GI's, but personally speaking, right now, he was about as effective as a hickey on a hemorrhoid, and apparently, I wasn't alone in my assessment.

Our two lines were actually moving quite smoothly as the medical personnel loaded and reloaded their inoculation guns, but this angry MP was still going up and down the lines yelling as he pleased. Then walked by *me*. I was standing behind my sister, a couple of feet to the left of the line, and looking up toward the front.

"Get in line, boy!" the MP yelled. So, I told him that I *was* in line, as was quite evident due to the fact that there was a person standing in front of me (my sister) and a person standing directly behind me (my father) and thus, three people constituted a 'line' (said with 'quotation fingers').

The MP looked closely at me. "Oh, I remember you," he said. "You're that little shit who likes to spy on all the goings-on around here." So I asked him how his meditation classes were progressing.

"Still the little smart ass, aren't we?" the MP said. He stepped toward me. My father started to step between us, but I put my arm out to stop him. The MP leaned into my face.

"I said, get in line, smart boy, and I do mean now," he yelled, veins in his forehead pumping, his eyes bulging. So I returned his pleasantries with a kissing sound. My sister started giggling and my mother, standing behind my father, began giggling as well. Then the giggling began to spread. I mean, what was this hard-on gonna do, shoot me in the face in front of 100 witnesses?

The angry MP raised his arm as if to backhand me, my father stepped between us, and then we heard 'The Voice'—and by 'we,' I mean everyone in the two lines, everyone in the two medical tents, everyone milling around outside the small terminal area (100 yards away)—everyone. A booming, commanding voice, a voice that could freeze a flock of starlings in mid-flight, a voice that could lance a crotch boil from 50 feet, a voice that shut the MP up completely (and I mean, *now*), a voice that in no way fit the shape and form from which it emanated.

"Stand down, Sergeant!" the voice said.

From directly behind my mother, a middle-aged man, perhaps two inches shorter than me, sporting a neatly trimmed mustache—a well-groomed man with fine, well cared-for olive skin and expertly clipped hair, roundish with small, but muscular, hands and forearms and sporting a loose-fitting, blue, short-sleeved, button down, collared cotton shirt that clung tightly to his torso due to the increasing heat that was coming off the gray tarmac, khaki-colored short pants, woven sandals, a short-brimmed, woven fedora-type hat and aviator sunglasses—stepped forward and squared himself to the much taller, much larger, angry MP. The MP sized up the smaller man quickly.

"Who in the fuck are you?" the MP asked.

The shorter man looked around at all the other waiting passengers who were in his vicinity which, to be honest, in an instant, had become all of us, then looked back at the MP.

He said, calmly, "Right now, Sergeant, I happen to be the one who currently has the tightest grip on that six-foot pearl-handled stick you've got jammed up your disrespectful ass." Okay, the MP took a breath with that one. A murmur began to rise from the passengers.

"Well, let me tell *you*..." the MP began, but the shorter man shut him down instantly—booming voice, commanding stance.

"Son!" the shorter man said, "You'll speak when I tell you to speak!" The shorter man continued to face the MP. With his aviator glasses, it wasn't possible to *see* the shorter man's eyes, but there was no doubt that the MP could *feel* the shorter man's eyes. The shorter man held his gaze on the MP, unmoving, unflinching.

"Are we clear, Sergeant?" the shorter man said. Then

he said, "Sergeant, tell me, do you see any clusters on these shoulders?"

The MP said nothing.

"No?" the shorter man asked. "And do you know *why* you don't see any clusters on these shoulders?"

The MP shook his head, no.

"Good," the shorter man said. "You see, the *reason* why you don't see any clusters on these shoulders is because I've been out of the country, just like everyone else here. And now I'm back, which means I'm here, right now. So, tell me, Sergeant, are *you* here?"

"Sir?" the MP asked. Classic confused dog look.

"I asked you a question, Sergeant. Do I need to repeat myself?" the shorter man said.

"You asked if I was here," the MP said.

"Sir," the shorter man said.

"Sir," the MP repeated.

"Well?"

"Yes, sir."

"Good," the shorter man said. "Good. Then perhaps you would be good enough to explain the nature of these inoculations we are all in line for?"

"Sir, it was determined that the water treatment plant for Royal Oaks had absorbed some contamination and the cholera shots are a mandatory precaution for all personnel," the MP said.

"I see, Sergeant," the shorter man said. "And what about those folks who do not reside in Royal Oaks?"

"Sir, there's a strong chance that the water supply for the base here has also been compromised, on account of the water supply tower," the MP said. I could feel everyone moving closer, up against my back.

"Compromised?" the shorter man asked. "Do you mean poisoned?"

"Yes, sir," the MP answered.

"Because of...?"

"On account of the graffiti found painted on it, sir."

"Graffiti?"

"Anti-war graffiti, sir."

"And what did this anti-war graffiti say, exactly, Sergeant?"

"It said, 'Stop the war,' sir."

"I see."

"It was most likely those hippie-type subversives that attend the high school. Them and those long-haired, bearded teachers, sir," the MP said. The MP looked directly at me and glared, so I pointed my thumb at the transport jet behind me to indicate that I wasn't here during the time in question. The MP still glared. Some people deserve idiot mountain. It's true.

"I see," the shorter man said. "So, Sergeant, one more question."

"Yes, sir!"

"Have you been inoculated yet?"

"No, sir."

"Well, then, don't you think it would be in this air base's best interests that our first line of defense against hippie subversives like say, maybe, my three daughters, who happen to attend that high school, be inoculated against potentially poisoned water?"

"Affirmative, sir," the MP said.

"Now would be good, don't you think?" the shorter man said.

"Sir, I'm supposed to..." the MP started.

[Booming voice] "*Now*, Sergeant, would be good! Head of the line," the shorter man barked.

The MP turned on his heel and began walking toward the medical tents.

"Sergeant?" the shorter man called after him. The MP turned around. "Has your partner had his shot yet?" The angry MP shook his head, no. "Take him with you. Then I suggest you both go find some shade. I'm sure we can handle this." Then, booming voice, once more. "That's a direct order, Sergeant!"

The angry MP motioned to his partner, who, like all of the rest of us, had been watching the exchange, and both MP's went to the front of the lines to receive their cholera shots. I think that was about the time everyone who had pushed up around behind me finally took a breath. I couldn't be sure, but I think a couple of the weary travelers actually applauded. The shorter man then gave a brief smile at everyone and got back in line behind my mother. My father turned and faced the shorter man and stuck out his hand.

"Thank you, Colonel," my father said. The shorter man took off his aviator sunglasses and his hat and wiped his sweaty brow with the top of his forearm. He took my father's hand and shook it, warmly.

"You're welcome," the shorter man said. Then he put his finger to his lips, "And call me, Sarge. Shhh..."

"Sarge?" my father whispered. A small smile had crept into the corners of my father's mouth—the same smile I'd seen on his face practically all day, on New Year's Day, after I'd heard him and my mother whispering in the kitchen and a few times in the ensuing days after the new base commander had totally botched the Air Force anthem on Armed Forces Radio.

"Master Sergeant Bonacetti," he said.

"But how..." my father started.

"I majored in acting at UCLA before I dropped out to join the Air Force," Bonacetti said.

"Quite a performance," my father said.

"You should see my *King Lear*."

"I bet it's over the top," my father replied.

"You know it," Bonacetti said, with a huge smile. The two men proceeded to converse like they'd known each other for 20 years as the two cholera shot lines moved forward.

When we got up to the front of our line, the doctors were changing the large vials of vaccine in their inoculation guns. My sister was next. Sgt. Bonacetti stepped in front of her. Now, there *is* some truth to the phrase, 'truth in advertising,' as well as to the tactic of 'point of purchase product placement,' but these concepts don't apply all that well when it comes to mandatory health treatment. The two doctors, both captains, were wearing short-sleeved, white T-shirts with their left sleeves rolled up. Their upper left arms revealed angry red bulges about the size of a golf ball if you were to cut the ball in half and tape it to your arm. The doctor at the head of our line locked and loaded his inoculation gun and turned to see Bonacetti giving him the once-over.

"Your left arm, Colonel," the captain said.

"So, tell me, Captain," Bonacetti said, "Did somebody *really* shit in the pool?"

The captain looked back at Bonacetti blankly.

"Just so we're clear here," Bonacetti continued, "This mandatory treatment came straight from the top, correct?"

"Directly from the commander, sir." the captain said. "A precautionary measure."

Bonacetti studied the captain's face briefly. Then he said, "And *all* this is, is a precautionary measure against *potential* cholera, nothing more. Is that correct?"

"Yes, sir. Your left arm, sir?" the captain said.

"So, in no way is this another one of those bullshit, Tuskegee-type experiments our fun-loving government is so fond of doling out. Is *that* correct, captain?" Bonacetti asked.

"I wouldn't know about that, sir," the captain said. He was clearly becoming agitated by Bonacetti's third degree.

"Captain, are you aware of how many of those men have died?" Bonacetti asked.

"That would be all rumor, sir," the captain replied.

"Oh," Bonacetti said, "So you have *heard* of it then, correct?"

"Yes, sir. All rumor, sir," the captain said.

"So, what you're saying is that these shots are perfectly safe?" Bonacetti asked. By now there were no more lines, just a crowd of people all clustered together behind Bonacetti, listening in.

"Yes, sir," the captain replied. "All of the medical staff received their shots first." The captain turned so Bonacetti (and everyone else) could see more clearly the results of the inoculation on his own arm—big, red, angry lump.

"And having already received our mandatory cholera shots before arriving in Spain makes no difference?" Bonacetti asked.

"It's precautionary, sir," the captain said. "Consider this a booster." Yeah, clearly agitated.

"So, in 10 or 20 years, none of these fine folk are going to contract some sort of brain cancer or be transmuted into some kind of catatonic stupor in the name of bullshit military science—is *that* correct?" Bonacetti asked.

"Begging the colonel's pardon, sir," the captain said.

"Yes, Captain?"

"Begging the colonel's pardon, but has the colonel always been such a candy-ass, sir?" the captain asked. A smile started at the corners of Bonacetti's mouth, but he quickly wiped it away. Everyone, I was convinced, could benefit from an acting lesson or two.

"I will disregard that remark, Captain.......?" Bonacetti said.

"Reynolds, sir. Captain Reynolds," the captain replied.

"Reynolds. Good. I will disregard that remark and just say that if any adverse effects crop up in me or my family, or in any of these other fine folks here, then I will come looking for *you*. Is that clear, Captain Reynolds?" Bonacetti asked, his voice rising just a bit.

"Understood, sir," Reynolds replied. "Your left arm, sir?"

Bonacetti rolled up his sleeve, Reynolds wiped his arm with an alcohol swab and administered the shot.

Bonacetti gave his arm a couple of quick rubs, rolled his shirt sleeve down, then looked at Captain Reynolds. "And if, for some reason, Captain, I should suddenly die, let it be known, here and now, that I will come back and haunt your ass until the end of your days."

"It would be an honor, sir," Reynolds said. "If it's any consolation, sir, that jovial MP you dressed down so wonderfully for us all, fainted when he got his shot. Just so you know."

"Captain Reynolds, you have a peculiar bedside manner," Bonacetti said.

"So I've been told, sir," Reynolds said. He motioned for my sister to step forward. I had to nudge her to get her to move.

"Oh, and, sir?" Reynolds said to Bonacetti, "You'll want to keep that arm free from anything rubbing against it. All personnel have been given the green light to go sleeveless for the next few days after their shots until the swelling goes down. It's also recommended that you try not to rub it too much. The swelling just means it's working, sir."

"Says you," Bonacetti said. He stepped aside and began to roll his sleeve back up as my sister stepped forward, got swabbed, got her shot, and promptly fainted. Bonacetti caught her before she went totally down, the big baby.

(coming soon)

Made in the USA
Columbia, SC
23 August 2017